Tor Books by Harry Turtledove

Gunpowder
Empire

Gunpowder Empire

Crosstime Traffic—Book One

Harry Turtledove

TOR®

A Tom Doherty Associates Book
New York

GUNPOWDER EMPIRE: CROSSTIME TRAFFIC—BOOK ONE

Copyright © 2003 by Harry Turtledove

This book is printed on acid-free paper.

Edited by Patrick Nielsen Hayden

Book design by Michael Collica

A Tor Book
Published by Tom Doherty Associates, LLC
175 Fifth Avenue
New York, NY 10010

www.tor.com

Tor® is a registered trademark of Tom Doherty Associates, LLC.

Library of Congress Cataloging-in-Publication Data

Turtledove, Harry.
    Gunpowder empire / Harry Turtledove.— 1st ed.
        p. cm.
    "A Tom Doherty Associates book."
    ISBN 0-765-30693-X (acid-free paper)
    1. Time travel—Fiction. 2. Teenage boys—Fiction. 3. California, Southern—Fiction. 4. Rome—Fiction. I. Title.

PS3570.U76G85 2003
813'.54—dc21

                                                            2003054334

First Edition: December 2003

Printed in the United States of America

0 9 8 7 6 5 4 3 2 1

To Robert A. Heinlein,
Andre Norton, and
H. Beam Piper

Gunpowder Empire

One

When Jeremy Solters found a note from his mother in his lunchbox, he started to laugh. He couldn't help it. So many ways she might have got hold of him—e-mail to his handheld, e-mail to his desktop, voicemail to his phone, a tingle on the implant behind his ear. But what did she pick? The most primitive comm mode she could find, and the one most likely to go wrong. That was Mom, all right. Maybe she'd spent too much time out in the alternates. She forgot to use technology when she had it at her fingertips.

He unfolded the note and made sense of her scrawl. *Stop at the store on the way home and pick up two kilos of apples,* she wrote. Jeremy laughed again and reread the note to make sure he had it right. He supposed he should have been glad she hadn't talked about pounds and ounces. He never could remember which was bigger. And he supposed he should have been glad she'd remembered to write in English. He could have read neoLatin. But if she'd used Koine or Great Serbian or any of the Indic languages, she wouldn't have got her precious apples.

"What's that?" Michael Fujikawa asked, as Jeremy wadded up the piece of paper and tossed it in the direction of the trash can.

"Note from my mom, if you can believe it," Jeremy told his friend. The crumpled note bounced off the front of the trash can. Jeremy sighed. He unfolded from his perch on a concrete bench, picked up the paper, and threw it out. He was tall and skinny, but he'd never made the Canoga Park High basketball team. This wasn't the first time he'd proved he couldn't shoot.

Michael only nodded. "Oh, yeah," he said. He was short and kind of round. Most of Jeremy's friends were short and kind of round. He sometimes wondered if that meant anything. Before he could do more than start to wonder now, Michael went on, "My dad will do the same thing. When he comes home from an alternate, it's like he has trouble remembering he's at the end of the twenty-first century, not stuck in a fifteenth-century equivalent or whatever."

"Maybe that's it," Jeremy agreed. "I was thinking the same thing about Mom."

The sun beat down on him. It was only May, but it was supposed to get up past thirty today. The Valley was like that. When real summer came, it could climb over forty for a week at a time.

Jeremy ate his sandwich and his yogurt and an orange from a Palestine that hadn't seen a century and a half of murder and war. That Palestine was a sleepy Turkish province where nothing much ever happened. The oranges and lemons were especially fine there. He didn't know whether that was better or worse than the Palestine in his own world. It sure was different, though.

Michael's lunch had a couple of golden plums of a sort Jeremy hadn't seen before. He pointed to the one his friend was eating. "Where'd that come from?" he asked.

"Safeway," Michael said unhelpfully.

"Thanks a lot," Jeremy told him. "Which world did it come from, I mean? It's not one of ours, is it?"

"I don't think so," Michael said. "But I don't know which alternate it's from. All I know is, Dad brought it home when he did the shopping the other day. Half the time, the store labels don't tell anyhow."

"They're supposed to," Jeremy said. "The EPA gets on 'em if they don't."

"Well, the EPA's pretty dumb if it bothers about these. They're good." Michael ate all the flesh off the plum. He tossed the pit at the trash can. It went in. He was a good shot. He took the second plum out of its plastic bag. Jeremy hoped for a taste, but Michael ate it all. He liked his food, which was no doubt why he stayed round.

The lunch bell rang just after Michael finished the plum. He jumped up. "I have to go to my locker. I left my history paper in there, and Ms. Mouradian doesn't let you print new ones in class."

Jeremy nodded sympathetically. "She's strict, all right. I've got mine." He slung his notebook and his handheld under his arm and headed off for U.S. History. "See you there." His grandfather told stories about lugging around a backpack full of ten or fifteen kilos' worth of books when he went to high school. It wasn't so much that Jeremy didn't believe him. He just thought old people remembered things as being much better or much worse than they really were, depending on what kind of message they wanted to get across.

Boys and girls hurried through the dark, narrow halls. Canoga Park High was almost 150 years old. Some of the buildings were newer, replacing ones knocked down in the earthquake of '27 or the bigger one of '74, but a lot of them went all the way back to the 1950s. As far as Jeremy could see, they hadn't known much about how to make schools back then.

Of course, compared to what people in the alternates had, this was heaven. But that wasn't how most kids looked at it. Jeremy didn't look at it like that most of the time himself. He compared Canoga Park High to new schools, fancy schools. Next to them, it didn't make the grade.

Michael Fujikawa slid—skidded, really—into his seat just ahead of the late bell. Ms. Mouradian sent him a fishy stare. That was all she could do, though. He *had* beaten the bell. She said, "Now that we're all here"—another fishy look for Michael—"we need to push. Only a couple of weeks left in the semester, and we still have a lot of ground to cover. First things first. Pass your homework papers to the front of the room."

Jeremy pulled his paper from his notebook. He sent it forward. Looking relieved that he'd remembered his, Michael did the same. Ms. Mouradian snatched up the homework with impatience she couldn't hide. Jeremy almost laughed, but managed to hold it in. He'd never had a history class where they didn't cover the last part of the material at a mad gallop.

Ms. Mouradian said, "Yesterday we talked about how energy problems started showing up as early as the 1970s." Jeremy's desktop came to life. It showed him a long line of incredibly old-fashioned–looking cars in front of a gas station just as far out-of-date. The history teacher went on, "Things only got worse as time went on. By the time we reached the 2040s, our oil reserves really did start running dry, the way people had said they would for years. Nobody knew what to do. Many feared that civilization would collapse from lack of energy, lack of transport, lack of food."

The desktop showed skinny people plundering a truck outside a supermarket. Jeremy's grandfather talked about those days, too. Jeremy hadn't taken him too seriously till he found out on his own how bad things had been. The video on the desktop looked a lot better than the stuff from the 1970s. It had started out digital. It wasn't so grainy, and the color and sound were better. Jeremy felt more as if he were really there, not watching something from ancient history.

"What caused the change?" Ms. Mouradian asked. "Why don't we have troubles like those now?"

A dozen hands shot into the air at the same time. Jeremy's was one of them. Behind him, a girl said, "Why doesn't she ask easy ones like that all the time?"

Two or three people couldn't stand knowing and not saying. Before Ms. Mouradian could call on anybody, they shouted out the answer: "The alternates!"

She nodded. "That's right. The alternates. Without the work of Galbraith and Hester, the world would be a very different place." When she suddenly smiled, she didn't look a whole lot older than the kids in her class. "And that's what the alternates are all about, isn't it? Look at your desktops, please."

Jeremy did, even though he'd already seen this video a million times. There were Samaki Galbraith and Liz Hester announcing their discovery to a startled world. He was tall and black and dignified. She was a little redhead who bounced and squeaked, excited at what they'd found. Considering what it was, she'd earned the right, too.

Then the desktop cut away from the chronophysicists. It showed some of the worlds they'd found—worlds where things had gone differently from the way they'd happened here.

Jeremy had seen a lot of these videos, too. Here was footage from a world where the Vikings had settled North America. Here was one where successors of Alexander the Great ruled half a dozen empires that stretched from Spain to the borders of China. Here were gaudy pictures from a world where civilization in the Old World had got off to a later start than it had here, so the Native American cultures were the most advanced anywhere.

Here was a triumphal procession through the streets of Rome in a world where the Roman Empire hadn't fallen. Jeremy smiled when that one came up. His folks spent a lot of their time trading there. He and his sister went there, too. Sometimes the locals needed to see a whole family. It added realism.

And here, quickly, one after another, were worlds with breakpoints closer to here-and-now. Here were Spaniards with bayoneted flintlocks swaggering through a town on the border between their empire and Russia in a world where the Armada conquered England. Here was a race riot in a town that didn't look too different from the ones Jeremy knew, but where the Confederate flag flew. And here was one in a world where nobody had discovered atomic energy. The United States and the Soviet Union were fighting World War VI there right this minute.

The desktop went blank. Jeremy knew how many more alternates it might have shown: the one where the Chinese had discovered the Americas; the one where the United States was a contented part of a British Empire that covered three-quarters of the globe; the nasty one where the Germans had won World War I; the even nastier one where they'd won World War II; and on and on.

Ms. Mouradian said, "How did finding the alternates change things for us?" Again, a lot of hands went up. Again, Jeremy's was one of them. Nobody yelled out the answer this time, though. It wasn't so simple.

The teacher pointed at him. "Jeremy."

"We aren't limited to the resources of one world any more," he answered. "We can get food and raw materials and ideas from a lot of different places, a little from here, a little from there. We don't take enough from any alternate world to hurt it." He'd known all that stuff long before he took this class. With his mom and dad both working for Crosstime Traffic, he had to.

Ms. Mouradian knew where his folks worked. Maybe that was why she'd picked him to answer. She nodded when he was done. "That's good," she said. "And what are some of the problems we've had since we started traveling to the alternates?"

Jeremy raised his hand one more time. He didn't want Ms. Mouradian—or anybody else—to think he didn't know there were problems. She didn't call on him again, though. She picked Michael Fujikawa instead. His folks worked for Crosstime Traffic, too. He said, "Probably contamination is the worst one."

"That's right," the history teacher said. "Please look at your desktops again." Jeremy looked down. He saw the video he thought he would. There were long lines of people waiting to get shots for Hruska's disease. An early explorer had brought it back from a world that was off-limits now. There were also pictures of the blank, idiotic stares on the faces of people who'd come down with the illness. Then the desktop showed some of the plant and animal diseases and parasites that had come back here from other alternates.

A girl named Elena Ramos raised her hand. When Ms. Mouradian called on her, she said, "The other big problem is keeping people in the alternates from knowing we're visiting them."

"Oh, yes." The teacher nodded again. "That is the other important one. Wherever we go where there's civilization, we have to keep the secret. That's why we always pretend to be part of the world where we trade. Some alternates are advanced enough that they might be able to use the technology if they got their hands on it. That could be very, very dangerous." The desktop showed another clip from the world where the Nazis had won the Second World War. It wasn't pretty. Ms. Mouradian went on, "That rule is also why we drill for oil and do our mining on alternates where there are only hunters and gatherers, or else worlds without any people at all. On worlds like those, we don't have to hide."

On the desktop, oil rigs stood like steel skeletons in the middle of a vast, golden desert. Antelope with enormous horns watched, wondering what the fuss was about. An oil worker in grimy coveralls walked up to one and stroked its nose. It stood there and let him. It had never learned to be afraid of men. In that alternate, there were no men to be afraid of.

The antelope disappeared from the desktop. Jeremy sighed, and he wasn't the only one. Ms. Mouradian said, "Now we're going to go over some of the Supreme Court decisions that center on crosstime travel." Jeremy sighed again, on a different note. Again, he wasn't the only one.

Amanda Solters stood under the awning at Canoga Park High. She stayed out of the sun while she waited for the bus and for her brother to show up. She hoped Jeremy would get there before the bus did. His last class this year was on the far side of campus, so sometimes he cut things close.

While she waited, she checked her handheld to see what she had to do tonight. She made a face at the thought of algebra homework. That was old-fashioned, boring drill and practice. She had to understand what she was doing to get it right. It wasn't like a foreign language, where she could soak it up in a few sessions with the implant. She'd learned Spanish that way, and French, and neoLatin and classical Latin for trips out to the alternate with her parents and Jeremy.

Here he came, as usual half a head taller than most of the kids around him. He'd tried out for the basketball team the autumn before, but he hadn't even got onto the JVs. Being tall wasn't enough. You had to be able to run and shoot, too.

He spotted her and waved. Amanda was tall herself, for a girl—one meter, seventy-three centimeters. Her grandfather, who was old-fashioned as well as old, sometimes said she was five feet ten. That meant next to nothing to her, any more than pounds or quarts or degrees Fahrenheit did.

"We've got to stop at the store and get apples," Amanda said importantly when her brother came up. He started to laugh. She scowled at him. "What's so funny?"

"Did Mom leave a note in your lunchbox, too?" he asked.

"She left me one, all right," Amanda said. "You mean she gave 'em to both of us?"

Her brother nodded. "She sure did."

"Why didn't she just carve the message on a rock and leave it here at the bus stop?" Amanda said. "Sometimes I think she's even more stuck in her ways than Grandpa is."

"I wouldn't be surprised." Jeremy pointed up the street. "Here comes the bus."

It was old-fashioned, too. The school district couldn't afford anything newer and cleaner. It burned natural gas, which meant it spewed carbon dioxide into the air. Most vehicles, these days, were either electric or ran on fuel cells that gave off only clean water vapor. Global warming hadn't stopped, but it had slowed down.

They got on the bus. As soon as it was full, the driver pulled off the side street where she'd picked up her passengers and turned north onto Topanga Canyon Boulevard. The bus rattled almost enough to drown out the trills of telephones as friends on other buses and in cars started catching up with people here. Kids on the bus made calls, too. Back in the old days, Amanda's grandfather said, everybody could listen to everybody else talking. She had trouble imagining that. It sounded like an amazing nuisance. Throat mikes let people keep conversations private, the way they were supposed to be.

Jeremy's phone trilled as the bus rolled past the green of Lanark Park on one side of the street and the rival green of an old, old nursery on the other. His lips moved. His Adam's apple bounced up and down. All Amanda could hear was a faint mumbling with no real words. Like everybody else, she and Jeremy had learned to use throat mikes before they got out of elementary school.

She had to poke Jeremy when the bus stopped in front of the Safeway. "Apples!" she said. He nodded and got up. He kept right on talking while they got off the bus. *Probably Michael,* Amanda thought. He and her brother had been best friends since the second grade.

When she and Jeremy went into the store, he asked, "Did Mom's note to you say what kind of apples she wanted?"

"I wish!" Amanda exclaimed. "No—we're on our own."

You could have too many choices. Amanda saw that when she walked into the produce department. This was a big store, even for a Safeway. It tried to stock some of everything. As far as fruits and vegetables were concerned, it couldn't. It couldn't even come close. Still, as Amanda peeled a plastic bag off a roll, she looked at a couple of dozen different kinds of apples, all in neat bins.

She eyed red ones, golden ones, green ones, golden ones with reddish blushes, red ones streaked with gold, green ones streaked with gold. The sign above one bin said RAISED RIGHT HERE, SO YOU KNOW WHAT GOES INTO THEM! Other signs announced the alternates from which those apples had come.

Amanda pointed to a bin full of apples that were almost the same color as the navel oranges across the aisle from them. "What are these?"

"They're weird," Jeremy said. He was suspicious of unfamiliar food.

Amanda wasn't. "Let's try them." She picked out two nice ones and dropped them into the bag. Even though petroleum didn't get burned much any more, it still had a million uses. Making every kind of plastic under the sun was one of the most important.

As if to make up for the orange apples' strangeness, Jeremy chose two golden deliciouses from the RAISED RIGHT HERE bin. He pulled off a bag of his own. In went the apples. Even so, he pointed at the sign and said, "That's really lame. We're so mixed up with the alternates by now, who can tell what started out here and what didn't? And who cares, anyway?"

"Some people don't like anything new. Some people probably didn't like TV and telephones when they were first starting up," Amanda said. She took an apple from a different bin.

Her brother grabbed another one, too. "I know, I know. They ought to look at what things are like in some of the alternates. That would teach them a lesson."

"I doubt it," Amanda said. "People like that don't learn lessons."

"Don't I wish you were wrong." Jeremy put another apple in his sack. "How much have we got?" They set both bags of apples on the tray of a produce scale, and added fruit till they had two kilos. Then they took the bags to the express checkout line.

The checker gave them a dirty look. "Why didn't you buy all the same kind?" he said.

"Because we like different kinds," Amanda answered.

"But they all have different prices per kilo," the checker grumbled. Jeremy probably would have got angry by himself. Amanda only smiled, which worked better. The checker muttered something, but he pulled out his handheld so he could see which kind cost what. He looked at the total on the register. "It comes to 557 dollars."

"Here." Amanda gave him five benjamins, a fifty-dollar piece, and a smaller ten-dollar coin. He ran the benjamins through a reader to make sure they were genuine, then put them and the coins in the register. He gave her back three little aluminum dollars. She stuck them in the hip pocket of her shorts.

Jeremy grabbed the apples. "Come on," he said, looking at his watch. "There'll be a northbound bus in five minutes."

They crossed the street and caught the bus. It wasn't a school bus, so they had to pay 125 dollars each for the ride.

From the stop where they got off, it was two blocks to their house. A squirrel was nibbling something under the mulberry tree in the front yard. Fafhrd watched it wistfully from a window. The big red tabby was an indoor cat. That kept him safe from cars and dogs and the occasional raccoon and coyote, to say nothing of fleas and other cats with bad tempers. He still knew what he was supposed to hunt, though. Every line of his body said, *If I ever get the chance, that squirrel is dinner.*

"Poor thing," Amanda said as she walked up the brick path to the front door. She didn't mean it. Fafhrd was an indoor cat because the last one they'd had hadn't looked both ways before he crossed the street.

She opened the door. She and her brother hadn't even got out of the front hall when their mother called from the kitchen, "Did you remember the apples?"

"Yes, Mother," Amanda said, and then, under her breath, "I knew she was going to do that." Jeremy nodded. Raising her voice again, Amanda went on, "Why didn't you call when we were on the bus, to make sure?"

She'd intended that for sarcasm. Her mom took it literally. "Well, I was going to," she said, "but your Aunt Beth called me just then, and I got to talking with her. I forgot what time it was till I saw you out front. I'm glad you remembered all by yourselves." She'd never believe they weren't still four years old.

As they took the apples into the kitchen. Fafhrd rubbed against their ankles and tried to get them to trip over him. Amanda bent down and scratched behind his whiskers. He purred for fifteen seconds or so, then trotted away. Yes, she still adored him. That was all he'd needed to know.

"What kind did you get?" their mother asked when they plopped the apples on the kitchen table. Melissa Solters looked like an older, shorter version of Amanda. Jeremy got his lighter brown hair and eyes that were hazel instead of brown from their father.

"You didn't say you wanted any kind in particular, so we bought a bunch of different ones," he said now.

"Don't be ridiculous," Mom said. "Apples don't—"

"Grow in bunches." Amanda waved a finger at her. "I knew you were going to do that." Mom made silly jokes. Dad, on the other hand, made puns. Amanda had never decided which was worse.

"Haven't seen these funny-colored ones before," Mom said, peering into the bag. "They must be from a newly opened alternate."

"Orange you glad we got them?" Jeremy asked, deadpan. He took after Dad in more ways than looks. Amanda felt like taking after him, preferably with a baseball bat.

"How was school today?" Mom asked. Either she hadn't noticed what Jeremy had said or she was pretending she hadn't. Sometimes it was one, sometimes the other. Amanda could never be sure which.

"Okay," she answered. "I got an A-minus on my lit paper."

"In my day—" Mom shook her head. "They've tightened up since my day. Most people got A's then. An A-minus meant you weren't doing so well."

"What's the point of having grades if everybody gets the same thing?" Amanda asked.

"I don't know. I guess that's why they tightened up. It's not the first time they've had to do it, either," Mom said. "Getting rid of grade inflation, they call it. The other kind of inflation, the kind with money, just goes on and on. When your grandfather was little, a dollar was worth almost as much as a benjamin is now."

Amanda thought about bygone days when people got good grades without working hard. She thought about even more distant days, when dollars were real money instead of afterthoughts in small change. The only answer she could see was that she'd been born in the wrong time.

The last day of school was always a half-day. When the final bell rang at twenty past twelve, soft whoops—and a couple that weren't so soft—came from every corner of Jeremy's homeroom. "Have a great summer," the teacher said. "See you in September."

Out trooped the students. They were saying, "Have a great summer," too, and, "See you senior year," and, "See you online," and all the other things Jeremy had said and heard ever since the first grade. Somebody from another class started singing,

"No more stylus, no more screen,
No more teachers—they're obscene."

Other boys and girls—mostly boys—joined in right away. People always did. Jeremy couldn't see why. Kids escaping school had probably sung that song since the days of the Pyramids.

Jeremy waved to Michael Fujikawa, who was coming out of a room a few doors down. When they were smaller, they'd got together almost every day during summer vacation. Not now. Now it was, "See you in September." They both said it at the same time, and not just because they didn't live two houses apart any more.

"Good luck in your alternate," Jeremy added.

"Same to you," Michael said. His parents traded in an Asian-dominated alternate world, the same as Jeremy's did in Agrippan Rome. In the alternate where the Fujikawas worked, Chinese fleets had kept Europeans out of the Indian Ocean. Trade patterns and all later history were very different there. These days, Japanese warlords dominated China in that alternate, as German warlords had dominated the Roman Empire here. Michael went on, "It'll be good getting back. I'm starting to know people over there, too."

Jeremy nodded. "So am I. But it's not the same. It can't be the same. Too many things we know, but we can't tell them."

"Yeah." Michael walked on for a few steps. Then he said, "Friends are one thing. I wonder what happens if you fall in love in an alternate."

"People have," Jeremy said. "They say people have, anyway. It's usually supposed to be a mess. I don't see how it can be anything else." He didn't even want to think about that. Instead, he changed the subject: "I miss the days when we could fool around together all summer long."

"Me, too. Text messages just aren't the same," Michael said. "I wish there was bandwidth enough for video between alternates."

"There is—if you're a gazillionaire," Jeremy said. That disgusted him. If you were rich enough, you could get whatever you wanted. If you weren't, you had to put up with e-mail as primitive as it had been a hundred years earlier. Even still-photo attachments were iffy.

"We'll be glad to see each other when school starts, that's all," Michael said.

"Sure." Jeremy nodded again. "You be careful, you hear?" That wasn't idle advice. Michael was going to a violent place. What warlords there wanted, they reached out and took. People who didn't like it could easily end up dead.

"You, too," Michael told him.

"Me? Don't worry about me. I'll be fine." Jeremy laughed. "Hardly anything ever happens in Agrippan Rome. The Empire's more than two thousand years old there, and they've spent all that time making it more complicated. You have to fill out sixteen different forms before you can swat a fly, let alone catch a mouse." He was exaggerating, but only a little.

"Be careful anyway," Michael said. "If you're not careful, you get in trouble." Jeremy's folks always said the same thing. He didn't mind it so much from his friend. Michael pointed. "There's your sister." He waved. "Hi, Amanda." When he and Jeremy were smaller, he'd done his best not to notice her. Now he was polite.

"Hi, Michael," she said, and then started, " 'No more stylus, no more screen—' "

"Not you, too!" Jeremy broke in.

"Why not?" Amanda said. "They sing the same kind of song in Polisso, where we're going." She started a chant in neoLatin.

"In my alternate, too," Michael said, and sang in the Japanese-Chinese pidgin merchants used there. That didn't mean anything to Jeremy, who'd never soaked up the language through his implant. Michael had taught him a few phrases, most of them dirty, but he didn't hear any of those. He'd done the same for his friend with neoLatin, which was an excellent language to swear in.

"Here comes our bus, Jeremy," Amanda said. "Last time this year. I like that."

"Everybody likes that," Michael said.

Jeremy grabbed his hand before getting on the bus with Amanda. "We'll message back and forth all the time."

"Sure," Michael said. "See you. So long, Amanda."

"So long," Amanda said. As she and Jeremy climbed into the bus, she added, in a low voice, "I didn't used to think much of Michael, but he's okay."

"He is the best of men," Jeremy said in neoLatin. His sister poked him in the ribs.

She sat down with a girl she knew. Jeremy sat in the seat right behind her. Somebody in the back of the bus sang out, "'No more stylus, no more . . .'" Jeremy stuck his fingers in his ears. The guy who'd sat down beside him laughed.

People called good-byes as their friends got off the bus. They waved through the windows. The ones who'd left waved back and then headed home. Some would go out to the alternates for the summer. Some would work here. Some would just take it easy till September. *Lucky,* Jeremy thought.

Jeremy and Amanda got out at their stop. He hurried up the street toward their house. "What's the rush?" Amanda called.

"Don't you want to finish packing so we can leave?" Jeremy asked. He wished they could have left weeks ago. Amanda didn't need to think very long. She caught up with him in three long strides. They went on together.

Amanda's stomach didn't have time to do more than lurch on the suborbital hop to Romania. Then weight returned, the sky went from black to blue once more, and down they came, outside of Bucharest. "Now for customs," Jack Solters said. "That'll take longer than getting here did."

Amanda thought her father was exaggerating. He turned out not to be. They stood in line for an hour and a half before a man in a muddy brown uniform examined their passports with microscopic care. He took their thumbprints and retinal prints and compared them to the data in the passports. "Purpose of your visit?" he asked. He spoke with a thick accent. Romania wasn't a wealthy country. Not many people here had implants. The customs man had learned English the hard way, the old-fashioned way. It showed.

"We are in transit," Dad answered. "We are doing business in an alternate."

"Papers," the customs man said.

"Right here." Amanda's father handed him a thick sheaf of them. Some were in English, others in Romanian. The official called over another man in a fancier uniform. They put their heads together and talked in their own language. Amanda thought she recognized a word here and there. Romanian and the neoLatin she knew both sprang from classical Latin, though they'd gone in different directions.

Dad spoke up in fluent Romanian. He'd learned it through his implant. The man in the fancier uniform answered him. They went back and forth for a minute or two. The Romanian gestured. He and Dad stepped off to one side. They talked some more. Then they smiled and shook hands. After that, everything went smoothly. The junior customs man stamped the Solters' passports. No one searched their bags. They went on to the rental-car counter.

As they drove the little, natural gas–powered Fiat north and west up Highway E-68, Jeremy said, "What did you do, Dad? Slip him a couple of hundred benjamins?"

"Of course not," their father answered. "That would be illegal."

At the same time, Mom pointed to the dome light. Jeremy looked blank. Amanda got it right away. She grabbed her stylus and scribbled on the screen of her handheld. She showed it to Jeremy: THE CAR'S BUGGED, DUMMY.

He stared at the dome light. Amanda couldn't figure out why he would do that. For somebody who was smart—and Jeremy was, no doubt about it—he could act pretty foolish sometimes. A microphone right out there in the open where anybody could see it wouldn't make much of a bug.

"Oh," Jeremy said—much later than he should have. "Sure."

From Bucharest to Moigrad, the little town by the site of what was Polisso in the alternate and had been Porolissum in ancient days, was a little less than four hundred kilometers. The Fiat wheezed and chugged going over the Transylvanian Alps. They drove through Cluj, the only good-sized town between Bucharest and Moigrad, an hour before they finally got where they were going.

In this world, Porolissum was a ruin, a place where archaeologists dug. A hundred years earlier, they'd rebuilt one gate to look the way it had back in Roman days. Amanda supposed they'd been trying to lure tourists. They hadn't had much luck. If Moigrad wasn't the middle of nowhere, you could see it from there.

The reconstructed gate didn't look much like the one in Polisso. That had bothered Amanda when she saw first one and then the other. It didn't any more. In the alternate, Polisso had been a going concern for two millennia. People there must have repaired or rebuilt the gate half a dozen times.

With a sigh of relief, Dad parked in front of the Crosstime Traffic office in Moigrad. Two men in the white, grays, and black of urban camouflage came out of the building. They both carried assault rifles. "Are they guards or bandits?" Jeremy asked.

"Guards," Dad said. In a low voice, he went on, "Romania's poor, and it's proud. Not everybody here likes multinationals."

Amanda eyed the rifles. *That sounds like an understatement,* she thought. Her father rolled down his window. He spoke to the guards in Romanian. They smiled, but the smiles didn't reach their eyes. One of them said something. Dad handed him his passport. The guard studied it, nodded, and gave it back. He spoke again.

"Show him your passports, too," Jack Solters said. Mom and Amanda and Jeremy got out the documents. They handed them to Dad, who gave them to the guard. He looked them over, then returned them. He nodded again. He and his partner stepped back and waved toward the office.

"Looks like we're okay," Mom said. She opened the car door. As she got out and stretched, the second guard said something.

Dad translated: "Our luggage will have to go through the sniffer. He knows we are who we say we are, but they aren't making any exceptions."

"I don't mind," Amanda said. "Have they had trouble here?"

After some back-and-forth with the guards in Romanian, Dad shook his head. "He says they haven't, and they don't want any, either. They've got some hotheads, some big talkers, and they aren't taking any chances."

"Don't people realize what a mess we'd be in without the alternates?" Amanda said.

"In a word," Dad answered, "no."

Two

Going from the home timeline to an alternate should have been dramatic. It should have been exciting. Jeremy had seen video of a Saturn rocket blasting off for the moon. This should have been something like that, all noise and flame. Why not? He and his family were traveling between worlds, too.

No drama here, though. They sat in the same kind of seats as they had for the suborbital hop from Los Angeles to Bucharest. They got even less leg room here than they'd had in the shuttlecraft. They couldn't see out. Jeremy had always wished you could see things change as you passed from one alternate to the next. Things didn't work out that way, though. When you traveled between alternates, you weren't properly in any of them till you stopped. That meant there was nothing to see, and no point to a window.

One by one, the family changed into clothes that wouldn't look out of place in Polisso. Tank tops and shorts wouldn't do. Sandals would, but not sandals of bright blue-and-red plastic.

Jeremy and his father put on knee-length woolen tunics. Jeremy's was undyed, his father's a dull blue. Both tunics had embroidery around the sleeves and the neck opening, Dad's more than Jeremy's. Jeremy's socks were also of wool, hand-knitted; his sandals were leather, with bronze buckles. His underwear came down to his knees. It was wool, too. It itched. A plain floppy felt hat finished his outfit. Dad's hat boasted a braided leather band and a bright pheasant feather sticking up from it.

Mom and Amanda wore tunics that fell all the way to their ankles. Amanda's was blue like Dad's. Mom's was saffron yellow, which showed the family had money. So did her shiny brass belt, the gold hoops in her ears, and her lace headdress. Amanda wore a brass belt, too, but not such a wide one. Her headdress was lower and flatter than Mom's. That meant she wasn't married.

A computer guided the transposition chamber. An operator sat in the chamber with the travelers. He didn't change, and looked like the odd man out. He had manual controls in case of emergency. Fortunately, emergencies were rare. Emergencies where the manual controls would do any good were even rarer. Jeremy chose not to dwell on that.

He tried to tell when the chamber reached the right alternate. He tried whenever he went crosstime, and he always failed. If he'd been waiting for the chamber, he would have seen it materialize. Inside it, he might as well not have left the home timeline.

The trip to the alternate seemed to take about forty-five minutes. When he got out and looked at the sun, though, it would be in the same place in the sky here as it had in the home line. Duration across timelines was a tricky business. Quantum physics seemed simple beside it.

Out of the blue—or so it felt to Jeremy—the operator said, "Okay, you're here." Jeremy muttered to himself. Caught by surprise again.

He got up and stretched. The ceiling of the chamber was only a few centimeters above his head. Tall in his own timeline, he would seem taller in the alternate. The locals weren't as well nourished as people back home. *I'd make the basketball team here,* he thought. *I'd play center, too.*

Somebody had scribbled something on the wall by the door. He leaned closer to get a better look. THE ONE AND ONLY HOMEMADE TIME MACHINE, it said. He grinned. That hadn't been there the last time he came to Agrippan Rome. Odds were it wouldn't be there when the chamber came back for his family. The company usually made that kind of stuff disappear in a hurry.

"Here you go." The operator opened the door, the way a steward would on a shuttlecraft. The air they'd brought with them from the home timeline mingled with what the locals breathed. That was cool and damp. The transposition chamber had materialized in a cave two or three kilometers from Polisso. The cave overlooked the road to the west. That road never had a whole lot of traffic. When video cameras in the cave showed it was clear in both directions, people could go down and head for town with the locals none the wiser.

Dad was the first one out the door. "Time to make the best deals we can," he said in neoLatin. He used English as little as he could while they were in the alternate. So did everybody else. What people in Polisso didn't hear, they couldn't wonder about.

Jeremy and Amanda followed their father around to the cargo compartment. The first things Dad got out were two swords in leather sheaths. He gave Jeremy one and buckled the other one on himself. No one here traveled cross-country unarmed. Then he pulled out four packs full of trade goods. Everybody in the family got one of those.

"A good thing bandits don't know we're coming, or we'd really have things to worry about," Mom said as she slung her pack on her back.

"Need more than swords to keep off bandits," Dad agreed.

Jeremy put on his own pack. Like the others, it was full of wind-up pocket watches almost the size of a fist, mirrors in gilt-metal frames, straight razors, Swiss army knives, and other examples of what would have been thoroughly outdated technology in his world. Here, though, no one could match it. No one could come close. Traders from Crosstime Traffic got wonderful prices.

If they'd been limited to what they could carry on their backs, they would have lost a lot of business. But they weren't. Another transposition chamber brought more trade goods to a subbasement under the house they used in Polisso. People hardly ever traveled through that one. If strangers appeared in Polisso from nowhere, the locals would wonder how they got there. Walking in and out through the west gate was a different story. Anybody could understand that.

Dad was checking the monitors to make sure nobody could see the family when they came out of the cave. Jeremy went over to look at the screens, too. They showed grassy hillsides. Motion and an infrared blip drew Jeremy's eye. It was only a rabbit hopping along. He relaxed. The Roman military highway arrowed off toward the west, as scornful of the landscape it crossed as any American interstate.

"Looks good," Jeremy said.

Dad nodded. "Yes, I think so, too." He raised his voice a little. "Come here, Melissa. See anything you don't like?"

Mom took a long, careful look at the monitors. She shook her head. "No, everything looks fine."

"Let's go, then," Dad said.

The mouth of the cave wasn't wide enough to let anyone in or out. A camouflaged trapdoor nearby took care of that. Jeremy and Amanda hurried down the hillside to the highway. When Jeremy got to it, the soles of his sandals slapped against the paving stones. That road had been there for two thousand years. It wasn't heavily traveled, but still. . . . How many others had walked it before him?

The breeze blew from out of the west. The grass on either side of the road rippled like seawater. A starling flew by overhead. It made metallic twittering noises. Jeremy didn't hate starlings here the way he did in California. They belonged here. They weren't imported pests.

"Cooler here than when we left," Mom said. Jeremy nodded. She was right. It didn't mean much, though. Weather changed randomly from one timeline to another.

"Let's go," Dad said. They started east toward Polisso, which lay not far past the curve of the next hill.

Amanda could see the walls of Polisso ahead when the wind shifted. She wrinkled her nose. Dad broke a rule: he dropped into English to say, "Ah, the sweet smell of successpool." The pun wouldn't work in neoLatin.

"Funny," Amanda said, meaning anything but.

Horse manure. Garbage—old, old garbage. Sewage. Wood smoke, thick enough to slice. People who hadn't bathed for a long time. Those were some of the notes in the symphony of stinks. The scary thing was, it could have been worse. People here knew about running water. There were public baths. But the pipes only went through the richer parts of town. The baths were cheap, but they weren't free. Not everybody could afford them.

After coughing, Amanda said, "Those who travel across time learn things about smells that those who stay home never imagine." It sounded more impressive in neoLatin. It would have been true no matter what language she spoke.

"In a few days, you won't even notice," Mom said. That was also true. Amanda wouldn't have believed it the first time she came to Polisso. She'd wanted to throw up. She hadn't, quite. Some people did when they first went crosstime. Living in cultures that knew little about sanitation and cared less took work.

Sandstone walls, lit by the sinking sun, seemed to turn to gold. The long black barrels of cannon stood on wheeled carriages atop the wall. More big guns poked out from the tall, narrow windows of siege towers that strengthened the fortifications. Some of those towers and parts of the wall were visibly newer than others. Polisso had stood siege before.

A wagon drawn by half a dozen horses came rattling and squealing out of the gate. The horses' iron-shod hooves and the iron tires on the wagon wheels banged and clanked against the paving stones of the highway. The horses strained against their harness. The wagon was full of sandstone blocks. Pulling it couldn't have been easy for the animals.

The driver was a swarthy little man with a big black mustache. He wore a tunic like Jeremy's, but shabbier and with less embroidery. "Gods look out for you," he said, as Amanda and her family stepped off onto the grass by the side of the road to give the wagon plenty of room to go by.

"And for you as well," Dad answered politely.

"Thanks, friend," the driver said. His neoLatin had an accent a little different from what Amanda had learned through her implant. That guttural undertone said he came from the province of Dacia—probably from right here in Polisso. Amanda sounded as if she came from Italy, or perhaps Illyricum or southern Gallia.

With a leer for Amanda, or for Mom, or maybe for both of them, the local flicked the reins. Men here weren't shy when they liked somebody's looks. Amanda stuck her nose in the air. So did her mother. The driver just laughed. You couldn't discourage them that way. The Solters family walked on toward Polisso.

A gate guard yawned, showing two broken teeth. He and his comrades wore surcoats of dull red linen over light mail-shirts. They tucked baggy wool trousers into rawhide boots that rose almost to their knees. Their helmets had a projecting brim in front and a downsweeping flair in back to protect their necks.

They all wore swords on their hips. Some of them carried pikes twice as tall as they were. The rest shouldered heavy, clumsy-looking matchlock muskets. A lot of them had nasty scars. They'd seen action somewhere.

"God look out for you," Dad called to the guards.

"Gods look out for you as well," answered the guard with the broken teeth. He had a small plume of red feathers sticking up from his helmet. That meant he was a sergeant. It also meant he could read and write, which many of the other guards couldn't do. And it meant he was going to ask nine million questions and write down all the answers. Sure enough, he pulled out an enormous book with pages made from parchment, a reed pen, and a brass bottle of ink. "Your names?"

"I am Ioanno Soltero, called Acuto," Dad answered.

Scratch, scratch, scratch, went the pen. "They call you clever, eh?" the sergeant said. "Should they?"

With a wry shrug, Dad answered, "If I were as clever as that, would I let people know I was clever?"

"Huh," the sergeant said. "And the people with you?"

"My son, Ieremeo Soltero, called Alto," Dad said. The sergeant nodded as he wrote that down. Jeremy *was* tall. Dad went on, "My wife, Melissa Soltera. My daughter, Amanda Soltera." Women didn't have semiofficial nicknames tacked on after their family names.

"Occupation?" the sergeant asked.

"We are merchants," Dad replied. "We work with Marco Petro, called Calvo, whom you will know. If you do not recognize us, some of your men will."

Several guards nodded. One said, "I remember the Solteri from last year and the year before that. Don't you, Sarge?"

"Of course I do. You think I'm stupid?" the sergeant snapped. "But that doesn't matter. We've got to have the records." He turned back to Dad. "Nature of your trade and merchandise?"

"Hour-reckoners, mirrors, knives with many attached tools, razors, and other such small things of great use, all at best prices." Dad got in a quick sales pitch.

Scratch, scratch, scratch. The sergeant wrote it down without changing expression. He paused to reink the pen, then asked, "Declared value of your merchandise?"

"Nine hundred aurei," Dan answered. Merchants bringing more than a thousand goldpieces' worth of goods into a town had to pay a special tax. Nobody admitted bringing in more, not if there was any way around it.

The sergeant grunted. He knew the rules at least as well as Dad. If he wanted to be difficult, he could search the Solters' packs. His broad-shouldered shrug made his mail-shirt clink. Merchants whose goods were worth more than a thousand aurei were rich enough to land a nosy sergeant in hot water. He seemed to decide snooping beyond what the law required was more trouble than it was worth. "Religion?" he asked. "Your greeting and your names make you Christians or Jews."

"We're Imperial Christians," Dad said. "We're peaceful people. We don't cause trouble."

Another grunt. "Yeah, that's what they all say." The sergeant wrote it down, though. "Now—your home province and birthplace?"

It went on and on. Agrippan Rome floated on a sea of parchment, papyrus, and, in recent years, paper. The Empire had been a going concern for more than two thousand years. Amanda wondered if anyone had ever thrown anything out in all that time. Somewhere in Polisso, were there records of travelers who'd come through this gate five hundred or a thousand or fifteen hundred years before? She wouldn't have been surprised. Had anybody looked at them since a bored guard took them down? *That* would have surprised her.

After what seemed like forever and was almost half an hour, the sergeant said, "All right. Everything seems in order. Entry tax for a grade-three town, a family of four, merchant class, is . . . Let me see." He had to check a sheet of parchment nailed to the guardhouse wall. Once he had checked it, he did some figuring on his fingers. "Eighteen denari."

Dad grumbled. Grumbling was good form. It said you weren't too rich to worry about money. Grumble a lot, though, and you risked annoying the guardsmen. "Here." Dad handed over the small silver coins. They weren't all quite the same size or shape, but they all weighed the same. The Empire was careful about its coinage.

The sergeant counted the denari. Twice. Then he nodded. "You have paid the entry tax," he said formally. "You do not have the seeming of Lietuvan spies. Enter, therefore, into the city of Polisso. May your dealings be profitable. You will report to the temple of the spirit of the Emperor for the required sacrifice. If not, your failure will be noted." He sent Dad a hard look.

In this paperwork-mad society, not sacrificing *would* be noticed. But Dad only said, "We will. I told you, we're Imperial Christians."

Christianity here had the same name as it did back home, but it wasn't the same thing. In this world, it never had become the most important faith in the Roman Empire. The Empire here hadn't gone through the troubles it had in Amanda's world. It had stayed strong and mostly prosperous. People hadn't worried so much about the next world. For most of them, this one had seemed enough. The new belief and the old ones had mingled much more here. Even the Christians who didn't call themselves Imperial were less strict about other gods than the ones in the home timeline.

Judaism here wasn't as different as Christianity, but it wasn't the same, either. Jews here didn't believe the Emperor was divine, the way most people did. But they did think of him as God's viceroy on earth. They would sacrifice to his good health and good fortune, but not to his spirit.

In this world, Muhammad had never been born. It was a different place, with a different history. Finding things in it the same as they were back home would have been the real shocker.

"Come on," Jeremy said. "Let's get moving."

"Why are you in such a hurry?" Mom asked. He didn't answer, but pushed on into Polisso. The rest of the family followed.

Once upon a time, the town had been a camp where a Roman legion stayed. It still kept the square layout and grid of main streets it had had then. In between those streets that joined at neat right angles, little lanes and alleys wandered every which way. Houses had their lower story of stone or brick, the upper floors of timber. Some of them had balconies that reached across the lanes toward balconies reaching from the other side. Amanda wondered how sunlight ever trickled down there. By the damp, nasty smell, it often didn't.

A triumphal arch sprouted in the middle of a square. Men on horseback, ox carts, and people on foot went past it or under it. They didn't look at it twice. Why should they? To them, it was just part of the landscape. Amanda pointed to the figure in relief above the keystone. "There's Agrippa."

Even after almost two thousand years of weathering, even with bird droppings streaking his face and his ceremonial armor, Marcus Vipsanius Agrippa still looked tough. The sculptor showed him as a burly, muscular man with bushy eyebrows, a big nose, and a chin that stuck out. Here, as in Amanda's world, he'd been a lifelong friend and helper to Augustus, the first Roman Emperor. In both worlds, Augustus had married his daughter to Agrippa. He'd given Agrippa his ring during an illness, showing he wanted Agrippa to be his heir.

Augustus was always getting sick—and always getting better. Agrippa was the picture of health—till, in Amanda's world, he died in 12 B.C. He was only fifty-one. Augustus kept right on getting sick—and getting better—for another quarter of a century before he finally died, too.

In this world, Agrippa had stayed healthy. It made an enormous difference. Augustus tried to conquer Germania, the way his great-uncle, Julius Caesar, had conquered Gallia. When the Germans rebelled, in Amanda's world Augustus had had to send a bad general against them. Agrippa was already more than twenty years dead. The other general—his name was Varus—got three Roman legions massacred. The German revolt succeeded. In Amanda's world, the Roman frontier stopped at the Rhine till the Empire fell.

Things weren't the same in this world. Here, Augustus had had Agrippa to use against the Germans. Agrippa was old by then—he was the same age as Augustus—but he knew his business. He beat the Germans and killed their chief. Settlers from the Empire came in, as they had in Gallia. Germania became a Roman province. Here, it still was a Roman province.

And when Augustus finally died here, who succeeded him? Agrippa. "My hair is white, but I am still strong," he said when he became Emperor. He proved it, too. He reigned for twelve years on his own, and he conquered Dacia—the land that had become Romania in Amanda's world. The Romans had conquered it in her world, too, but not for almost another hundred years. They'd never held it very firmly there. Here, it was still called Dacia, and it still belonged to Rome.

One man, Amanda thought, looking up at Agrippa. *One man made all that difference.* In her world, the German invasions helped bring down the Roman Empire. In this one, the people of Germania became Romanized. They came to speak and read and write Latin. Cities sprang up there, Roman cities. Some great Roman Emperors and some great scholars and writers—and a lot of good soldiers—here had had German blood. The same held true for Dacia, though not quite to the same degree.

With the lands and people it hadn't had in her world, the Roman Empire here never fell. It went on and on, staying itself and not changing much, the way China had in her world. It had known a couple of dynasties of nomad conquerors from off the steppe, but in time it had swallowed them up. They were like a drop of ink in a lake. They couldn't turn all that water black. There weren't enough of them.

Dad pointed to a sign. LUCERNARIUS, it said: lamp-seller. Sure enough, the little shop stocked lamps of pottery and polished brass. "There's a man trying to rise above his place here," Dad remarked.

"How come?" Amanda said, and then, "Oh! The sign's in classical Latin."

"You bet it is," Dad said. "In neoLatin, it'd just be *lucerno*."

The sounds of neoLatin had changed less from the old language than those of Italian or Spanish or French. But its grammar worked like theirs—and like English's, too, come to that. Word order told who did what in a sentence. *Man bites dog* meant something different from *Dog bites man*.

Classical Latin had another way of doing things. You could use almost any word order you wanted, because word endings were what counted. If a lamp-seller bit a dog, he was a *lucernarius*. If the dog bit him, he was a *lucernarium*. If you gave him a dog, you gave it to a *lucernario*. After that, it was his dog, *canis lucernarii*—or, if you preferred, *lucernarii canis*. And if you wanted to speak to him about it, you called out, *Lucernarie!* All nouns changed like that. Adjectives changed with them. Verbs had their own forms.

It made for a language more compact than English. Classical Latin didn't need a lot of the helping words English used. Its word endings did the job instead. If you didn't have an implant, classical Latin was probably harder to learn than English.

And classical Latin wasn't dead in Agrippan Rome. Far from it. People spoke neoLatin in their everyday business. But the men who mattered—the bureaucrats who kept the Empire going whether the ruler was a genius or a maniac or a murderer or all three at once—wrote in the classical language. So did scholars and historians and poets. They looked down their noses at neoLatin. Learning the old tongue, learning to be elegant in it, was a big part of what raised a man to the higher classes of society here.

Sometimes the upper crust even spoke classical Latin among themselves—usually when they didn't want ordinary people to know what they were talking about. In Amanda's world, the Catholic Church had used Latin the same way into the twentieth century.

"The lamp-seller won't get in trouble for writing his sign like that, will he?" Jeremy asked.

Dad shook his head. "It's not against the rules. Just— snooty. Maybe he sells to rich people. Maybe he wants poor people to think he sells to rich people, so he can get away with charging more."

"Snob appeal," Mom said.

Agrippan Rome had its share of real snobs, its share and

then some. Aristocrats here carried on an old, old tradition, and boy, did they know it. They looked down their noses at anybody who wasn't one of them. In a way, that made Amanda want to laugh. For all his gold and all his slaves, even the richest aristocrat here didn't have a car or a phone or a computer or a refrigerator or air-conditioning or a doctor who knew much or any of a million other things she took for granted when she was home.

But people were people, in her timeline or any of the alternates. Knowledge changed. Customs changed. Human nature didn't. People still fell in love—and out of love, too. They still schemed to get rich. They squabbled among themselves. And they needed to feel their group was better than some other group. Maybe they had more money. Maybe they had blond hair. Maybe they spoke a particular language. Maybe they had the one right religion—or the one right kind of the one right religion. It was always something, though.

And they showed off. A woman stood in the middle of the street holding up a puppy. Her friends gathered to pet it. It snapped at one of them. She smacked it in the nose. It yipped. The woman who owned it smacked it, too. People here didn't worry about cruelty to animals. That was custom, not human nature. *Too bad,* Amanda thought.

She and her family went up the main street that led into Polisso from the west gate. At the third good-sized cross street, they turned left. All the houses and shops and other buildings had numbers on them. That let the *vigili*—the police—find any place in town in a hurry. It let the city prefect collect taxes more easily, too. The numbers didn't look just like the ones Amanda was used to, but they used the same system. What she thought of as Roman numerals were for display here, the same as they were in her world.

Dad turned right on the next big cross street. The important streets, like that one, were paved with cobblestones. You had to be careful when you walked, or you could turn an ankle. The lanes and alleys that branched off from the main streets weren't paved at all. They were dusty when it was dry and streams of stinking mud when it rained.

"Here we are—24 Victorious Emperor." Dad looked pleased with himself for remembering the way. The house—an upper story of whitewashed wood above a lower one of white-washed stone—showed little to the street. Only narrow windows with stout shutters and a door with heavy iron hinges interrupted the stonework. All the display would go on the inside, in the rooms and in the courtyard.

The door also had a heavy iron knocker. Before Dad could grab it, Jeremy did. He raised it and brought it down three times. *Bang! Bang! Bang!*

"Welcome, welcome, three times welcome!" Marco Petro, called Calvo, was a stout man with blue eyes and a big nose. His bald head gave him his nickname. In Jeremy's world, his name was Mark Stone. He clasped hands with Dad and Jeremy and blew kisses to Mom and Amanda. "Come in, come in, come in." People here liked saying and doing things in threes. They thought it was lucky. That way why Jeremy had knocked three times.

"Thank you, thank you, thank you," Dad answered. Jeremy shot him a suspicious look. Marco Petro had sounded normal. He was just . . . talking. The way Dad said it, he might have been poking fun at the custom he was following.

Or, then again, he might not have. You never could tell with Dad.

By the way Marco Petro boomed laughter, *he* thought Dad was sending up local customs. He stood aside to let the Solters family come in, then closed the door behind them. It was close to ten centimeters thick, of solid oak. He set a stout iron bar in brackets to lock it.

Closing the door cut off most of the light in the entry hall. Jeremy blinked, trying to help his eyes adapt. Marco Petro laughed again, on a different note. Now he too sounded like somebody gently—or maybe not so gently—mocking the culture in which he'd been living. "Good to see you folks," he said. He kept on using neoLatin, but in a way that suggested he would rather have spoken English. "Messages by thinking machine are fine, but real live people are better."

Mom curtsied. "Thank you so much for the generous praise. Better than a thinking machine!" She couldn't come out and say *computer.* It wasn't just that the word didn't exist in neoLatin. The idea behind the word didn't exist, either.

Marco Petro bowed to her. "More sarcastic than a thinking machine, too. Take your packs off. Make yourselves at home. You *will* be at home for the next three months. Come out into the courtyard, why don't you? We'll get you something wet."

Bees buzzed among the flowers in the courtyard garden. A fountain splashed gently. This house had running water. It was cold, and the germs in it would give you stomach trouble in nothing flat if you weren't immunized, but it ran. A statue of Agrippa's son and successor, the Emperor Lucius, stood not far from the fountain. It was a small recent copy of a famous piece in Rome. It wasn't all that well carved, but the gilding on the armor and the lifelike paint on the flesh and face helped hide flaws.

Jeremy thought painted statues were gaudy, to say nothing of tacky. But the ancient Greeks and Romans had always done that. In Jeremy's world, the custom had died out. It lived on here. When in Agrippan Rome, you did as the Romans did.

"Lucinda!" Marco Petro called as he hurried into the kitchen. "Bring out some wine, will you, dear? The Solteri are here." He wouldn't serve the guests himself. He was the head of a family. That would have been beneath his dignity. He had his daughter do it instead.

In most households this wealthy, a servant or a slave would have brought the wine. But Crosstime Traffic rules prohibited owning or dealing in slaves. Even if they hadn't . . . Jeremy shook his head. He'd seen slavery here, and it sickened him. How could one person buy, sell, *own* another? The locals did, though, and it bothered them not a bit. Some—not all, but some—slaves seemed contented enough. That puzzled Jeremy, too.

Servants also weren't a good idea here. Along with the transposition chamber in the subbasement, this house had other gadgets and weapons from the home timeline. The locals thought the merchants who lived here were eccentric for doing their own housework. But there was no law against being eccentric.

Marco Petro came back out into the courtyard. His wife came out, too, from another door. Her name was Dawn. Here, she went by Aurora, which meant the same thing. "Welcome, welcome, three times welcome!" she called. "Marco, are you getting something for them?"

"Lucinda's taking care of it, dear," Marco Petro answered.

He sounded like someone holding on tight to his patience. His wife nagged. Jeremy had seen that before. The merchant turned toward the kitchen. "How are you coming, Lucinda?"

"Ill be right there, Father."

Lucinda Petra came out carrying a big tray of hammered copper. On the tray were an earthenware jar of wine, seven hand-blown glass cups, a loaf of brown bread, and bowls of honey and olive oil for dipping. In this world, only Lietuvans and other barbarians ate butter.

Lucinda was Jeremy's age. She had blue eyes like her father. She didn't have a big nose, though, or, as far as he could see, anything else wrong with her. She was the main reason he'd hurried into Polisso. He never had got up the nerve to tell her how cute he thought she was.

Even without his saying anything, Amanda could tell what he was thinking. "Stop staring," she whispered.

"Stifle it," Jeremy answered sweetly.

After Lucinda set the tray on a table, she poured wine for everybody. Agrippan Rome thought of wine the way a lot of Europeans did in Jeremy's world. Babies here started drinking watered wine as soon as they stopped nursing. As children got older, they watered it less and less. It was probably safer than drinking the water.

In his own world, there were good reasons not to let kids drink wine. They had plenty of other things to drink: water and milk that wouldn't make them sick, fruit juices, soda. They could get behind the wheel of a car and kill themselves and other people. And they were just starting out in life. Who his age or Amanda's was ready to take a place in the grown-up world?

There wasn't much else to drink here. There were no cars.

People started working at twelve or thirteen—sometimes at eight or nine—and worked till they dropped. The line between children and adults blurred. It was a different world. One whiff of the ripe, ripe air told how different it was.

Marco Petro splashed a little wine on the paving stones of the courtyard. "To the spirit of the Emperor," he murmured.

Everyone else imitated the ritual. The traders would have done it with their customers. They did it among themselves, too, to stay in practice. The paving stones showed plenty of stains, some old, some new, If they hadn't, the locals would have wondered why. The most obvious answer was that the people here didn't wish the Emperor well. That would have been dangerous.

"By what you've sent back home, business has been good here," Dad remarked, dipping a chunk of the brown bread into olive oil.

"Not bad at all," Marco Petro agreed. "Hour-reckoners and mirrors, especially. Everybody who's anybody wants to pull out an hour-reckoner and see what time it is. All the people with hour-reckoners want everybody else to see them seeing what time it is. They want to show off, you know. And if you've been looking at yourself in polished bronze, or not looking at yourself at all, a real mirror seems like a miracle."

Lucinda smiled. "They do wonder why we'd rather have grain than gold."

"They always have," Jeremy said. Talking about trade with Lucinda was easier than talking about other things. "As long as they don't wonder where it goes, everything's fine."

"We make sure of that," Aurora Petra said. Jeremy nodded. Most of the grain went back to the home timeline through the transposition chamber in the subbasement. Some went out in wagons, though: enough to make it look as if more did. That grain didn't go any farther by road than the chamber outside of town. The locals saw it leave Polisso. That was what counted.

"It'll be funny, going back to Cincinnati after living here for a while," Lucinda said. "Do without things for a while, and they don't seem real any more."

"It's like jet lag, only more so," Jeremy said.

"That's just what it's like," Lucinda agreed. Jeremy felt proud. His sister made a face at him. He ignored her.

"I hope things stay quiet with Lietuva," Mom said.

"The guard at the gate was talking about Lietuvan spies," Amanda put in.

"They aren't keeping Lietuvan merchants out of the Empire, so it should be all right," Marco Petro said. The kingdom to the north and east ruled what were Poland and Belarus and Ukraine and the Baltic countries and some of European Russia in Jeremy's world. Every generation or two, it fought a war with Rome. Neither side ever gained much, but they both kept trying. No, human nature didn't change much across timelines.

Three

"Safe trip! God go with you!" Amanda called as Marco Petro and Aurora and Lucinda Petra left the house and strode toward the west gate of Polisso. They would leave Agrippan Rome through the other transposition chamber. As long as they were seen to leave the town and weren't seen to go out of this alternate, everything was fine.

"Thank you. See you before too long," Marco Petro answered. He had a sword on his belt and carried a bow. He wore a quiver of arrows on his back. A leather pouch on his hip hid a pistol. That was for real emergencies, though. They had pistols here—long, clumsy, single-shot pistols. His neat little automatic was something else altogether.

A couple of skinny little boys in ragged tunics watched the traders leave. No one else paid much attention. They looked like ordinary people. Why get excited?

The Petri tramped down the street. They walked carefully because of the cobblestones. Tripping and breaking an ankle just when they were leaving would have been awful. The surface would get better on the flat paving stones of the highway. Still, the Petri didn't have to go very far.

Next to Amanda, Jeremy blew Lucinda a kiss. Her back was turned, so she didn't see it. Amanda sighed. Jeremy was socially challenged. He even knew it, but knowing it and doing something about it were two different beasts.

Mom called, "Safe journey!" too. Marco Petro turned and waved. So did his wife. They rounded a corner. Marco Petro started singing a song. Amanda could pick it out for a little while. The the noise of Polisso swallowed it up.

"Just us now." Dad sounded cheerful about it.

Amanda wasn't so sure she was cheerful. Maybe Dad hadn't intended to, but he'd reminded her how alone they were here. Jeremy seemed to have the same feeling. He went into the house without looking at anybody else.

A gray cat darted up the street. It gave Amanda and her parents a wary green glance and kept on running. Mom said, "Maybe I'll leave some scraps in front of the door and see if we can make friends."

"Good luck," Amanda said. Cats here were more like wild animals than pets. They lived in towns because towns were full of rats and mice. They didn't want much to do with people.

"It could happen." Mom was a born optimist.

"Let's go in and set up," Dad said. "It's late now, so we may not have any new business today. If we don't, we will tomorrow."

They took a few watches and mirrors and razors and Swiss army knives and arranged them on a display stand in a room near the front door. Most of the trade goods went into a strong room by the kitchen. A lot of houses in Polisso had strong rooms. This one was special. Local thieves couldn't come close to winning against technology from the home time-line. Burglar alarms with infrared sensors meant traders were waiting for them even before they tried beating modern alloys and locks that read thumbprints.

"We'd better get supper started," Mom told Amanda.

Amanda made a face, but she went off to the kitchen. Like most alternates, Agrippan Rome had rigid gender roles. At home, Dad and Jeremy did at least half the cooking. Not here, even though the work was a lot harder here.

Supper was barley porridge. It had mushrooms and onions and carrots chopped up in it. It also had bits of sausage. The sausage came from a local butcher shop. Amanda carefully didn't think of what all might have gone into it. Whatever it was made of, it didn't taste bad. It had a strong fennel flavor, like Italian sausage on a pizza, only more so. Since the rest of the porridge was bland, that perked it up.

Washing dishes was another pain. You couldn't get anything clean, not the way it would have been back home. Scrubbing a bowl with a rag in cold water without soap would have frustrated a saint. Going back to the home timeline for most of the year had let Amanda forget how tough things were here. The first evening reminded her in a hurry.

After the sun went down, the only lights in the main part of the house were olive-oil lamps and candles. The traders couldn't show anything different from what other people in Polisso had. Trouble was, those lamps and candles didn't give off a whole lot of light. Shadows lurked in corners. They reared when flames flickered. And, when a lamp ran dry or a candle burned out, they would swoop.

Amanda found herself yawning. You didn't get sleepy right after sundown back home. Electric lights held night at bay. Not these feeble lamps. Here, night was *night*, the time to lie quiet. Like somebody out of a fairy tale, Amanda carried a candle to bed. It gave just enough light so she didn't trip and break her neck, but not a dollar's worth more.

She yawned again when she got to the bedroom. The bed,

she remembered, was all right. Leather lashings attached to the frame weren't as good as a box spring, but they weren't bad. The mattress was stuffed with wool. It got lumpy, but you could sleep on it. The blanket was wool, too. No one here knew about sheets. The pillow, now, the pillow was full of goose down. That would have cost a pile of benjamins back home.

Before Amanda went to sleep, she rubbed on insect repellent. It came in a little pottery jar, so it looked like a local medicine. Unlike local medicines, it really worked. Bedbugs and fleas and mosquitoes were bad enough. Lice . . . Amanda shuddered and slathered on more repellent. She'd found out the hard way why *lousy* meant what it did.

She blew out the candle. The darkness that had been hovering poured down on her. She could hardly tell the difference between having her eyes open and closed. She didn't keep them open very long anyway. Sleep hit her over the head like a rock.

Next thing she knew, the new day's first sunlight was trickling in through the shutters. That wasn't what woke her, though. The new day's first wagon was clattering past outside. A second one followed, and a third, and a fourth. Like a lot of towns in Agrippan Rome, Polisso had a law against wheeled traffic at night. That let people sleep. But as soon as it got light . . .

She'd slept in her tunic. On a hot night, she would have slept nude. Nude and regular clothes were the only choices you had here. Nobody'd thought of pajamas or nightgowns or anything of the sort.

For breakfast, Amanda ate leftover porridge from the night before. It had sat in the pot all night. *Pease porridge in the pot, nine days old* wasn't a nursery rhyme here. It was a way of life. No refrigerators in Agrippan Rome. No ice at all in summertime. (No ice cream, either. She sighed. Thinking of food could make her homesick like nothing else.)

No one had finished eating before somebody knocked on the door. Jeremy said something rude in English. "Try that in neoLatin," Dad said. The knock came again. It was louder and more insistent. He muttered a few words that might have been neoLatin—or might not, too. "People go to bed with the sun here. They wake up with the sun, and they're ready to do business."

Bang! Bang! Bang! Whoever was out there sounded ready to break down the door.

Amanda rose from her stool. "I'll get it," she said. "I'm almost done here."

When she opened the door, the man outside was reaching for the knocker to pound some more. He dropped his hand. He also gave back a step in surprise. People in Polisso often did the first time they saw Amanda. She was five or six centimeters taller than this fellow, for instance.

"Bono diurno." she said sweetly. "What can I do for you, sir?"

He didn't return her *good day*. Instead, still staring, he blurted, "You're not Marco Petro!" A moment later, he added, "You're not even part of his family," which made a little more sense.

"No, sir," she agreed, still polite. The man was olive-skinned, but he still turned red. Sometimes the best way to make someone feel foolish was to pretend not to notice how foolish he was. She went on, "The Petri have taken a load of grain out of Polisso. I'm Amanda Soltera. We Solteri are from the same firm. We'll be staying in town for a while." She waited. When the man kept on standing there with his mouth hanging open, she prompted him by repeating, "What can I do for you, sir?"

Hearing it a second time seemed to make him notice her as a person, not just a phenomenon. He said, "I am here to do business. Let me see your father." Then he paused and asked in a small voice, "Is he nine feet tall?"

The Roman foot was a little shorter than the one the USA had used till it went metric. Even so, nobody in the world was nine Roman feet tall. Amanda didn't like the rest of what the local had said, either. "You can do business with me, sir. What do you need? An hour-reckoner? A razor? A knife with many tools? One of the special mirrors we sell?"

"You . . . do business?" the man asked. In Polisso, women didn't, except those on their own or too poor not to. Amanda didn't fit either of those categories. He could see that much. Under his breath, he said, "Well, you are an Amazon in size— why not in manner?"

Amanda pretended not to hear that. If she didn't hear it, she didn't have to decide whether it was compliment or insult. She said, "Please come in," and then, as he walked past her, "Whose man of affairs are you?"

He stopped and gave her a funny look. Not only was she a person, she was a person with a brain. "How do you know I am anyone's man of affairs?"

"By the way you dress. By the way you talk. If you were a merchant on your own, you would have a different way of speaking. If you were a noble, your tunic would have more embroidery." It would be of finer wool, too, but Amanda didn't mention that.

"Well, girl, you are right," the local said. He tried to get some of his own back with that faintly scornful *girl* and with the way he went on: "I am Lucio Claudio, called Fusco. I have the honor to serve the most illustrious Gaio Fulvio, called Magno—and he is great indeed."

Amanda knew who Gaio Fulvio was. He had probably the largest estate of any noble who lived in Polisso. He'd dealt with Crosstime Traffic traders before, but never with the Solters family. "We are pleased to have the most illustrious Gaio Fulvio for a customer," she said. "I ask you again, what would he like?"

"An hour-reckoner," Lucio Claudio answered. "He has seen those that other men in the city have. They are more convenient than water clocks. He can carry one with him, and he does not have to keep a slave boy filling and emptying basins."

"True," Amanda said gravely. So it was. A lot of nobles in Polisso had figured out the same thing years before. Some still hadn't, though. If their grandfathers hadn't had watches, they didn't want them, either. Things changed slowly in Agrippan Rome. That made people want to think they didn't change at all. But things always changed, whether people wanted them to or not.

She led Gaio Fulvio's man to the room where the trade goods were on display. His eyes went from one big pocket watch to another. Before he spoke or pointed, she told herself she knew which one he'd choose. When he said, "That one," she almost hugged herself with glee. She'd hit it right on the money.

He'd picked the biggest, gaudiest watch the merchants carried. To Amanda, it looked like a bright blue enamel turnip with gilding splashed here and there. The back had a gilded relief of Cupid shooting an arrow into Paris as he gazed at Helen of Troy. It couldn't have been more tasteless if it tried for a week.

But it was popular as could be in Polisso. People here

liked things that were big and bright and overdecorated. They admired them. Two hundred years before Amanda's time, the Victorians in her world had been the same way.

She took the watch off the stand and wound it. It started to tick. Lucio Claudio heard the noise, too. He leaned forward. "You should wind it once a day," Amanda told him. "This is how you set the hour. It is now near the end of the first hour of the day." In Agrippan Rome, the first hour of the day began at sunrise, the first hour of the night began at sunset. Day and night always had twelve hours each. Daytime hours were longer in summer, nighttime in winter. Water clocks measuring steady bits of time had already begun to dent that idea. Mechanical clocks would probably kill it, the way they had in Amanda's world.

Lucio Claudio held out his hand. Amanda gave him the pocket watch. He held it up to his face to look at the dial (it had Roman numerals on it, which was as old-fashioned here as it would have been in the home timeline) and listen to the ticking. "There are gears and springs inside to make it work?" he asked.

"That's right," Amanda said. The locals knew about such things. The ones in the watch were smaller and finer than any they could turn out for themselves, though.

"How is it that no one else can make such things?" Lucio Claudio inquired.

"That's our trade secret," Amanda answered, not quite comfortably. "Everyone who makes or sells things has trade secrets. Others would steal if we didn't." People stole in the home timeline. They stole in every alternate ever found. They were people, after all. They had an easier time here than some places. No one in Agrippan Rome had ever thought of patent laws.

"Only you," the local said musingly. "How very lucky for you. I wonder if we should not ask for a report—an official report, mind you—on how you came to be so lucky."

Alarm trickled through Amanda. Official reports were trouble. They meant the ponderous bureaucracy of Agrippan Rome had noticed the crosstime traders. Amanda supposed that was bound to happen sooner or later. She wished it hadn't happened while she was here. It would make life a lot more complicated.

Letting Lucio Claudio see that wouldn't help. "If the city prefect asks us for an official report, I'm sure we'll give him one," Amanda said. "In the meantime, do you want to buy the hour-reckoner for the most illustrious Gaio Fulvio?"

Lucio Claudio's nickname meant *dark*. His scowl certainly lived up to it. Why? Had he hoped the threat of an official report would scare Amanda? (It did, even if she didn't show it.) He looked at the pocket watch again. "Yes, the most illustrious nobleman does want it," he said. He wasn't nearly so good at hiding unhappiness as Amanda was. "What is your price?"

"You know you've chosen the finest hour-reckoner we have," Amanda said. She vastly preferred a plain old five-benjamin wristwatch herself, but nobody'd asked her. "That one costs five hundred modii of wheat." A modio—in classical Latin, a modius—was a little less than nine liters.

"That is too much," Gaio Fulvio's man said. "The most illustrious nobleman will give you two hundred fifty modii." Haggling was a way of life here. Offering half the opening price was a standard opening move—so standard, it was boring.

But Amanda shook her head. "I am sorry, sir. Our prices are firm. You will have heard that, I think." Lucio Claudio scowled again, which meant he had heard it. He just hadn't believed it. Amanda added, "We have fixed prices for all our hour-reckoners. If the most illustrious Gaio Fulvio would like something cheaper—"

That did it. She'd hoped it would. The locals were vain. They showed off, and took pride in showing off. Lucio Claudio turned red. "No!" he snapped. "Nothing but the best, the finest, for the most illustrious nobleman. Your price is outrageous, but he will pay it."

Yes, he would have tried to dicker more if he hadn't known about the fixed-price policy. Amanda hid a snicker, imagining how Gaio Fulvio would have lost face if he'd gone out in public with a cheap watch. She said, "I thank you, and I thank the most illustrious nobleman. I will write out a contract for the sale—"

"You write the classical tongue? You read it?" Lucio Claudio said.

"Oh, yes, sir," Amanda answered. "Many merchants do. It helps us in our business." Literacy wasn't all that unusual in Agrippan Rome. In a town like Polisso, perhaps a quarter of the men had their letters. More knew neoLatin than the old language, though.

"But you are a girl—a woman—a female," Gaio Fulvio's man sputtered. Far fewer women could read and write, even in neoLatin. It was a sexist society, no doubt about it. And neoLatin wasn't valid for most business deals, which made life harder still.

Amanda enjoyed poking just because the society was so sexist. "I am a merchant," she said proudly.

The pen, like most, was a reed with a hand-carved nib. Penknives really were *pen* knives here. Amanda neatly printed a standard sales contract. She gave it to Lucio Claudio to sign.

He read it over, looking for anything wrong. To his obvious disappointment, he found nothing. "Let me have the pen," he said, and scrawled his name in the space she'd left for it.

"I hope the most illustrious nobleman gets good use from his hour-reckoner," Amanda said, letting him down easy. Not too easy, though: "He can have it as soon as he pays."

"Of course. Payment will come to you soon. I'm sure he will be pleased to carry the hour-reckoner." Lucio Claudio got out of there in a hurry. Amanda closed the door behind him, then went back to finish her breakfast.

A skinny stray dog gnawed at something in a pile of garbage near Polisso's main square. It growled as Jeremy and his family walked by. When they didn't bother it, it lowered its head again.

"Poor pup," Amanda said.

She was right. By the standards of anybody from the home timeline, everybody here was poor. Jeremy knew all the things the locals didn't have. But *they* didn't know, and so it didn't bother them. Some of them thought they were rich. They tried to keep what they had, and to get more. The ones who didn't have so much wished for more, schemed for more. People, again.

In the square and in the roofed colonnades to either side, farmers and craftsmen and traders sold everything under the sun. Here a man hawked cups. Another man carried a tray of sweet rolls and shouted about how good they were. A craftsman displayed wooden buckets on a stand. A storyteller told a fable about the Emperor Agrippa and the beautiful Queen of China. Agrippa had never gone anywhere near China, but that didn't stop the storyteller. Every so often, someone would toss a coin into the bowl at his feet. A blank-faced peasant woman stood behind a big basket of onions she'd carried from her farm. Come evening, she'd go home with the ones she hadn't sold.

On the far side of the square stood the prefect's palace and the temple to the spirit of the Emperor. The clerks and secretaries and nobles who ran Polisso worked in the prefect's palace. Soldiers stood guard in front of it. Nobody was going to give the rulers any trouble. Just for a moment, Jeremy remembered the guards in front of the Crosstime Traffic office in Moigrad.

Dad pointed to the temple. "We'll make our offering. We'll get our certificate. Then nobody will worry about us any more."

"That sounds good to me," Jeremy said. They were in public, so he couldn't come out with what he really thought. He felt like a hypocrite, sacrificing to a spirit he didn't believe in. Dad insisted that hypocrisy greased the wheels between people. *If you always said just what you thought, nobody could stand you,* he'd say. *And you'd hate everybody who did it to you.* Jeremy wasn't convinced.

A big blond man in a linen shirt with billowing sleeves and baggy breeches tucked into boots held up some furs. "You want pelts?" he asked in accented neoLatin. That accent and his clothes showed he came from Lietuva. "Make fine fur jacket. Marten? Sable? Ermine?"

"No, thank you." Jeremy tried not to look at the pelts as he walked by. He couldn't have been much more revolted if the Lietuvan had tried to sell him a slave. No one in the home timeline had worn furs for more than fifty years. The mere idea turned his stomach. True, furs were warm, and this alternate had no substitutes. But Jeremy couldn't get over his disgust—and he couldn't sell pelts in the home timeline anyway. He sneaked glances at his sister and his parents. They all had that same tight-lipped look. They were trying not to show what they thought, too, then.

Up the stairs of the temple they went. The guards nodded to them. "In the name of the gods, greetings," one of the soldiers called.

"Greetings to you," Dad replied. He didn't have to mention the gods. That wasn't the custom for what Agrippan Rome called Imperial Christians. He went on, "We've just come to Polisso. We need to make an offering to the Emperor's spirit."

"Go ahead, then, and peace go with you," the guard said.

Before they entered the temple itself, they paused in an anteroom called the narthex. Several clerks stood there behind lecterns. Only the very most important people here worked sitting down. Dad steered the family to a clerk who was talking to a woman and had no one else waiting in line. That did him less good than he'd thought it would. The woman had a complicated problem, and took what seemed like forever to get it settled.

"You pick the shortest line, you take the longest time," Mom said. "It's just as true here as it is at home."

"I know," Dad said gloomily. "You wish some of the rules would change when you travel, but they don't." The locals who might overhear him would think he meant traveling from town to town. His own family knew better.

At last, the woman flounced off. Jeremy didn't think she'd settled anything. She seemed to be giving up. The clerk spent the next couple of minutes making notes on her case—or, for all Jeremy knew, doodling. Only after he'd used that time showing how important he was, did he look up and ask, "And how may I be of assistance to you?"—in classical Latin.

Most newcomers wouldn't have understood him. They would have had to ask him to repeat himself in neoLatin. He would have done it—and looked down his pointy nose at them while he was doing it. But Dad answered in the classical language: "Having arrived at the famous city of Porolissum"—using the ancient name was especially snooty—"we should like to make a thanks-offering to the spirit of the Emperor."

"Oh." Upstaged, the clerk seemed to shrink a few centimeters. "All right. Give me your name and the day you came into town." That was in neoLatin. Since he couldn't score points with the old language, he stopped using it. Dad also returned to the modern tongue. The clerk went off to a wooden box full of papers and parchments and papyri. He finally found the one he wanted. "Ioanno, called Acuto; Ieremeo, called Alto; Melissa; and Amanda. Yes, you are all here, and as described." He didn't seem happy about that. Dad had proved more clever than he would have liked. "You are Imperial Christians?"

"That's right," Dad said.

"Then you will offer incense, not a living sacrifice?"

"Yes," Dad said.

"Very well. That is permitted." By the way the clerk sounded, he wished it weren't. But he didn't decide such things. He just did what the people set over him told him to do. After scribbling several notes on his forms, he said, "You do understand, though, that you will pay as large a fee for the incense as people who believe in the usual gods pay for a sacrificial animal?"

"Yes," Dad said again, this time with resignation. *Why wouldn't the government tolerate Imperial Christians?* Jeremy thought. *It makes money off them.*

"The fee for four pinches of incense, then, is twelve denari," the clerk said. Dad paid. As far as Jeremy was concerned, the rip-off was enough to incense anyone. The clerk wrote some more. He handed Dad a scrap of parchment.

"Here is your receipt. Keep it in your home in a safe place. It is proof that you have offered sacrifice." He pulled four tiny earthenware bowls from a cabinet behind him and handed one to each member of the Solters family. The bowls held, literally, a pinch of waxy incense apiece. "You may proceed into the sacred precinct. Set the bowls on the altar, light the incense, and offer the customary prayer. Next!"

That last was aimed at the woman standing behind the crosstime travelers. The clerk reminded Jeremy of someone who worked for the Department of Motor Vehicles, not a man who had anything to do with holiness. But then, for most people here religion was as much something the government took care of as roads and public baths.

As he walked into the temple proper, he brought the bowl up to his nose so he could sniff. The incense smelled faintly— very faintly—spicy. It was, no doubt, as cheap and as mixed with other things as it could be and still burn.

Sunbeams slanting in through tall windows lit up the interior of the temple. Mosaics on the walls and statues in niches showed every god the Agrippan Romans recognized, from Aphrodite and Ares to Zalmoxis and Zeus. One small statue pictured Jesus as a beardless youth carrying a lamb on his back. That kind of portrait had gone out of favor in Jeremy's world, but not here. Here, for most people, Jesus was just one god among many. Mithras the Bull-slayer had a more impressive image.

One of the sunbeams fell on the bust of the Roman Emperor behind the altar. Honorio Prisco III was a middle-aged man with a big nose, jowls, and a bored expression. As far as Jeremy could tell, he wasn't a very good Emperor. He wasn't a very bad Emperor, either. He just sort of sat there.

The sunbeam also highlighted a line around his neck that looked unnatural. The lower neck and top part of the chest on the bust never changed. The head and upper neck did whenever a new Emperor took the throne. A peg and socket held the two parts of the bust together. A new Emperor? Take the old ruler's portrait off the peg, pop on the new. There you were, easy as pie, ready to be loyal.

Several pinches of incense already smoked on the altar. Off to one side, a priest in a white toga—only priests wore togas these days—wrung the neck of a dove for a man who wasn't a Christian of any sort.

Dad set his incense bowl on the altar. Jeremy and Amanda and Mom followed suit. Several lamps burned on the altar. By each one stood a bowl full of thin dry twigs. Each member of the family took a twig and lit it at a lamp. They used the burning twigs to light their incense, then stamped them out underfoot.

Four thin twists of gray smoke curled upward. Along with his parents and sister, Jeremy said the prayer required of Imperial Christians: "May God keep the Emperor safe and healthy. May his spirit always be the spirit of truth and justice. Amen." They all bowed to the bust of Honorio Prisco III, then turned away from the altar.

That prayer didn't say the Emperor was divine. It did say that the people who made it cared about him and wished him well. It was hardly religious at all, not in the sense Jeremy would have used the word back home. It was more like pledging allegiance to the flag. It showed that the people who did it willingly took part in the customs of this country.

Not far from the altar, two ordinary-looking men stood talking in low voices. They weren't being rude. They were quietly making sure the prayers were made the way they were supposed to be. People who didn't like being watched couldn't have stood living in Agrippan Rome.

That was one of the traders' biggest problems here. The locals weren't just curious. They were snoopy. About everything. Jeremy glanced over at Amanda as the family left the temple. That fellow to whom she'd sold the blue-plate special—that was how he thought of the big blue pocket watches—had talked about making them submit one of the Empire's dreaded official reports about how they could turn out such things when nobody else here knew how. Dad would have to figure out a way around that.

Out in the market square, a herald was shouting, "Hear ye! Hear ye! The great and mighty Emperor of the Romans, Honorio Prisco III, has declared that the Roman Empire will keep the peace with the Kingdom of Lietuva for as long as King Kuzmickas chooses to keep it!"

"What's that supposed to mean?" Jeremy asked. "It doesn't sound like it means anything." A lot of the proclamations the government put out didn't sound as if they meant anything.

But Dad said, "It means we're liable to have a war. Lietuva has wanted to take this province away from Rome for years. And if King Kuzmickas does decide to go to war, the Emperor is saying he'll get all the fight he wants."

Border provinces like Dacia did sometimes change hands between Agrippan Rome and Lietuva. In the Middle East, Mesopotamia—Iraq in the home timeline—and Syria went back and forth between the Romans and Persians every so often. But the heartland of each great empire was too far from its neighbors to be conquered. The ruling dynasties might change, but the empires went on and on.

Oddly, gunpowder made that more true, not less. Hearing

as much had puzzled Jeremy at first. But it made sense if you looked at it the right way. Cannons could knock down the strongest fortress or city wall. And cannons, here, were also very, very expensive. Only central governments pulling in taxes from huge tracts of land could afford to have a lot of them. That meant anybody who rebelled against the central government was likely to lose. He wouldn't be able to get his hands on enough cannons to fight back well.

There had been gunpowder empires in Jeremy's world, too. The Ottoman Turks, the Moguls in India, and the Manchus in China had all run states like that. In his world, though, Europe had had lots of countries, not one big, overarching empire. They'd competed, kicking technology and thought ahead and leading to the scientific and industrial revolutions.

Competition here was weaker. The dead hand of the past was stronger. *This is how they did it in the good old days* carried enormous weight in Agrippan Rome . . . and in Lietuva, and in Persia, and in the two gunpowder empires that split India between them in this alternate, and in China. The Japanese here were pirates who raided China's coast, the same as the Scandinavians did in Europe.

A beggar with a horrible sore on his face held out a skinny hand to Jeremy and whined, "Alms, gentle sir?"

Jeremy gave him a sestertio, a little copper coin. "That was a mistake," Dad said with a sigh.

"How come?" Jeremy asked. "Look what happened to the poor man."

"For one thing, that sore is probably a fake," Dad said. "And if it's not a fake, he probably picks at it and rubs salt in it to keep it looking nasty. Beggars' tricks are as old as time. And for another . . . Well, you'll find out."

And Jeremy did, in short order. He'd given one beggar money. All the other beggars in the market square hurried toward him. He might have been a magnet and they bits of iron. They showed off blind eyes, missing hands and feet, and sores even uglier than the first man's had been. None of them had bathed in weeks, if not years. Most of them called for coppers. Some, the bolder ones, screeched for silver.

"I can't give them all money," Jeremy said in dismay.

"Which is why you shouldn't have given it to any of them," Dad said. "Just keep walking. They'll get the message."

Little by little, the beggars did. By ones and twos, they drifted back toward their places in the square. Some of them cursed Jeremy, as much for getting their hopes up as for not giving them any coins. Others didn't bother. They might as well have been merchants. If business in one place didn't suit them, they'd look somewhere else.

"Did they try to slit your belt pouch?" Dad asked.

After checking, Jeremy shook his head. "No."

"You're lucky."

"I *am* lucky," Jeremy said slowly. He didn't mean it the way his father did. "I don't have to live the way they do." A day in Polisso taught more about human misery than a year in Los Angeles. "Most of what's wrong with them, a doctor back home could fix in a hurry. I've always had plenty to eat, and a house with a heater that works."

"Coming here can make you feel guilty about living the way we do at home," Amanda said.

Jeremy nodded. That was what he'd been trying to say. His sister had done a better job of putting it into a few words.

"There's nothing wrong with the way we live," Dad said. "Anybody who says poverty makes you noble has never been poor—really poor, the way these people are. But you were right. We are lucky that we don't have to live like this all the time."

"Yeah," Jeremy said. Even when they were in Polisso, they didn't live just like the locals. They had links back to the home timeline. If something went wrong, they could get help or leave. They had a swarm of immunizations. They couldn't come down with smallpox or measles or typhoid fever or cholera. Smallpox didn't even exist any more in the home timeline. They had antibiotics against tuberculosis and plague. The locals didn't—they had doctors who believed in the four humors and priests who prayed. One was about as much use as the other—as much, or as little.

A drunk lurched out of a tavern. He stared around with bleary, bloodshot eyes, then sat down next to the doorway. He wasn't going anywhere, not any time soon. Some things didn't change from one timeline to another. Jeremy's also had its share of drunks, and probably always would.

"Make way! Make way! In the name of the city prefect, make way!" bawled a man with a loud voice.

Up the street came a gang of slaves carrying firewood to heat the water in the public baths. They were skinny, sorry-looking men, all of them burdened till they could barely stagger along. They belonged to Polisso, not to any one person. That made their lives worse, not better. Because they didn't serve anyone in particular, no one in particular cared how they were treated. The overseer shouted out his warning again.

Neither Jeremy nor anybody else in his family said much the rest of the way back to the house. That gang of slaves reminded them again all how lucky they really were.

Four

The smith's name was Mallio Sertorio. He used his dirty thumbnail to pull one tool after another out of the Swiss army knife. Big blade, small blade, file, corkscrew, awl . . . When he found the little scissors, an almost comic look of surprise spread over his face.

"How do they do that?" he muttered, more to himself than to Amanda.

"I am only a trader," she answered. "I do not have the secrets of the men who made these knives."

"Of course you don't—you're only a girl," Mallio Sertorio said. That wasn't what Amanda had said, and didn't endear him to her. He extracted a screwdriver blade. That puzzled him. Screws here were made by hand, and uncommon. But he poked at the blade with his thumb. "Fine workmanship. And very fine steel, too."

"We sell only the best." Amanda nodded.

"Oh, yes. Oh, yes." The smith nodded, too. "I want to buy this one and take it apart, to see if I can learn the secrets these fellows know." He pulled a tweezer out of its slot. "Isn't that clever?" he crooned.

"I'll be glad to sell it to you," Amanda said. "What you do with it afterwards is your business." She didn't think he would learn much. A couple of smiths in Polisso had already started selling imitation Swiss army knives. They were bigger and clumsier and held fewer tools.

"Do I have to pay grain?" Mallio Sertorio asked. "Grain is a nuisance. I'll give you silver. I'll even give you gold. You can buy grain yourself, or anything else you want."

"Grain is what we want," Amanda answered. Grain and other food from the alternates helped feed the crowded home timeline. Oil fed the petrochemical industry. The list went on and on.

"I have to have this," Mallio Sertorio said. "Do you understand? I *have* to have it. I am not a young man. You, you have your whole life ahead of you, but I am not young." He scratched at his mustache. Like his hair, it was grizzled. "I have spent thirty years learning my trade. I am good at it, as good as any man in Polisso, as good as any man in the whole province of Dacia."

"I'm sure you are," Amanda said softly. People in Agrippan Rome liked to swagger and brag. They often made themselves out to be richer or more clever or more skilled than they really were. This didn't sound like that. Mallio Sertorio was stating the facts as he saw them.

"Thirty years." The smith set down the Swiss army knife. His hands—hands callused from work and scarred by cuts and burns—bunched into fists. "Thirty years, and I see this, and I also see I might as well be an apprentice in my first day at a smithy. How did they *do* this work?"

Machinery your culture won't invent for quite a while, if it ever does, Amanda thought. But she couldn't tell him that. Instead, she had to repeat, "I don't know." She felt embarrassed, even a little ashamed. How was a man with nothing but hand tools supposed to match this mechanical near-perfection? And even if he did somehow do it once, how could he keep on doing it again and again?

Mallio Sertorio saw that, too. People in Agrippan Rome were ignorant, yes. They weren't stupid. He said, "You have dozens of these knives, don't you? Hundreds of them, even? But each one has to take months, maybe a year, to make. *How?*"

Amanda didn't say anything. She didn't see anything she could say. It probably wouldn't have mattered. Mallio Sertorio was talking to himself—to himself, and to the Swiss army knife. "How?" he said again. "Whatever the answer is, by the gods, I'll find it." He picked up the knife and held it out to Amanda. "I will buy this. Write me up a fancy contract in old-fashioned Latin. You want grain? I'll get you grain. I must have this. I've got so much to learn."

The smith had to make his mark on the contract. Amanda witnessed it. "You know how many modii of wheat?" she asked.

"Oh, yes," he answered. "I know numbers. Words—especially in the old language—words I'm not so good with."

At supper that evening—bread, cheese, and a stew of rabbit, onions, garlic, and parsnips—Amanda mentioned the smith's driving urge to know. Her mother nodded. She said, "That's one of the things we want here."

"You bet," Dad said. "That's why we sell them things that aren't impossibly far ahead of what they can make. There's a story about an African who saw an early airplane, but it didn't mean anything to him—it was magic. Then he saw a team of horses pulling a carriage. He laughed and clapped his hands and said, 'Why didn't I think of that?' It was beyond what his people knew how to do then, but not too far beyond. This culture has been stuck in a rut for a long time. Along with everything else we're doing, maybe we can help shake it loose."

"Then what happens?" Amanda asked.

"With luck, things go forward here," her father answered. "By themselves, gunpowder empires don't change very much or very fast. A poke here and a poke there, though, and who knows? In a few hundred years, this may be a different place." He sounded as if he were sure he would come back here to see the changes.

To Amanda, a few hundred years didn't begin to seem real. She had enough trouble trying to figure out where she'd be and what she'd do when she got out of high school year after next. She wasn't going to worry about whether Agrippan Rome had its own industrial revolution a long, long way down the line.

One of the reasons Jeremy's folks brought him and Amanda to Agrippan Rome with them was so they'd look normal. Everyone here expected grownups to have children. Who else could take over the family business after they were gone? That meant he and his sister had to go out into Polisso and do the things kids their age did here. They had to be seen doing them, too. If they weren't out there being visible, what point to bringing them along?

The trouble with that was, Jeremy didn't like most of what the kids his age in Polisso did. A lot of those kids were already working hard at their trades. When they weren't working, they gambled with dice or knucklebones. They played sports different from the ones he knew, and they didn't seem to care if they maimed one another. Or they went to the amphitheater. Jeremy didn't have the stomach for that.

Here, the Roman Empire had never lost its taste for blood

sports. People swarmed into the amphitheater to watch bears fight wolves. They gave condemned criminals to lions. Thousands cheered as what they called justice was done. And they set men against men. Gladiators who won their matches were heroes here, the way running backs and point guards were at home. Gladiators who didn't win were often dragged from the arena feet first.

People here said seeing bloodshed made for better soldiers. Of course, people here also said the sun went around the Earth. They said some men were slaves by nature. They said there were one-eyed men and men with their faces in the middle of their chests off in some distant corner of the world. They said the streets in China were paved with gold. (In China in this alternate, they said the streets in the Roman Empire were paved with jade. The Chinese were no less ignorant than anybody else.)

That Jeremy was a visitor in Polisso didn't make things any easier. People picked on him because he came from somewhere else. It could have been a farm more than ten kilometers from town as easily as Los Angeles in the home timeline. And Polisso had its street gangs, too.

Things could have been worse. By local standards, Jeremy was very large. That made some of the town's less charming inhabitants think twice. Unfortunately, they often hunted in packs.

As much as he could, he stayed out of the alleys and lanes that wound between the main streets. Anything could happen there. The bigger streets, on the other hand, were pretty well patrolled. Gangs mostly steered clear of men with muskets, armor, and short tempers.

Mostly, though, didn't mean always. And the vigili couldn't

be everywhere at once. Three locals came up to Jeremy on the street just around the corner from where he was staying. They were his age or a little older: one of them had the fair beginnings of a beard. None of them would ever belong to the Polisso Chamber of Commerce. The one with the shaggy chin said, "You're not from here, are you?"

That was a loaded question. If he said yes, they'd call him a liar and jump on him. If he said no, they'd call him a stranger—and jump on him. Even if none of them came up much past his chin, one against three made bad odds. Sometimes people didn't come back from summer trading runs. He said, "No," but then, before they could jump on him, "But I've got some new jokes from Carnuto." The town to the west was a reasonable place to say he'd come from.

And the prospect of jokes was enough to make the punks pause. They could find people to beat up any old time. Jokes were something else, something special. In a world without the Web, TV, radio, movies, and recorded music, entertainment was where you found it. "All right, let's hear 'em," said the gangbanger with the whiskers. The other two nodded, trying to look tough. Plainly, they followed his lead. He leaned forward and stuck out his jaw. He was better at being menacing than his pals. "They better be good."

"They are." Jeremy hoped he sounded more confident than he felt. The jokes came from a real Roman joke book called *The Laughter-Lover*. Dad had got it so the family could have jokes to tell that came from Rome, not from Los Angeles. Trouble was, by Los Angeles standards, they were some of the lamest jokes in the world. With luck, things were different here. Without luck . . .

"Go on, then," Whiskers said.

"A halfwit wanted to see what he looked like when he was asleep, so he stood in front of the mirror with his eyes closed."

Jeremy waited for the punks to commit literary criticism on his person. Instead, they grinned. They didn't laugh out loud, but they didn't start kicking him, either. The skinnier one of the pair behind Whiskers got up the nerve to speak for himself: "Tell us another one."

"Sure." Jeremy flogged his memory. "'That slave you sold me died yesterday,' a man told a halfwit. The halfwit said, 'By the gods, he never did anything like that when *I* owned him!'"

Whiskers did laugh this time, which seemed to be the cue for his pals to do the same. "Not bad," he said. "Keep going."

How many can I remember? Jeremy wondered. The ancient Roman joke book did seem better suited to Polisso than to Los Angeles. He brought out another one: "An astrologer cast a horoscope for a sick man and said, 'You'll live another twenty years.' The man said, 'Come back tomorrow, then, and I'll give you your fee.' 'But what happens if you die tonight?' the astrologer said."

They needed a couple of seconds to get it. When they did, though, they howled scandalized laughter. Despite common sense, some people in Los Angeles believed in astrology. Here, people *believed* in astrology. They didn't know all the things about the way the universe worked that people in the home time-line did. Astrology let them think they knew more than they did.

"Not bad," Whiskers said. "Not bad at all. I knew a guy like that. He said he knew everything there was to know, but he didn't even know his girl was seeing somebody else on the side. You got any others?"

"Sure." Jeremy told as many jokes as he remembered. Some got laughs. Some were groaners—but if you told a lot of jokes, some would always be groaners. The three punks slapped him on the back. Whiskers reached out and affectionately messed up his hair. After that, they paid him the best compliment they could—they went off and left him alone.

From then on, he knew he wouldn't worry when he haggled with people in Polisso. How important was haggling over money or grain, really? He'd just won a dicker for his own skin.

Mom dug a big blob of bread dough out of an earthenware bowl. She slammed it down on the countertop and started to knead it. Half a meter away, Amanda was chopping cabbage. There was an odd sort of pleasure in making the family's food from scratch. If it was good, you deserved all the credit. (If it wasn't, you deserved all the blame. Amanda didn't like to think about that. *If I make it, it* will *be good,* she told herself.)

Pleasure or not, making food from scratch was much more work than cooking at home. No microwaves here. No computerized ovens that did everything but blow out the candles on a birthday cake. They had a wood-burning oven for baking, and the fireplace for soups and stews and for roasting. That was it.

Mom paused. "I'm going to bring in a stool," she said. "I'm sick and tired of standing up."

"It's all right with me." Amanda hoped she didn't show how startled she was. Local women always worked standing up in the kitchen. Always. And Mom had always been a stickler for doing things the way people here did them. To see her changing her ways was a surprise.

Even after she got the stool, she didn't seem comfortable. She kept shifting her weight, leaning now this way, now that. Watching her made Amanda nervous.

Finally, when she couldn't stand it any more, she asked, "Are you all right, Mom?"

"I'm fine," her mother said quickly. Too quickly? Her right hand rubbed her stomach and got bits of cabbage on her tunic. "I've had kind of a stomach ache the last couple of days, though."

"Probably getting used to what Polisso calls food again," Amanda said.

"I guess so," Mom said, but then she contradicted herself: "It doesn't feel like that." She shrugged then. "I don't know what else it could be." She went back to kneading what would be a loaf. If the dough wasn't well kneaded, the bread would be dense and chewy.

"Antibiotics don't always get everything," Amanda said. You could catch almost anything from food in Polisso. The only way to be perfectly safe would have been not to eat or drink. Unfortunately, that had drawbacks of its own.

"It doesn't feel like food poisoning," her mother said. "Only an ache. It's not bad. Just—annoying." She hardly ever complained. When she did, Amanda worried.

But there wasn't time for much worrying. There wasn't time for anything except chores from dawn till dusk: cooking and washing and cleaning and doing business. After the bread went into the oven, you couldn't walk away and forget about it till it was done. No thermostats here. Amanda had to watch the fire and feed wood into it at the right rate to keep it from getting too high or too low. Otherwise, the loaves would come out scorched or soggy. Either way, they wouldn't be worth eating. All the work that went into making them, starting with grinding grain into flour, would be wasted.

Mom used a flat wooden peel to slide the loaves out of the

oven: the same tool a cook at a pizza place used in the home timeline. After the bread had cooled, Amanda ate a piece. She wished she could have said it was far better than anything she could get at home because she'd helped make it herself. She wished she could, but she couldn't. It was gritty. The quern that ground the grain was made of stone, and tiny bits of it got into the flour. The bread was also coarse-grained; the quern didn't grind as fine as modern milling machines. And, in spite of everything, it had stayed in the oven a couple of minutes too long. It was okay, but nothing to get excited about.

Her mother had some, too. Amanda watched to see if she had trouble eating. She didn't seem to, even if she also looked disappointed at how the bread turned out. Amanda asked, "How do you feel?"

"I'm all right," Mom answered. "Like I said, a nuisance, that's all."

"Have you told Dad?"

"Yes, I've told your father. He's the one who wouldn't tell me. He wouldn't want me to worry." Mom rolled her eyes. "I don't want him to worry, either, but I want him to know what's going on."

"What if it . . . really is something?" Amanda didn't want to say that. She didn't even want to think it. She knew something about loss. Two of her grandparents had died. But Mom and Dad were different. They were supposed to *be there,* no matter what; they were the rocks at the bottom of her world.

Part of Amanda knew her parents were people. She knew things could happen to people. The rest of her recoiled from that like a nervous horse shying from a rattler. Move the rocks at the bottom of the world and you made an earthquake.

Mom came over and gave her a hug. "The very worst that

can happen is that I go back to the home timeline for a little while and get it fixed, whatever it is. Then I come back here again. Okay?"

"Okay." Amanda hugged her back, hard. She was very, very glad for the transposition chamber down in the subbasement here, just in case. Doctors in Agrippan Rome not only didn't know anything, they didn't even suspect anything. The really scary part was, they were better than doctors other places in this world. Roman doctors got fat salaries teaching medicine in Lietuva and Persia.

That evening, Jeremy got into an argument with Mom over nothing in particular. He would do that every once in a while, mostly because he couldn't stand admitting he might be wrong. He was right most of the time. That made it harder for him to see he was wrong some of the time. It also made him a first-class pain in the neck.

And tonight, it made Amanda furious. "You leave Mom alone!" she yelled at him. "Don't you know anything?"

Nothing made Jeremy madder than even hinting that he was dumb. "I know what a miserable pest you are," he said.

He would have gone on from there, too, but Dad held up a hand. "That will be enough of that," he said. "That will be enough of that out of both of you, as a matter of fact. There are four of us here, and thousands of people in Polisso. If we can't count on each other, we may as well go home."

It wasn't that he was wrong. He was right, and Amanda knew it. And he knew Mom wasn't feeling right, so he'd taken that into account. But so did Jeremy. And he kept steaming. He hadn't said all he wanted to, and he was itching to let out the rest. He pointed at Amanda. "She started it."

"That's the oldest excuse in the world—in any world,"

Dad said. "She got the first word, you got the last word, and that's plenty. If it goes on from there, the only thing you'll both do is get angrier. What's the use? Answer me, please."

Jeremy didn't. Maybe he wanted to. He probably did, in fact. But arguing with Dad was usually like playing chess against the computer at the high level. You could try it, and it would make good practice, and you'd even learn something, but you wouldn't win.

Mom sat quietly through the whole thing. She often did during squabbles. Dad enjoyed stamping on fires, and she didn't. But she seemed *too* quiet tonight.

Or maybe I'm imagining things, Amanda thought. She knew she sometimes borrowed trouble. She couldn't help it, any more than Jeremy could help being a know-it-all. But she feared this trouble didn't need borrowing. It was really here.

Most of the house the merchants from Crosstime Traffic used would have seemed ordinary to the people of Polisso. Most, but not all. That was why they had no servants. Servants would have seen things that couldn't be explained to anybody from this alternate. The basement and subbasement were cases in point.

Part of the basement wouldn't have seemed strange to the locals. A lot of houses here had storerooms under them. This one did, too, but its were different.

Jeremy took a lamp with him when he went down the wooden steps into the storeroom that held sacks of grain, baskets of onions, strings of garlic, and big clay jars full of olive oil and wine and the fermented fish sauce that went into every kind of cooking here the way soy sauce and salsa did back home. As usual, the lamp didn't defeat darkness. It did push back the hem of its black cloak. Jeremy could walk around without banging his head.

There was a smooth patch on the wall above one particular jar of wine. Jeremy let his hand rest on it for a moment. Software scanned his palmprint and fingerprints. A well-camouflaged door silently slid open. The camouflage was all the better down here, with only lamplight to see by.

As soon as Jeremy walked through the door, it closed behind him. Real lights, electric lights, came on in the ceiling. High-capacity batteries powered them—and everything else down here. The flickering flame of the lamp was suddenly next to invisible. Jeremy blew it out. He would light it again when he left the basement.

The wall behind the palm lock was reinforced concrete. So was the ceiling. The locals might be able to blow them open, but they wouldn't have an easy time of it. The subbasement where the transposition chamber came and went had another layer of shielding. But the most important shield was making sure nobody in Polisso suspected the house had a special basement, let alone a subbasement.

On a table sat a PowerBook. It was sleeping to save power. Jeremy touched a key to rouse the laptop. It was the house's link to the home timeline and all the alternates Crosstime Traffic visited. "Michael Fujikawa," he said into the microphone, and then an eight-digit number that defined the alternate where his friend was spending the summer.

"Go ahead," the computer told him.

"You around, Michael?" Jeremy asked. "It's me, Jeremy." He didn't really expect that Michael would be there. North China, where his parents traded, was six hours ahead of Romania. Michael would probably be snoring in the wee small hours. "How's it with you? What you been up to? Give me a yell when you get a chance. 'Bye."

The PowerBook turned Jeremy's spoken words into written ones. Text took up a lot less bandwidth to send than voice did. Jeremy knew he ought to go back up into the world of Agrippan Rome. Instead, he started a game. The computer, which was playing the aliens invading Earth, was knocking the snot out of him when the incoming-message bell rang.

"Quit. Don't save," Jeremy said with relief. The twisted World War II vanished from the screen. He wouldn't lose tonight, anyway. A human player would have screamed at him for grabbing the excuse to bail out. The PowerBook didn't care.

Words formed on the monitor. *Hey, Jeremy,* Michael said. *Good to hear from you. I was wondering when I would.*

"We've been getting settled in," Jeremy said. "You could have messaged me, too, you know. And what are you doing up so early?"

Sunrise ceremony today—yawn, Michael answered. *We've been busy, same as you. It happens. How's business?*

"Pretty good," Jeremy said. "The locals are starting to wonder how come we can do things they can't, though. One of them gave my sister a hard time about it. They may start trying to snoop harder. That wouldn't be so good, not when traders have spent so much time making connections here."

If you have to pull out, you have to pull out. Plenty of alternates, and they're all easy to get to. Crosstime will find one that's not too different, and you'll start over. Michael could be practical to the point of cynicism.

"I suppose so." Jeremy knew Crosstime Traffic had had to abandon some alternates. Most of those had technology a lot higher than Agrippan Rome's, though. And that wasn't really what was on his mind, anyhow. After a pause, he said, "Other thing that's been going on here is, Mom doesn't feel good."

What's wrong? The question came back at once. Michael had spent so much time at the Solters' house, Mom sometimes seemed to be almost as much his mother as Jeremy's.

"Some kind of stomach trouble," Jeremy said.

Something she ate?

"Maybe. I hope so. That would be the easiest to fix and the least to worry about," Jeremy answered. As he spoke, the dictation program on the PowerBook put his worries on the monitor, where he could see them as well as think them. He didn't like that. It made them seem more real. When he said, "The antibiotics she took didn't do much," the words on the screen took on a frightening importance.

They also must have seemed important to Michael, who was reading them not just in another place but in another universe. *That doesn't sound so good,* he said. *Do you think she'll have to go back to the home line to get it looked at?*

"I don't know," Jeremy said. On the monitor, that looked very bald and very helpless. "As long as she's all right, nothing else matters."

Sure, Michael replied. *Listen, tell her I hope she's feeling better.* He wasn't somebody who talked for the sake of being polite. What he said, he meant. He went on: *I wish I were close enough to do something. You let me know what's going on, you hear? You don't, you're in big trouble when I see you this fall.*

"I will," Jeremy said. "Thanks." Michael wouldn't tell him anything like, *If you need somebody to talk to, I'm here.* Coming right out with something like that would only embarrass both of them. But there were ways to get the message across without saying the words.

Take care of yourself. I've got to go. The rising sun is call-ing me. Like Jeremy, Michael took part in rituals he didn't fully believe in. The locals believed in them, and that was what counted.

"You watch yourself, too." Jeremy waited for an answer . . . and waited, and waited. Michael really had gone, then. Jeremy softly said something else—softly, but not quite softly enough. The words formed on the PowerBook's screen. He laughed. "Erase last six," he said, and they disappeared.

He wanted to say something that would make the monitor burst into flames. But that wouldn't help, either, even if it might make him feel better for a little while. He didn't know what would help. He didn't know if anything would help.

He was seventeen. He took care of most things on his own. Some of them, his folks never found out about. Taking care of your own troubles—learning how to take care of your own troubles—was a big part of what growing up was about. But having Mom and Dad there as backups felt awfully good. And when the trouble was that something was wrong with one of them . . . He said some more things he had to tell the computer to erase.

A water jug on her hip, Amanda walked down the street to the public fountain a couple of blocks from her house. She didn't have to bring water back, not when it was piped into the place. But she or Mom went every few days anyway. Women didn't just fill up their jars and walk away. They stood around and chatted, the way men were more likely to do in the market square. Locals said *I heard it by the fountain* when they meant *I heard it through the grapevine.*

The last couple of times, Mom had sent Amanda to get water and listen to the chatter. Mom liked to go herself. That she stayed home gnawed at Amanda. Mom kept insisting everything was all right now. Trouble was, she didn't act as if everything were all right.

A girl about Amanda's own age came out of a house not far from the fountain. "Hello, Maria," Amanda said. "How are you this morning?" She'd got to know the local the last time her family was in Polisso.

"I'm fine, thank you, Mistress Amanda," Maria answered. She was short and skinny and dark. She had a delicately arched nose and front teeth that stuck out and spoiled her looks. In the home timeline, braces would have fixed that. Here, she was stuck with it. Her smile was sweet even so. "God bless you," she told Amanda. She was a Christian, and not one of the Imperial sort. She clung tight to her beliefs, not least because she had little else to cling to. She was a slave.

"What do you know?" Amanda said uncomfortably. She had tried and failed to imagine what it would be like to own somebody, or to be owned. If the prosperous potter Maria belonged to ever ran short of cash, he could sell her as if she were a second-hand car. And he could visit indignities on her no car ever suffered. Under local law, every bit of that was legal, too.

"I know God loves me." Maria did sound convinced of it. Maybe believing that helped keep her from fretting about her fate in this world. She went on, "And I know my master is worrying about the godless Lietuvans again."

"Is he?" Amanda said. Maria nodded. The Lietuvans weren't really godless. But they did have their own gods. They didn't much like the traditional Roman deities. And they really didn't like the Christian God. In Lietuva, Christians still became martyrs. There weren't many of them there. The handful who did live in the kingdom lived secretly, and in fear. Even in Amanda's world, Lithuania had been the last European country to accept Christianity.

Maria said, "He thinks they will go to war with the Empire. There have been more Lietuvan merchants and traders in town than usual. He says they are all spies."

The guard at the gate had talked about Lietuvan spies when Amanda and her family came into Polisso. Had he known something? Or had the city prefect or the garrison commander started worrying for no good reason? That could make everybody in town jumpy.

"Why doesn't your family have any servants, Amanda?" Maria asked. "You traders must be rich. You could afford them. Then you wouldn't have to do work like this." She didn't say *a slave's work*—it wasn't, or wasn't always, anyhow—but she meant something like that.

"We like taking care of things for ourselves," Amanda answered. It was an un-Roman attitude, but she couldn't explain the real reasons.

Maria looked puzzled. "But you don't mind doing this?" She sounded puzzled, too.

"It's just something that needs doing," Amanda said. If it were something she had to do every day of her life, she probably wouldn't have felt that way about it. It wouldn't just have been work. It would have been drudgery. Most of the year, she didn't have to worry about it. Maria did.

Other women at the fountain were talking about the Lietuvans, too. Maybe that meant there was something to Maria's master's alarm. Maybe it just meant they'd all heard the same rumors. Either way, Amanda knew she'd have to tell her folks about it. They didn't want to get trapped in a war.

A lot of the chatter at the fountain, though, could have happened in front of the lockers at Canoga Park High. The women and girls talked about who was seeing whom. They talked about who was cheating on whom. They traded news on where the prices were good, and on who had the best stuff. A couple of them asked Amanda about the mirrors her family was selling.

"How do they give such good reflections?" a plump woman asked. "Nobody in town has ever seen anything like them."

Amanda went into her song and dance about buying the mirrors from people who lived a long way away. The less she admitted knowing about them, the fewer really pointed questions she'd get.

"It's too bad you won't tell," the plump woman said.

"Oh, leave her alone, Lavinia," another woman said. "You mean to tell me your kin haven't got any trade secrets?"

"Well, of course we do," Lavinia said. "But not everybody's so interested in ours."

That made Amanda want to fill up her jar and get back to the house as fast as she could. But the women took turns, and cutting ahead would get her talked about much more—and much more nastily—than any trade secrets. She had to wait and smile and pretend she didn't know what Lavinia was talking about.

While she was waiting, though, Jeremy came up the street calling, "Amanda! Amanda, come home quick!"

Ice ran through her. "What's the matter?" she said, afraid she already knew the answer.

Her brother didn't come right out and say it, not in front of all the women. He did say, "Mom needs you," in a way that could only mean one thing.

"I'm coming." Amanda started away without a backwards glance.

Quietly, Maria called, "I'll pray for you," after her. Amanda had told her Mom wasn't feeling well. The rest of the women would soon know the same thing.

Once Amanda got out of earshot of them, she asked, "What is it? How bad is it?"

"Dad thinks it's her appendix," Jeremy answered. "All the pain is here now." He rested his hand between his right hipbone and his belly button, then went on, "She'll have to go back and have it out. That's not something to take care of here. They're sending a chamber now, down in the subbasement. He'll go back with her, then come here again as soon as she's okay."

Amanda nodded. "That's fine. We can manage by ourselves for a couple of days, or whatever it takes. I just want to make sure Mom's all right."

Her mother didn't look all right, or anywhere close to it. By the dark circles under her eyes, the pain wasn't just in one place now. It was worse than it had been, maybe a lot worse. But she tried hard to stay cheerful. She kissed Amanda and said, "I'll be fine. If it is appendicitis, they won't have any trouble fixing it once I get back to the home timeline."

Dad and Jeremy and Amanda all helped her down to the subbasement. The chamber appeared in the room fifteen minutes later. Dad and the operator eased Mom inside. Dad said, "I'll send a message as soon as we know for sure, and I'll be back as fast as I can."

"Okay," Amanda and Jeremy said together. The chamber door slid shut. A moment later, the chamber disappeared. Amanda looked at Jeremy. He was looking back at her. For a little while, they were on their own.

Five

Jeremy thought people were looking at him. He had to go out in Polisso and pretend everything was normal. Mom and Dad had been gone for only a few hours. Jeremy felt as if his shield against the world were gone, too. Responsibilities weighed a million kilos. If he made a bad mistake, he couldn't pass any part of it on to someone else. It was *his*.

And he worried about Mom. Appendicitis was something simple enough to fix on the home timeline. But all the same, even doctors said the only minor surgery was surgery you didn't have to have. If something went wrong . . . Or if it turned out not to be appendicitis, but something worse . . .

He wouldn't think about that. He told himself so, again and again. It was like trying not to think of a green-and-orange zebra. You could tell yourself you wouldn't. You could tell yourself all sorts of things. The thought kept returning just the same.

"Furs! I have fine furs!" a Lietuvan trader shouted. Jeremy kept on walking through the market square. He didn't want furs. He wanted to tell the Lietuvan what he thought of him for selling them. He couldn't. A real Agrippan Roman might not have bought fur, but he wouldn't have minded anyone selling it.

And the locals call the Lietuvans barbarians, Jeremy thought. *They're more alike than they are different.*

They had reason to be, of course. Rome and Lietuva had lived next door to each other for a thousand years. They'd fought wars against each other. They'd traded. Ideas had gone across their border along with trade goods. NeoLatin had words for things like *amber* and *wax* and *slave* that were borrowed from Lietuvan. Lietuvan had more words taken from classical Latin and neoLatin: a whole host of technical terms, as well as words like *wine* and *wheel* and *ship*.

Another Lietuvan in a fur jacket called, "Here! You are a young man! Buy yourself a slave girl! She's well trained. She'll do what you tell her." He leered.

The girl he pointed at was blond and skinny and broad-faced, with high cheekbones. She couldn't have been more than twelve years old. Her threadbare tunic was filthy. She didn't look well trained. She looked scared to death.

"You want her?" the Lietuvan asked. "I'll give you a good price."

"No." Again, Jeremy kept on walking. Behind him, the Lietuvan said something in his own language. Whatever it was, it wasn't praise. Jeremy didn't care. He discovered he'd only thought being offered furs was disgusting. Now he found the real thing. If he gave the trader enough silver, the fellow would sell him the girl.

He couldn't. Dealing in slaves, even to set them free, was as illegal as could be for crosstime traders. Setting her free wouldn't do her much of a favor, anyhow. What was called freedom here was often only the freedom to starve. Keeping her was just as much out of the question. She would ask questions the traders couldn't answer, see things she wasn't supposed to see, and learn things the locals shouldn't know. Whatever happened to her would just have to happen.

"Good luck," Jeremy whispered. She would need it. He hoped she got an easy master. There were some: quite a few, in fact. That wasn't really the problem with slavery. The problem with slavery was that there *were* masters, period.

"Plums! Peaches! Who'll buy my plums and peaches?" a peasant woman called. She wore a bright scarf wrapped around her head. Years of weathering had left her cheeks almost the same color as the plums in her basket. The peaches here were smaller and paler than the ones Jeremy knew from the home timeline. They didn't taste just the same, either. They weren't quite so sweet, but they had a spicy flavor he liked.

He haggled long enough to look normal, then took a small basket full of them back to the house. He'd brought the basket himself. Nobody here gave out shopping bags or anything like them.

Amanda opened the door as soon as he knocked. Smiles wreathed her face. "You've heard from Dad!" Jeremy exclaimed.

His sister nodded. "It was her appendix, and now it's out, and she's going to be fine."

Some of the weight fell from Jeremy's shoulders. "That's . . . about the best news there is," he said. "Did Dad say how long he'll stay back there?"

"A few days," Amanda answered. "He can't be quite sure yet, 'cause he has to see how Mom's doing. But he said he'd get back here as soon as he could. And Mom shouldn't be more than a couple of weeks—but she'll have to wear a patch of false skin over the scar when she goes to the baths."

"I hadn't thought of that," Jeremy said, but it made sense

when he did. Nobody here had a scar like that. Agrippan Rome knew no anesthetics. It had no antibiotics. It had never heard of sterile operating techniques. A wound in the belly meant sure death from infection.

"It doesn't matter," Amanda said. "She's going to be okay. That does."

"Yeah." Jeremy nodded. Yes, some of the weight was off. Things would get back to normal pretty soon. Now he could concentrate on how much business he and Amanda did before Dad came back to Polisso.

And he could tell Michael Fujikawa the good news. He stayed up late to try and catch Michael getting up. When he went to the laptop in the hidden part of the basement, he found a message waiting for him. *How's your mom doing?*

"She went back to the home timeline," he answered, as if his friend were standing there in front of him. The computer transcribed his words. "It was appendicitis. Dad was right about that. They took out her appendix. She'll be back in a couple of weeks. Dad says he'll be back in a few days—as soon as he's sure she's all right. She should be. The operation went fine."

He waited. He didn't have to wait long. Michael must have been sitting at the laptop that connected them across the skein of alternates. *That's terrific!* he said. *I'm sorry she had to have the operation, but now she'll be okay. So you and Amanda are by yourselves? How you doing?*

"We're okay," Jeremy said. "We can manage on our own for a little while, anyway. I want to see how much we can sell before Dad gets here again."

There you go, Michael told him. *Show him what you can do by*

The message stopped there. Jeremy frowned, waiting for Michael to go on. But only the incomplete sentence stared at him. After half a minute or so, new words formed on the screen: TRANSMISSION INTERRUPTED. NO CONTACT WITH HOME TIMELINE.

"What's that supposed to mean?" Jeremy asked. The message program was still running, so those words went up on the monitor, too. "You there, Michael?" That appeared, too. What didn't appear was an answer from Michael Fujikawa.

Muttering, Jeremy ordered the computer to send the message. He got the same error report as before: TRANSMISSION INTERRUPTED. NO CONTACT WITH HOME TIMELINE.

"But I'm not even trying to send to the home timeline," Jeremy protested. He really did swear when he saw those words go up on the screen. Then a chill ran through him. He wasn't trying to send to the home timeline, but everything went through it. He called up the address code for the Crosstime Traffic office in Moigrad. That was the home timeline's counterpart of this place. "Is everything all right there?" he asked, and told the laptop to send.

TRANSMISSION INTERRUPTED. NO CONTACT WITH HOME TIMELINE.

That wasn't good at all—not even slightly. Something had gone wrong somewhere between here and the world where he'd been born.

He tried Michael one more time, and got the same error message. Really scared now, he left—fled—the basement. The secret door closed behind him.

Amanda was not someone who gave in to panic. She was someone who always tried to look on the bright side of things.

That was one reason her brother sometimes drove her crazy. Of course, Jeremy had woken her out of a sound sleep to tell her about the error message. She was not at her best yawning in the middle of the night.

She went down to the basement to try to send messages to the home timeline herself. When she found she couldn't, either, she went back to her bedroom. "It'll be fine in the morning," she said.

"How do you know that?" Jeremy demanded.

"Because nothing's ever as awful when the sun comes out as it is at three in the morning, or whatever time it is now," Amanda answered. Then she shut the door in his face.

The computer still wouldn't send messages when she got up in the morning. That wasn't good news. It was, in fact, very bad news. With the sun shining down brightly on the court-yard, though, it didn't *seem* so bad.

Before long, Amanda was too busy to worry about it anyway. She and her mother had had all they could do to keep the house in some kind of order and to keep everybody fed without help from servants or slaves. Now she had to do it without Mom around. It was more work than one human being could do.

She tried to get Jeremy to help. He didn't want to. That made her lose her temper. "You listen to me, Jeremy," she snapped. "If you don't do what needs doing, I'll tell Dad when he gets back here. Then you'll catch it. And you know what else? You'll deserve it, too."

He helped. He was surly about it. He helped less than he would have if he'd known what he was doing. Sometimes just having an extra pair of hands and an extra pair of eyes made a difference, though.

Breaking off from the housework to deal with customers every once in a while didn't help, either. The one good thing about that was that nobody asked them, *Where are your mother and father?* The locals probably thought they would get better deals from the younger people in the family. They were wrong, but it kept them from being too curious.

Two days passed. Three days. Four. Five. The computer kept giving the same error report whenever Amanda and Jeremy tried to send a message. No message from any of the other alternates or the home timeline came in.

And Dad didn't come back to Polisso.

At first, Amanda wondered whether that was because something had gone wrong with Mom. No way to know for sure, not when the message system was down. As one day followed another, though, she began to realize that probably wasn't the problem.

"I think something's wrong with the transposition chamber," she said to Jeremy at supper the sixth night.

When she put it that way, it didn't sound so bad. If she'd said, *I'm afraid we're stuck here forever,* it would have seemed much worse. But it would have meant the same thing.

Her brother was sucking marrow out of a lamb shank. Amanda thought that took realism too far, but Jeremy really did like marrow. Air and marrow going through the center of the bone made a gross noise. He smacked his lips.

"You may be right," he said, scratching his chin. He was growing the scraggly beginnings of a beard. Razors here, even the straight razors the traders sold, were nothing but long, slim knives. No neat blades in plastic safety housings. You could do yourself some serious damage if you weren't careful. From what he said, the beard itched coming in.

"Maybe we ought to go out to the chamber outside of town," Amanda said.

"We can if you want to," Jeremy said. "I don't think it'll do much good, though."

"Why not?"

"Because if that one were working, Dad would have come through it by now, along with technicians to fix whatever's wrong with this one."

"Oh." Amanda winced. That made more sense than she wished it did. She tried to stay optimistic. "We ought to check anyway."

"All right. I'll go tomorrow," Jeremy said.

Amanda wished he didn't make sense there, too, but he did. Anyone on the road was much less likely to give a large young man trouble than a young woman. That was unfortunate, which didn't make it any less true. She said, "What could make both transposition chambers stop working at the same time?"

"I don't know," her brother answered bleakly. "I've been chewing on that for three or four days now, and I haven't got any sure answers."

Three or four days? That was a day or two longer than Amanda had been worrying. Jeremy hadn't let on how worried he was till now. Amanda said, "What are some of the things you've thought of?"

"Maybe there was an earthquake in the home timeline." That could have been true. Quakes happened randomly across timelines. "Maybe the transposition operators are out on strike." That was a joke; the chambers could go automatically 99.999 (and probably several more nines after that) percent of the time. Jeremy went on: "Maybe the operators are still filling out Agrippan Roman forms." That was a joke, too—sort of.

"What are we going to do if a chamber . . . doesn't show up for a while?" Amanda asked.

"The best we can," her brother answered. "What else can we do?"

"Nothing," she said unhappily.

"When people do come back for us, we'll be the richest pair in Polisso," Jeremy said.

"That sounds good," Amanda said. Her brother grinned at her. She knew he was trying to keep up her spirits along with his own, and liked him for it. After a second, she stuck a finger in the air—the sign she'd thought of something. "From now on, we'd better take money for everything we sell."

"How come?" Jeremy asked. Then he looked foolish. "Oh."

"Yeah," Amanda said. "What would we do with all that grain if we couldn't ship it back to the home timeline? It'd start coming out of our ears."

"Uh-huh." Jeremy nodded. "Then when things do get straightened out again, that'll make things more complicated, because the locals will keep wanting to buy for cash. But we can worry about that later. Right now, we'll just do what we've got to do to keep going."

Do what we've got to do to keep going. That made a lot of sense to Amanda. It was simple. It was practical. And it meant she didn't have to think about nasty possibilities. If the transposition chamber couldn't come back for a few weeks, that was one thing. If it couldn't come back for a few years, that was something else again. No matter how much energy the batteries stored, they'd run dry sooner or later. Then Amanda and Jeremy would be on even terms with the locals, and they'd stay that way till they got rescued.

And if for some reason the chamber couldn't come back at all . . .

Then we're stuck here, Amanda thought. The chill that ran through her was colder than winter at the South Pole. Polisso was a nice enough place to visit; plenty of alternates were worse. But to live here? To speak neoLatin the rest of her days and forget English? To have to forget that women were just as good as men and could do anything men could? To say good-bye to doctors and dentists and ice cream and deodorant and malls and Copernicus and the SPCA and everything she'd grown up with?

Jeremy said something under his breath. She thought it was *Robinson Crusoe.* She didn't want to ask him, for fear she was right. Why wouldn't he be thinking along with her, though? They would be even more isolated from their homes than Robinson Crusoe ever was. At least he'd stayed in his own world.

"We know Mom's all right. That's the important thing," Jeremy said.

"Sure." Amanda made herself sound perky. If her brother didn't want to think about getting stuck here, how could she blame him? She didn't want to think about it, either.

A literate soldier poised pen over papyrus. "Reason for leaving the city?" he asked.

"I'm just going out for a walk," Jeremy answered. "It's a nice day. And I'm sick of smelling smoke and garbage in here."

"Reason for leaving the city: constitutional." The guard at

the western gate wrote that down, then laughed. Jeremy realized the fellow wasn't much older than he was himself. When the local smiled, he looked like a kid. He said, "The city stink does get to you, doesn't it? But when you get out of it for a while, it's even worse when you come back."

"I've noticed that, too," Jeremy said.

"You'll be back by sunset?" the soldier asked. "There's another form if you stay out longer."

"By sunset," Jeremy promised.

"All right," the guard said. "If you come in late, now, there's a fine for giving false information."

"There would be," Jeremy said. The guard laughed again. He thought Jeremy was kidding. Jeremy knew he wasn't. Life in Agrippan Rome broke down into a million separate boxes. If you stepped outside any of them, or if you stepped into one where you'd said you wouldn't go, you had to pay.

Even the law here worked like that. For two thousand years and more, lawmakers and lawyers had tried to take life apart and look at each possible deed. If you were accused of doing something wrong, they would fit it into a pigeonhole—stealing sheep worth between twenty and forty denari, for instance. Then they would decide whether you'd done it. If they decided you had, another pigeonhole told them exactly how to punish you. To Jeremy, that kind of precise control felt like a straitjacket. The locals took it for granted.

"Pass on," the gate guard said, and Jeremy did.

A hawk wheeled overhead. There were rabbits in the fields. The hawks weren't the only ones to eat them. Sometimes the locals would hunt them with dogs and nets. Rabbit stew could be tasty. No matter what people in the home timeline said, it didn't taste like chicken.

Jeremy realized he hadn't been outside Polisso since coming here. The town couldn't have been even a kilometer square. He traveled several times that distance every day he went to high school. When you were on foot all the time, though, distance stretched dramatically.

A few tombstones poked up through the tall grass on either side of the road. Time had blurred the carvings on them. The locals didn't bury people inside the walls. That wasn't because they thought dead bodies left there might spread disease; they'd never heard of germs, and had no idea how disease spread. The only pollution they worried about was the religious kind.

As Jeremy reached the bend that put Polisso out of sight behind him, he stopped in the middle of the road. Except for the faintest ripple of the wind through the grass and a starling's distant, metallic call, silence was absolute. That kind of quiet was something he didn't get to know in Los Angeles. There was always a murmur of traffic noise there, of airplanes and helicopters overhead, and of the neighbors' TVs or radios or computers or stereos. There was also the sixty-cycle hum of electricity. You didn't constantly notice it, but it was around whenever you went indoors.

Not here. This was just . . . nothing. The starling fell silent. All Jeremy could hear was the blood rushing in his ears. He hardly ever realized it was there, but it seemed very loud now.

When he started walking again, each thump of his sandal on the paving stones might have come from a giant's heavy boots. He tried to go on tiptoe to be quieter. It didn't seem to do much good.

He concentrated so hard on being quiet, he almost

walked past the cave that hid the transposition chamber. That would have been great. He looked ahead. He turned around and looked behind. No one coming either way. He left the road and went over to the mouth of the cave. He had to cast around a bit before he found the hidden trapdoor close by. Grunting with effort, he lifted it and went down the tunnel pathway that led back into the cave.

Almost everything inside the cave seemed the same as it had when his family got here. Only one thing was missing: the transposition chamber. He hadn't expected to find that there. It would have been nice, but he hadn't expected it.

He turned on the PowerBook sitting on a table in a niche farther back in the cave. The computer came to life right away. He sent a message to the Crosstime Traffic electronic monitor in the home timeline that checked this machine's output. He tried to send one, anyway.

TRANSMISSION INTERRUPTED. NO CONTACT WITH HOME TIME-LINE.

Jeremy said several choice things, in neoLatin and in English. Again, he wasn't really surprised, but he was disappointed. Whatever had gone wrong had gone wrong here as well as at the chamber inside Polisso. He'd feared that was true. As he'd told Amanda, Dad—or somebody—would have come out of a chamber here and fixed the problem with the one under the house if it weren't.

After running out of curses, Jeremy said one thing more: "Well, I tried." Now he and Amanda knew help wasn't right around the corner. They'd already been pretty sure of that. Finding out they were right was news they needed, not news they wanted. For the time being—however long the time being turned out to be—they were on their own.

He thought about growing old and dying in Polisso. Then he thought about *not* growing old but dying in Polisso. There was a lot more wear and tear here than back in Los Angeles. There were a lot fewer ways to fix anything that went wrong, too.

Filled with such gloomy thoughts, he went to the monitors to make sure he could safely leave. He got a surprise then, and not a pleasant one. An army was coming up the highway toward Polisso.

It was a Roman army. The standard-bearers carried gilded eagles above the letters SPQR. Those stood for *Senatus populusque Romanus:* "the Senate and people of Rome" in classical Latin. The Senate, these days, was a powerless rich men's club. The people had no voice in politics, and hadn't for two thousand years. The slogan lived on.

Some cavalrymen were heavily armored lancers. Others were archers, with quivers full of arrows on their backs. The big, clumsy matchlock pistols they had here weren't practical for horsemen. Behind the cavalry squadrons marched troop after troop of foot soldiers. Some men carried tall pikes. Others shouldered matchlock muskets. They laughed and joked and sang as they tramped along.

Their being here said they were liable to see action before long. The government wouldn't reinforce Polisso if it didn't think trouble likely. That kind of trouble could come from only one place: Lietuva.

Jeremy remembered the gate guard who'd asked if he and his family were Lietuvan spies. The soldier had been kidding, but he'd been kidding on the square. Were some of the Lietuvan traders in town real spies? Jeremy would have been surprised if someone in Polisso weren't looking into that right now. He wouldn't have wanted to be a Lietuvan trader here. No one in this world had ever heard of laws against illegal search and seizure.

The army's baggage train followed the foot soldiers. Cannon rattled along on wheeled carriages. Wagons carried food and gunpowder and lead for bullets and stone or iron cannonballs. Other wagons held surgeons and their supplies, clerks to keep track of pay records and such, and farriers and blacksmiths and veterinarians to care for the horses.

Those cannon made Jeremy especially thoughtful. Polisso already had a lot of artillery. The central government wouldn't move more in unless it really worried about an attack.

Normally, Jeremy and his family wouldn't have had to fear a war. If it got bad, they could hop into a transposition chamber and leave it behind. But, at least for now, he and Amanda were stuck here. That made him take things more seriously than he would have otherwise.

He was also stuck *here*—in this cave—till the army marched past and went into Polisso. He couldn't come out while soldiers might spot him. They would wonder what he'd been doing there. Spying on them? The way things were, that would have to occur to them. They would ask questions. They wouldn't be polite about it—or gentle, either.

Up till then, he'd never worried about how long an army took to pass any particular place. While he was waiting, it seemed like forever. In fact, it was several hours. He kept looking down at his wrist to find out just how long. That would have worked better if he'd worn a wristwatch. In Agrippan Rome, he couldn't. Even the big mechanical pocket watches Crosstime Traffic traders sold here were way ahead of the state of the art.

At last, the coast was clear. Jeremy scooted out of the cave and made it to the road before anybody coming from Polisso spotted him. He sauntered toward the city as if he had not a care in the world. Pretending to be carefree took more acting than anything else he'd done since coming to this alternate.

Pretending to be carefree also proved the wrong role. Travelers in Polisso hadn't been allowed to leave while the army was going in. A gray-haired merchant leading a train of mules was the first man who came up to Jeremy. The merchant stared at him and said, "Boy, don't you know there's a gods-cursed army just ahead of you?"

Jeremy couldn't very well claim he didn't know. The horses and oxen of the cavalry and baggage train had left unmistakable hints an army was on the move. So he smiled and shrugged and nodded.

The merchant's eyes got bigger yet. "Well, then, don't you know you're an idiot?"

If he'd smiled and shrugged and nodded again, the older man would have been sure he was one. Instead, he asked, "What are you talking about?"

"What am I talking about? What am I *talking* about?" The merchant seemed convinced he was an idiot anyway. "The gods must watch over fools like you, even if you are a big, strong fool. Don't you think those soldiers would have grabbed you and put you in a helmet if they'd spotted you?"

"Gurk," Jeremy said. The man with the mule train seemed to think that was the first sensible thing to come out of his mouth. He got his mules going again and left Jeremy standing in the middle of the road. After a couple of minutes, Jeremy walked on to Polisso.

Other travelers coming out of the city sent him strange

looks. They too must have wondered what he was doing ambling along in the army's wake. None of them asked him any questions, though. They just went on about their own business.

When he got back to Polisso, the gate guard who'd let him out of the city checked him back in. He too said, "You're lucky the soldiers didn't see you." After a moment, he took off his helmet and scratched his head. "How come they didn't?"

"I'd gone off the road when they came. I was trying to knock over rabbits with rocks," Jeremy answered. He spread his hands. "No luck."

"I wouldn't think so." The gate guard laughed at the idea. "You'd need a cursed lot of it to hit one." Then he laughed again. "And when you saw the soldiers, I'll bet you bloody well made sure they didn't see you."

"Well—yes." Jeremy had been inside the cave. Of course they hadn't seen him. But he could agree without actually lying. The guard clapped him on the back and waved him into Polisso. He didn't have good news for Amanda: no sign of the transposition chamber and no contact with the home timeline. But he was happy just the same. The good news was, he would be able to tell her the bad news in person. He hadn't been pulled into the army.

What would happen if there really was a war? He did his best not to think about that.

In the Declaration of Independence, Thomas Jefferson complained that the King of England quartered his soldiers on the American colonists. Amanda remembered that from the U.S. History class she'd taken two years before. It hadn't meant anything to her then except one more fact she had to know for a test. People in the United States hadn't had soldiers quartered on them for a long, long time.

But she wasn't in the United States any more. Some of her neighbors had soldiers living in their houses and eating their food. She and Jeremy were lucky it hadn't happened to them.

"I wonder why they didn't try to give us any soldiers," she said at breakfast, two days after the army came to Polisso.

"They like what we sell, and they don't want to make us so angry we'll go away and won't come back," Jeremy answered, spooning up barley mush. "That's the only thing I can think of."

"What do we do if they say, 'Here, take these four'?" Amanda asked.

"I'm going to give the city prefect a couple of thousand denari," Jeremy said. "Why not? Silver's not much more than play money for us. I'll tell him to use it to buy food for the reinforcements. We'll do that instead of letting them in here."

"Can you be smooth enough to get away with it?" Amanda asked.

Her older brother shrugged. "I can—because I have to. Dad would probably do a better job of it, but he's not here. That leaves me."

"I'm not a potted plant, you know," Amanda said.

"No, but you're a girl," Jeremy answered. "As far as the locals are concerned, you might as well be a potted plant."

That stung, especially because it was true. Amanda's chin went up. "So what?"

Jeremy held up a hand. "Look, I know it's no big thing. Everybody you've skinned on a deal here knows it's no big thing. But if you go try to talk to the city prefect, what will he and his flunkies see? A girl. Guys like that are like principals—they can't see past the end of their noses."

The principal at Canoga Park High was a woman. That didn't spoil Jeremy's point: Ms. Williams definitely couldn't see past the end of her nose. Amanda sighed. "All right," she said. "No, not all right, because it isn't. But I can see why you've got to be the one who goes. Macho!" She spat that out as if it were the dirtiest word ever invented. Right then, she felt it was.

"Most alternates that haven't had an industrial revolution are like this," Jeremy said. "If you don't have machines, size and strength count for more than they do with us. Guys don't have babies, either."

"It's still not right," Amanda said.

"Did I tell you it was?" Her brother gave her a don't-blame-me look. "But even if it's not—even though it's not—it's real."

And that was also true, and also stung. But the next day, Jeremy went to see the city prefect. Amanda went to the public water fountain with a jug on her hip to listen to the talk there. *That's what people here think women are good for,* she thought. *Carrying water and gossip. And I can't even rock the boat.*

There was gossip, too—plenty of it. A plump woman with an enormous wart on the end of her nose spoke in important tones: "I hear the city prefect ordered all the Lietuvan traders out of Polisso last night."

"No, that isn't true," the slave girl named Maria said. "A lot of them are leaving, but they're leaving on their own."

"How do you know so much?" The woman with the wart—not a regular at the fountain—looked down her nose past it at the slave.

Maria didn't get angry. Amanda had never seen her get angry. Maybe that was because she was a slave and couldn't afford to. Maybe it was because she was a Christian—what they called a strong Christian here, not an Imperial Christian—and didn't believe in it. Or maybe she was just a nice person. She said, "I pray with a girl who serves at the inn where the Lietuvans stay. That's what she told me."

"Well, I heard my news from someone who heard it from the city prefect's second secretary's cousin's hairdresser," the plump woman said.

Amanda laughed out loud. If that woman thought her account trumped what an eyewitness said . . . But a couple of the other ladies filling water jugs were nodding, too. They must have believed it did. Both of them were free and fairly prosperous. As far as Amanda could see, both of them were also fairly dumb.

"Too bad they'll let the Lietuvans go," one of those ladies said. "We could hold them for hostages in case the barbarians attack."

"What would the Lietuvans do to Romans they caught, then?" Amanda asked. She didn't call the woman a jerk, no matter what she thought.

"Well, they'd do that anyway. They *are* barbarians," the woman answered. All the women gathered around the fountain nodded this time. Maybe the Lietuvans really did do horrible things to any Romans they caught. Maybe the Romans just thought they did. How was anybody supposed to know for sure? Go out and let the Lietuvans capture you? That didn't seem like a good idea to Amanda.

A squad of soldiers marched by. Nobody in Agrippan Rome had ever heard of the wolf whistle, but the men in the dull red surcoats had no trouble getting the message across. Guys in Los Angeles usually weren't so crude. Amanda turned her back on the soldiers. That only made them laugh.

Some of the other women just ignored the men's leers and gestures and suggestions. A few of them smiled back, though. That horrified Amanda. If they encouraged the soldiers, those men would go right on acting that way. They would think they were right to act that way.

How could she say that, so someone who'd spent her whole life in Agrippan Rome would understand? It wasn't easy. People here took lots of things for granted that nobody in the home timeline would have put up with for a minute. The best Amanda could do was, "If you give them a smile, they'll only want more."

"Maybe I will, too, dearie," a woman twice her age said. Everybody except Amanda laughed. And she didn't push it any more. What was the use? She wasn't going to change this alternate single-handed.

She wished she hadn't had that thought. If she really was stuck here, how much would this alternate end up changing her?

Six

The city prefect was a moon-faced, middle-aged man named Sesto Capurnio and nicknamed Gemino, which meant he was one of a set of twins. As far as Jeremy knew, the other half of the pair didn't live in Polisso. Jeremy didn't know whether that meant he lived in some other town or wasn't alive at all.

Sesto Capurnio collected modern art. That meant something different here from what it would have in Los Angeles. Nobody in Agrippan Rome would know what to make of abstract painting or sculpture. Hardly any cultures that hadn't invented the camera produced art that didn't try to represent reality. Photographs reproduced the real world more exactly than painters and sculptors could hope to do. That let them in fact, it almost forced them to—try other things.

What the city prefect called modern art were pieces done by artists of Agrippan Rome from the past couple of hundred years. Even that made him unusual. For most collectors here, the older, the better. If they had an early Roman copy of an ancient Greek original, that was good. If they had the Greek original itself, that was heaven. But Sesto Capurnio was different.

Several busts of recent Emperors stared at Jeremy from behind the city prefect. The effect was eerie, not least because they were painted to look as realistic as they could. Eyes of ivory and colored glass added to the effect. Jeremy had seen the head of Honorio Prisco III in the temple. He still had trouble getting used to the style.

Sesto Capurnio also had several paintings on his wall. Some were landscapes, others scenes taken from mythology. One showed Christ and Mithras beating back a demon together. Official Roman belief mixed faiths in a blender.

And he had a pot made in the shape of a dog's head with a rabbit in its mouth. You drank from the dog's left ear. Jeremy was no art critic, but he knew what he liked. The best thing anyone could have done with that pot was break it. Into little pieces. Lots of them. The more, the better.

"It is good to see you, young Ieremeo," Sesto Capurnio said. Jeremy could have done without that *young*. But then, Sesto Capurnio was a pompous fool. He spoke neoLatin in a way that suggested he'd start spouting the classical language any minute. He never quite did, but still. . . .

"I thank you, most illustrious prefect of the great municipality of Polisso." Jeremy laid it on with a trowel, too. If he sounded as educated as the prefect, Sesto Capurnio couldn't score any style points off him. He went on, "I am glad to see that city garrison has been reinforced. The barbarians will surely know better than to trouble us now."

"Of course they will," Capurnio said. They were both lying through their teeth. They both knew it, too. Nobody wanted to see new soldiers coming into the city. If they were here, that meant Polisso was liable to need them.

Jeremy picked up a heavy leather sack full of silver. "I know these men will need supplies," he said. "Here is my family's small gift to the city, for the sake of the soldiers who have just come." He set the sack on the table behind which Sesto Capurnio sat.

"You are generous." The city prefect picked up the sack. One of his eyebrows jumped in surprise at the weight. "By the gods, you *are* generous."

He didn't seem to want to set the money down. Jeremy wondered how many denari would stick to his fingers. Some, no doubt. This was a world that ran on nudges and winks and greased palms. Come to that, most worlds did. This one, though, was more open about it than a lot of them.

With a small sigh, Sesto Capurnio said, "I am sure the soldiers will be grateful for your bounty." That meant he knew he couldn't get away with lifting the whole sack. If Jeremy told an officer he'd given Capurnio money and the soldiers had seen none of it, that could make the prefect's life difficult.

"It is the least we can do," Jeremy said. By that, he meant, *It is the most we can do. Don't ask us to do anything else.*

"Very generous. Very kind. A gift whose like I wish we had from every prosperous citizen of Polisso," the city prefect said. By that, he probably meant, *I will have a gift like this from every man who doesn't want soldiers in his house, drinking the best wine and coming on to the slave women—or to his wife and daughters.*

"The town needs to be as safe and secure as it can," Jeremy said. "And now, most illustrious prefect, if you will excuse me . . ."

Instead of going through the usual polite good-byes, Capurnio said, "Wait one moment, Ieremeo Soltero, if you would be as generous with your time as you are with your silver. There is something I would like to know from you, and I hope you will be kind enough to tell me."

"If I can, I will," Jeremy said. "I should not speak about the secrets of my trade, any more than any other merchant would."

"Of course not," the city prefect said. "What I want to know is, why are you making this generous gift, and not your father?"

"Oh," Jeremy said, as if he'd expected just that question. In fact, it did not surprise him all that much. "My father and mother went out of Polisso a few days ago. That is why."

"I see." Sesto Capurnio shuffled through sheets of papyrus and paper and parchment. "I have no record of their leaving the city."

Jeremy gulped. In Agrippan Rome, not to have a record of something was serious business. Records proved a person was real. They proved that things had really happened. By contrast, not having records meant something hadn't happened at all. That could be a problem. If Jeremy and Amanda were stuck here in Polisso with no escape through a transposition chamber, it could be a big problem.

"I don't know anything about that," Jeremy said. "They had to go back to Carnuto, and so they did. If your guards don't know about it, they can't have been keeping up with things very well, can they?"

The city prefect had poked him, so he poked back. Accusing the gate guards of not keeping the proper records was like accusing Sesto Capurnio of sleeping on the job. Capurnio glared. "You will give me an affidavit concerning this?" he asked in a harsh voice.

An affidavit would give him the record he wanted. Jeremy nodded. "Sure I will," he said. He didn't like lying, but he liked being cut off from the home timeline even less.

"Very well." By Sesto Capurnio's scowl, it was anything but. Jeremy wished he hadn't angered the city prefect. But if Capurnio didn't believe Mom and Dad had left Polisso, what was he going to believe? That Jeremy and Amanda had killed their parents? The punishment for that was putting each guilty person in a sack with a dog, a cock, and a snake and throwing all the sacks in the river. In some ways, Agrippan Rome had changed very little from ancient days.

Sesto Capurnio called in a secretary. The man took down Jeremy's statement, using a stylus to write the words on wax that coated one side of a wooden tablet. That was what the locals used for a scratch pad. When the secretary made a mistake, he rubbed it out with the blunt end of the stylus and wrote over it.

"Let me have that," Capurnio said when Jeremy was done. The secretary gave him the tablet. He read the affidavit aloud. "Is this the truth, the whole truth, and nothing but the truth?" he asked at the end.

"It is," Jeremy answered. Some of it *was* true: his mother and father *had* left Polisso, and he didn't know when they'd be back. If they hadn't gone out by way of the west gate . . . the locals didn't need to know that.

"Do you swear by . . ." Capurnio paused. "You are an Imperial Christian, is that not so?"

"Yes, illustrious prefect."

The illustrious prefect's face said he had a low opinion of all Christians, Imperial or otherwise. His words, though, were all business: "Do you swear, then, by your God and by your hopes for the Emperor's health, long life, and success that what you have stated is true and complete?"

"I do, illustrious prefect."

"Go on, then—and thank you again for your generosity," Sesto Capurnio added grudgingly.

"Thank you for your kindness, illustrious prefect," Jeremy said. Sesto Capurnio turned around and looked at his collection of imperial heads. The Emperors stared back without a blink. Jeremy left the city prefect's house in a hurry. He had the feeling Capurnio might not have let him go if he stayed much longer.

Amanda sat in the courtyard with a customer. They both enjoyed the warm summer sun. House sparrows sat on the edge of the red roof tiles and chirped. A starling hopped around in the herb garden. Every now and then it plunged its banana-yellow beak into the dirt. Sometimes it got something good to eat. Sometimes it had to try again.

She could have seen house sparrows and starlings in Los Angeles, of course. Neither was native to North America. She didn't know how house sparrows had got there. At the end of the nineteenth century, a mad Englishman who wanted America to have all of Shakespeare's birds had imported ten dozen starlings to Central Park in New York City. He'd brought in nightingales, too. The nightingales promptly died out. There were millions and millions of starlings all over the continent. It struck Amanda as a bad bargain.

Her customer was a matron named Livia Plurabella. She was a little older than Mom, and would have been a beauty if smallpox scars hadn't slagged her cheeks. She took the scars in stride, much more than she would have in Amanda's world. Here, plenty of women—and men, too—had their looks ruined the same way. Men could hide pockmarks with a beard. Women had to make do with powder and paint. Livia Plurabella didn't even try. She must have known a losing battle when she saw one.

"Let me have a look at that one, if you please," she said, pointing to a straight razor with a mother-of-pearl handle. "I like the way it gives back the sunlight."

"Here you are, my lady," Amanda said. The older woman was the wife of the richest banker in town. He wasn't a noble. In fact, he was the son of a freedman. Banking wasn't a high-class profession in Agrippan Rome. But, here as everywhere else, money talked. And money Marco Plurabello had.

His wife opened the razor. "Isn't that something?" she murmured. She seemed to admire the glitter of the sun off the edge even more than the way it brought out the pink and silver of the mother-of-pearl. She shaved a patch of hair on her arm. "Well!" she said. "Isn't *that* something?" The blade was of better steel and sharper than anything local smiths could make.

"If you strop it regularly, it will last you a lifetime," Amanda said. That was true, even though women in Agrippan Rome shaved more places than they did in California. The notion of shaving with a straight razor made Amanda queasy anyway. Jeremy hadn't wanted to try it, either. A mistake with that thing wasn't a nick. It was a disaster.

Livia Plurabella looked at the bare spot on her forearm. She felt of it. "I believe you," she said. By the way she brought those words out, she didn't use them every day. She closed the razor. It clicked. She waited, one eyebrow raised.

"A hundred fifty denari." Amanda answered the unspoken question.

"Well!" the banker's wife said again. "I thought you would put the price in grain."

"We've changed our policy there," Amanda said.

"Sensible. Very sensible." Livia Plurabella nodded. "I'll give you eighty for the razor."

"I'm sorry, but no. We haven't changed our policy there at all," Amanda said. "We don't haggle." She still wondered how much trouble they would get into for taking money instead of grain. If Crosstime Traffic wanted to yell about that, the company was welcome to yell as much as it cared to. She and Jeremy had nowhere to store grain if they couldn't ship it out of Polisso. But they were trying to bend as few rules as they could.

Livia Plurabella frowned. It was the sort of frown that said, *You can't possibly mean what you just said, kid.* It was meant to intimidate Amanda. Instead, it made her mad. The matron said, "I don't know that I want this razor enough to pay one hundred fifty denari for it."

"That's for you to decide, my lady," Amanda said politely. "We've sold several at that price—or the equivalent in grain—and nobody's complained. If you want to keep on using something ordinary, though, go right ahead."

Livia Plurabella frowned again. This time, she looked worried. Amanda hoped she was imagining other women having something she didn't. Amanda also hoped she was imagining the other women laughing at her because she didn't have it. Advertising was one more place where the home time-line had a long lead on Agrippan Rome. Amanda had seen a million commercials. Almost without thinking, she knew what buttons to push. And Livia Plurabella didn't know what to do when Amanda pushed them.

"I don't think you're being reasonable about the price," she complained. But her voice lacked conviction.

Amanda pounced: "Oh, but I am, my lady. You admired the mother-of-pearl. It comes all the way from the Red Sea." What little mother-of-pearl the Romans had did come from there. She went on. "And if you can find an edge like that on any other razor—"

"Any razor you don't sell, you mean," the other woman broke in.

"Yes, that's right." Amanda nodded proudly. "Everything we sell is of the best quality. If you can find something to match it anywhere else, go ahead and do that."

She pushed another button there. People in Polisso couldn't get anything to match what the crosstime traders sold, and they knew it. Livia Plurabella's face said just how well she knew it. "Oh, all right." She sounded angry—more angry at the world than angry at Amanda. "A hundred fifty denari. We have a bargain."

"I'll write up your contract," Amanda said, and she did. She hoped Livia Plurabella could read. Otherwise she would have to witness the local woman's mark. Even if she did, Marco Plurabello might still raise a stink and claim she'd cheated his wife. That wouldn't be true or just, but he was a power in Polisso. He wouldn't need truth or justice on his side to get what he wanted.

But Livia Plurabella proved to have her letters, as Amanda had hoped she would. If any woman in Polisso was likely to, a banker's wife would. "Let me have that pen, please," the matron said, Amanda gave it to her. She wrote her name on both copies of the contract. "Here."

"Thank you very much, my lady," Amanda said.

"I'll send a slave with the money," the banker's wife said. Her father-in-law had once been a slave. That didn't keep her from owning them. Amanda wondered why not. One of the harder things about living in Agrippan Rome was that there were so many questions she couldn't ask. One of these days—one of these years—scholars would look at history and literature and law and custom here and figure out some answers to questions like those. But Amanda wanted to know *now*.

The trouble with finding the alternates and visiting so many of them was that there were always more questions than answers. There probably always would be. There sure were now. Too many alternates, not enough people exploring them. The last time anything this important happened in the home timeline, Columbus discovered the New World. The alternates were far, far bigger than North and South America, and they'd been known for less than a lifetime. No wonder there were still so many things to learn. The wonder was that people from the home timeline had found out as much as they had.

Then Livia Plurabella said, "I've heard you people don't keep slaves. Can that be true?" She wasn't shy about indulging *her* curiosity.

"Yes, it's true," Amanda said. That was no secret.

"Really?" The local woman's eyes, their edges outlined with powdered antimony, went wide. "By the gods, dear, how do you ever get anything done without other people to do it for you?"

"We do it ourselves," Amanda answered. She didn't mention that they had gadgets here no locals could see. Aside from the wrongs of slavery—and its being illegal for people from the home timeline to have anything to do with—having the gadgets made it impossible for the traders to have slaves, too. Too many questions they would have to answer.

Amanda laughed at herself. There'd been answers she wanted to get. But there were also answers she couldn't give.

She'd certainly puzzled Livia Plurabella. "How do you manage that?" the banker's wife asked. "When do you sleep? When do you bathe?"

"We just do what needs doing, as best we can." Amanda thought she could ask one of her questions now: "How do you own people who are just like you?"

"They aren't people just like me. They're *slaves*," Livia Plurabella said, completely missing Amanda's point. This had to be the first time anyone had ever questioned slavery in the matron's hearing. She hesitated. She was polite, too, in her own way. Then she asked, "You're Christian, aren't you, dear?"

"Yes," Amanda said. "Imperial Christian."

"I know Christians have some . . . some different ideas." Yes, Livia Plurabella was working very hard to be polite. She went on. "Do Christians have some sort of . . . interesting notion that slavery is bad? I never heard they—you—did."

"No, they—uh, *we*—don't," Amanda answered. That was true for all kinds of Christians in Agrippan Rome. It had also been true for Christians in the Roman Empire of Amanda's world. The New Testament didn't say one thing about putting an end to slavery. People hadn't really started opposing it till the rise of democracy in England and America and France suggested that all men should be equal under the law—and till machines started doing work instead of slaves. Even then, America had needed a war to get rid of slavery.

But Amanda had only perplexed Livia Plurabella more. "What have you got against it, then?" she asked.

"We just don't think it's right for anyone to be able to buy and sell someone else," Amanda said. "And it's always worse for women—everybody knows that. If the Lietuvans took Polisso, would you want them selling and buying *you*?"

Such things did happen after cities fell. Livia Plurabella turned pale. She leaned towards Amanda and set a manicured hand—a hand probably manicured by a slave—on her forearm. "Is there going to be a war?" she whispered, as if she didn't dare say it out loud. "Is there? What have you heard?"

She'd missed the point again, or most of it. But war was no small thing, either. "I haven't heard anything new," Amanda said. "All I know is, everybody's worried about it."

Some of the matron's color came back. "Gods be praised," she said in a voice more like her own. "A sack is the worst thing in the world. Pray to your own funny God that you never have to find out how bad a sack can be." She got to her feet. "I will send the slave with the money. No, you don't need to show me out, dear. I know the way." Off she went, the hem of her long wool tunic sweeping around her ankles.

Amanda wanted to know how she knew about sacks. She also wanted to ask her more questions about slavery now that she had the chance. But Livia Plurabella had done all the talking she intended to do. She opened the front door, then closed it behind her. Amanda sighed. The chance was gone.

Jeremy was tossing a ball back and forth in the street with a boy named Fabio Lentulo and nicknamed Barbato—the guy with the beard. Fabio was Jeremy's age, more or less. He was a skinny little fellow, a head shorter than Jeremy. He'd been apprenticed to the silversmith whose shop stood a few doors down from Jeremy's house. Jeremy had got to know him the summer before. Even then, Fabio had had this thick, curly, luxuriant beard on cheeks and chin and upper lip. Jeremy didn't know if his own beard would be that heavy when he was thirty—or ever.

Playing catch in the street here was an adventure. They had to do it over and through traffic, which paid no attention to them. The ball was leather, and stuffed with feathers. It wasn't especially round. It would have made a crummy baseball. For throwing back and forth, though, it was all right.

Jeremy dodged a creaking oxcart. He lofted the ball over the sacks of beans or barley piled high in the back of the cart. Fabio jumped to catch it. When he came down, he almost got trampled by a horse with big clay jars of wine tied to its back. The man leading the horse called him several different kinds of idiot. Fabio gave back better than he got. Grinning, he sent Jeremy running after the ball with a high lob.

His foot splashed down in a smelly puddle the instant he made the catch. The dirty water—he hoped it was water, anyway—splattered him and three or four people around him. They all told him just what they thought. Since he was as disgusted as they were, he couldn't even yell back.

He flung the ball right at Fabio's nose, as hard as he could. It wouldn't have hurt much had it hit. But it didn't. The apprentice snatched it out of the air. He grinned. His teeth were white, but crooked. "Got you!" he said, and threw the ball back.

This time, Jeremy caught it without disaster. So Fabio thought landing him in trouble was fun, did he? "Why aren't you at work?" Jeremy shouted.

"My boss is down sick, so he didn't open up," Fabio answered. "Why aren't you?"

"I will be pretty soon, if you don't get me killed first," Jeremy said, and Fabio Lentulo's grin got bigger. Jeremy threw the ball high in the air. Fabio had to look up to follow its flight. That meant he couldn't watch where he was going. He caught it—and staggered back into one of the four big men carrying a sedan chair. Jolted out of step, the man swore and boxed Fabio's ear. The woman sitting in the sedan chair screeched at the apprentice. Now Jeremy was the one who grinned. "Two can play at that game!" he called.

From then on, it was who could land whom in a worse pickle. How they didn't get killed or badly hurt, Jeremy never understood. That they didn't lose the ball might have been an even bigger marvel.

And then everything, even the ball game, came to a stop. A herald went through the streets shouting, "All who are not Roman citizens or legal residents have two days to vacate Polisso! By order of the most illustrious city prefect Sesto Capurnio, and the most noble and valiant garrison commander Annio Basso, all who are not Roman citizens or legal residents have two days to vacate Polisso! After that, they may be arrested. Their property may be seized. They may be sold as slaves. Hear ye! Hear ye! All who are not . . ." He started over again, as loud as he could.

"That doesn't sound good," Jeremy said.

"Sounds like a war, all right," Fabio Lentulo agreed. "Don't want any stinking Lietuvans around to open the gates at night or something."

"Why would they want to do that?" Jeremy asked.

The silversmith's apprentice looked at him as if he'd just lost his mind. "Because they're Lietuvans," Fabio said with exaggerated patience. "They'd rather have their stupid King rule here than the Emperor, gods bless him. They'd rather have everybody bow down to their stupid gods, too—Perkunas and all the others nobody ever heard of. What do you want to bet they're throwing Romans out of their ugly old towns, too?"

What Jeremy would have bet was that Fabio had never been more then ten kilometers outside of Polisso in his life. He had no way of knowing whether the towns in the Kingdom of Lietuva were ugly. For that matter, he had no way of knowing whether King Kuzmickas was stupid, either. But he believed those things, because he lived in the Roman Empire. If he'd lived in Lietuva, he would have thought the Emperor was stupid and Roman towns were ugly and Roman gods were stupid. Nationalism wasn't as strong in this world as it was in the home timeline, but it existed.

Fabio Lentulo suddenly looked like a ferret that had spotted a mouse. "I know where some of those lousy Lietuvans live," he said. "They won't be able to take all their stuff with them—not if they've only got two days to pack. The plundering ought to be juicy."

"No, thanks," Jeremy said. "Leave me out."

"Why not?" Now Fabio really couldn't believe what he was hearing. "Who knows what all they'll have to leave behind?" But Jeremy shook his head. The apprentice stared. "You *are* weird. What's wrong with plundering a bunch of rotten foreigners?"

"I don't care that they're foreigners," Jeremy answered. "They're merchants. So am I. I wouldn't want anybody plundering me if I had to get out of town."

"Is that the Golden Rule thing Christians go on and on about?" Fabio asked.

"Well—yes," Jeremy said, surprised the local had heard of it.

Fabio Lentulo might have heard of it, but he wasn't much impressed. With a scornful wave, he said, "Bunch of crap, if you ask me. You do your friends all the good you can and your enemies all the harm you can, and that's how you come out on top."

The ancient Greeks and Romans had believed the same thing. Plenty of people in Jeremy's world still did, but they mostly pretended they didn't. In Agrippan Rome, Christianity hadn't changed morals as much as it had back home. People here were more openly for themselves than they were in the home timeline.

Maybe that explains why they don't worry about owning slaves, Jeremy thought. If somebody was a slave, didn't he have it coming to him? Jeremy liked the idea—for about half a minute. Then he remembered all the men who'd owned slaves in the South before the Civil War . . . and who'd called themselves good Christians. He sighed. Things weren't so simple as they looked at first.

He saw things like that more and more often as he got older. He'd begun to suspect that no small part of growing up was seeing that more and more things weren't so simple as they looked at first. Trouble was, he liked being sure. Watching certainties disappear under the magnifying glass was a jolt every time.

You could, of course, pretend things were as simple as you'd believed when you were a kid. You could—if you didn't mind living a lie. Or maybe if you just refused to look facts in the face. Some people did. Lots of people did, in fact. Jeremy wondered how.

Then he had to make a quick grab to keep the ball from hitting him in the eye. Fabio Lentulo screeched laughter. "I thought you'd gone to sleep there," he said. "If you had, I was going to slit your belt pouch."

Jeremy threw the ball back. "To the crows with you," he said, an insult the locals often used. "Good to your friends and bad to your enemies, you said? Am I your enemy, if you want to steal from me?"

"My enemy? Nah." The silversmith's apprentice shook his head. "But you sure were acting like a dopey friend there." He heaved the ball high in the air.

After a run that involved dodging two women and almost tripping over a dog, Jeremy caught it at his belt buckle. Willie Mays had invented that kind of catch a century and a half before his time. He'd seen old video. He wasn't so smooth as Willie Mays, but he was plenty smooth enough to impress Fabio Lentulo. "Let me try that!" the apprentice called.

Jeremy flung it high. Fabio staggered—he almost tripped over that dog, too—and tried his own basket catch. The ball thudded to the cobbles at his feet. Jeremy jeered. Fabio Lentulo came back with something just as nasty. They both laughed. The game went on.

Every day, Amanda would go into the secret part of the basement, hoping to see a message on the PowerBook's screen. Every day, she would be disappointed. Every day, she would try to send her own message. Every day, the computer would tell her she couldn't. And every day, she would go back up to the main level wishing none of this were happening.

Wishes like that were worth their weight in gold. Amanda

knew as much. Knowing didn't keep her from making them. Every day no message came, every day she and Jeremy remained cut off in Polisso, was an argument no message would ever come, an argument they'd stay cut off forever. She thought about Livia Plurabella. If she *was* stuck here, would she turn into someone like that in another twenty-five years? Wondering what you would be like when you grew up was scary enough when you were doing it in your own world. When you might be stranded forever in a place where you didn't want to live . . .

Then again, *stranded forever* might be stretching things. The Lietuvan traders still left in Polisso got out of town the day after the city prefect and the garrison commander finally issued the order expelling them. Some of their wagons rattled past the house where Amanda and Jeremy were staying.

Amanda peered out through one of the handful of narrow windows that opened on the street. Traffic in Polisso was as insane as usual. That meant the Lietuvans couldn't get out of town in a hurry, no matter how much they wanted to. It also gave the locals the chance to pay them a not so fond farewell.

"Get out!" "Never come back!" "Gods-cursed blond barbarians!" Those were a few of the nicer good-byes people yelled. The rest . . . Amanda had heard some vile things at Canoga Park High. What the people of Polisso called the departing Lietuvans would have made the toughest kid there turn green.

They didn't just call them names, either. They threw things. They had nastier things to throw than they would have in Los Angeles. Squishy vegetables and balls of manure were bad enough. But the stench of rotten eggs seemed ten times worse. Amanda couldn't get away from it, either. The windows had no glass. Closing the shutters didn't do a dollar's worth of good.

The worst of it was, the Lietuvans had to take the abuse. If they'd tried to hit back, they wouldn't have got out of Polisso alive. If they'd tried to hit back, the people in the street wouldn't have thrown dung and rotten eggs. They would have thrown rocks and jars instead. They probably would have mobbed the foreigners, too. And so, stone-faced, the Lietuvans pushed on toward the gate. They tried to keep the flying garbage from spooking their horses and mules and oxen too badly. They also tried to duck so they didn't get too filthy.

Some of the Lietuvans had been in Polisso a long time, long enough to have brought their wives down from their own country. The fair-haired women, tall by the standards of this world, left the town with their men. The locals spattered them with filth, too. Some of the things they called them made the names they gave the Lietuvan men sound friendly by comparison.

At last, after what seemed much too long, the hubbub moved closer to the gate. Amanda retreated to the courtyard, but the stink of hydrogen sulfide lingered there, too. Jeremy walked into the courtyard a minute or so later. He looked grim. He must have been watching the Lietuvans leave from another window.

"Nice people," he said. He didn't mean the Lietuvans. He meant the locals who had harried them on their way.

Amanda nodded. "Really."

"*We* wouldn't do anything like that," Jeremy said.

"Oh, I don't know." Amanda remembered her U.S. History class again. "Look what happened to the Japanese-Americans during the Second World War."

"So?" Her brother didn't buy the argument. "That was a hundred fifty years ago. Are you saying we'd keep slaves because they kept slaves in the South before the Civil War?"

"Well . . . maybe not," Amanda admitted. "But the Second World War was a lot closer to now than the Civil War was. People acted more like us."

"A little, maybe, but not a whole lot," Jeremy said. "It was still a long time ago. They didn't have any computers. They only had one telephone for every seven people in the country. You ask me, that's *backward*."

He'd just finished a high-school U.S. History course. Now that he reminded her of it, Amanda remembered running into that statistic, too. But she never would have thought of it on her own. She asked, "How do you come up with that stuff?"

She'd asked him questions like that before, so he knew what she meant. He'd never been able to give her a good answer, though. He couldn't now, either. He said, "I don't know. I just do," which told her nothing whatsoever. But then he said, "How do you know what people are feeling? I can't do that, or not very well."

"No?" Amanda said in surprise—surprise that vanished when she thought it over and realized Jeremy was right. He didn't just *see* how people worked. He always had to work it through inside his mind. Sometimes he didn't come up with the right answers even then. Maybe that was the other side of the coin to being able to remember how many telephones the United States had during World War II. Given a choice, Amanda knew which one she would rather be able to do.

But people didn't get choices like that. They were what they were, and had to make the most of it. Some remembered better and thought straighter than others. Some felt more clearly than others. A lucky handful, maybe, could do all those things well. Whatever you were good at, though, you needed to make the most of it. If you did, things wouldn't turn out too bad most of the time.

Amanda wished that hadn't occurred to her just then. Every once in a while, things happened to you where it didn't matter how smart you were or how well you remembered or how clearly you felt. Getting stuck in Agrippan Rome sure looked like one of those things. Amanda didn't see what she or Jeremy could have done to stop that.

He started to say something else, but some more noise outside the house made him stop. "What now?" Amanda exclaimed. "Lietuvans again?"

"Doesn't quite sound like that," Jeremy answered, and he was right. These shouts sounded happy and excited. They didn't have the fierce, baying undertone that had been there when people jeered the Lietuvans out of Polisso. He said, "We'd better go find out." Amanda nodded. Her brother didn't need to think very clearly to have that straight.

She got to a window just in time to see and hear another herald coming up the street. "War!" he shouted. "Lietuvan soldiers have crossed the border. We have begun the fight to drive them back. Because the gods love us, we will win. War! Hear ye! Hear ye! War is declared!"

Seven

Jeremy had thought bullets and cannonballs would start flying as soon as war between Rome and Lietuva was declared. That was how things worked in his world—not that people there bothered declaring war any more. They just launched missiles and sent tanks over the border. Things were more formal here. The gunpowder empires clung to rituals and customs that had their roots in the days of ancient Greece. And even if bullets and cannonballs flew fast here, too, armies didn't. They were tied to the speed at which a man could march and a horse-drawn wagon could roll. Nobody went anywhere in a hurry, not in the world of Agrippan Rome.

The people of Polisso took advantage of the time they had before the Lietuvans arrived. More soldiers came into the town, these troops tramping up from the south. More wagons full of wheat and barley came with them. As far as men and supplies went, Polisso was ready to stand siege.

Whether the walls were ready was another question. They were made of thick stone, sure enough. But even thick stone walls fell down if enough cannonballs hit them. In the home timeline, people had solved that by building huge earthen ramparts instead of stone walls. They weren't so impressive, but they worked better. A cannonball that hit piled-up earth didn't go *crash!* It went *thud!* and buried itself without doing much harm.

Nobody here had figured that out yet. It had taken two or three hundred years to see in the home timeline, and wars there had been a lot more common than they were here. There, in the centuries right after the invention of guns, Europe had been crowded with a whole slew of kingdoms and principalities and duchies and independent archbishoprics and free cities and even the occasional republic. Somebody was always fighting somebody else, and either coming up with new tricks on his own or stealing the almost-new tricks somebody else had come up with a few hundred kilometers away.

It wasn't like that here. Almost all of Europe belonged to either Rome or Lietuva. Almost all the Near East belonged to either Rome or Persia. The gunpowder empires did fight among themselves. But they usually fought once a generation, more or less. There wasn't the unending strife that had lit a fire under change in the home timeline.

And now is the time, Jeremy thought. *Joy and rapture.*

The first Lietuvan cavalrymen reached the outskirts of Polisso eight days after news of the declaration of war. They attacked a wagon train bringing still more grain into the town. Jeremy heard the details only later, in the market square. At the time, all he noticed were a few distant bangs, like Fourth of July fireworks at a park a couple of kilometers away. The big, clumsy matchlock pistols cavalrymen here carried couldn't be reloaded on horseback. The Lietuvans did most of their damage with bow and sword and lance.

Most of the time, they would have set fires all through the fields around Polisso. Not much point to that today, though, because it had rained the day before. The horsemen trampled long swaths through the green, growing wheat, then rode back the way they'd come.

Several of the wagons rumbled past the house where Jeremy and Amanda were living. Some of the animals that pulled them had been hurt. Some of the men who drove them had been hurt, too.

Jeremy gulped at the sight of bandages strained—soaked—with blood. He gulped even more at the sight of flesh punctured by bullets or split by swords. Some of the wounds had been roughly stitched up in the field. The drivers and guards who'd been hurt moaned or wailed or screamed.

In Los Angeles in the home timeline, Jeremy saw gore at the movies or on TV or in video games. He'd hardly ever run into the real thing himself. Oh, he'd gone past a restaurant once not long after a shooting, and he'd seen a few traffic accidents where people got hurt. But he'd never seen so many men other men had hurt on purpose before. And he'd never had the feeling, *This could happen to me.* He did now.

Doctors ran toward the wounded drivers and guards. They might do a little good. They had long-handled probes for digging out bullets. They could sew up sword-cuts and set broken bones. But all they had to fight pain while they worked was opium, which wasn't nearly enough. And all they had to fight infection was wine.

Injured men screamed louder when the doctors splashed it on their wounds. Jeremy would have screamed, too. Rubbing alcohol stung like the devil when you put it on a little scrape. Splashing something full of alcohol on a gaping cut . . . Just the idea made him shudder.

Wine wasn't that good a disinfectant—better than nothing, but not great. And there was more filth in this world than in the home timeline—far more. Some of those wounds *would* fester. When they did, there was nothing to do but drain them and hope for the best. A lot of the time, that wouldn't be enough, either. Some men would die of fever. No one in this alternate could do a thing about it.

About half an hour after the wagons came into Polisso, someone knocked on the front door. Jeremy opened it. Waiting in the street was a lean, dark man in a tunic of good wool but without too much embroidered ornament. After a second or two, Jeremy recognized him. "Good day, sir," he said politely. "You're Lucio Claudio, aren't you?"

"Called Fusco. Yes, that is correct." Lucio Claudio nodded. He had the air of somebody who liked to dot every *i* and cross every *t*. "I have the honor to act as man of affairs for Gaio Fulvio, called Magno."

"Yes, I know. Won't you come in?" Jeremy stepped inside. "We can sit in the courtyard, if you like. Would you care for some wine and honey cakes?"

"Thank you. That would be pleasant." By the frown ironed onto Lucio Claudio's face, he had trouble finding anything pleasant. But he was being polite, too.

Jeremy sat him down on a bench in the courtyard. He—politely—admired the flowers. Jeremy went into the kitchen to get wine and cakes for the two of them. While he was there, Amanda came in and hissed, "What's *he* want?"

"Don't know yet," Jeremy answered. "He hasn't said."

His sister looked daggers in the direction of Lucio Claudio. "He's a snoop."

"Well, who here isn't?" Jeremy said. "He's Gaio Fulvio's

man, too, and Gaio Fulvio is a big wheel in this town. People say he's got Sesto Capurnio in his back pocket. I wouldn't be surprised. I can't just ignore his man of affairs."

"Don't trust him," Amanda said fiercely.

"I don't intend to." Jeremy picked up the tray. "No matter what you think, I'm not dumb."

"Don't be, that's all." Amanda scowled at him.

He carried the refreshments out to Lucio Claudio. Gaio Fulvio's man of affairs praised the cakes—once more, politely. He spilled out a small libation for the gods and muttered a prayer before he drank any wine. He waited for Jeremy to do the same. Jeremy did, but in place of the prayer said only, "To the spirit of the Emperor."

"You are a Christian?" the local asked, frowning.

"Yes, we're Imperial Christians," Jeremy answered.

"It is permitted," Lucio Claudio admitted. His face said it wouldn't be if he had anything to do with the way things worked. He took another sip of wine, then gave a grudging nod. "Not bad."

"Glad you like it," Jeremy said, even if the man of affairs hadn't gone that far. "I hope your principal is pleased with his hour-reckoner?"

"He is." Again, Lucio Claudio sounded as if he was admitting something he would rather not have. "He is," he repeated, "though he does still wonder how you few merchants are the only ones who sell such marvelous devices."

"Hour-reckoners are not the only things we sell, you know," Jeremy said proudly. "We have fine razors, too, and mirrors of wonderful quality, and knives with sharp blades and many attached tools."

Amanda had told him to be careful. He'd said he would,

but he hadn't. He'd started bragging instead. And that turned out not to be such a good idea just then. He couldn't even blame the wine. He'd had only a sip.

Lucio Claudio smiled. It was the sort of smile an evil banker in a bad movie might have given when he foreclosed on a widow's mortgage. "Yes, I do know about these things," he said. "So does Sesto Capurnio."

Uh-oh, Jeremy thought, too late. He did his best to cover up: "I'm sure he hasn't got any complaints about quality or value."

"No." Lucio Claudio didn't like admitting that, either. But the shark's-teeth smile didn't slip from his face. "Because of the many, ah, unusual matters pertaining to your family, he now requests and requires an official report on your activities."

What Jeremy thought this time wasn't, *Uh-oh.* It was, *Damn!* An official report meant imperial bureaucrats were going to take a long, close look at the traders from Crosstime Traffic. That was the last thing he wanted. Well, no. He shook his head. The *last* thing he wanted was to be cut off from the home timeline. He had that. Now he had this, too. Talk about adding insult to injury. . . .

Maybe he could stall if he couldn't get out of it. He said, "Regulations state that an official report must be requested in writing."

"So they do. And why am I not surprised that you know those regulations very well?" Lucio Claudio had a nasty sarcastic streak. He also looked to be enjoying himself. From his belt pouch he pulled a rolled-up sheet of papyrus sealed with a ribbon and a big, blobby red wax seal. He aimed it at Jeremy as if it were a pistol. "Here."

"Thank you," Jeremy said, meaning anything but. He

broke the seal and unrolled the papyrus. It was what the local had said it was. In the most complicated classical Latin at his command, Sesto Capurnio—or more likely his secretary—ordered an official report on the deeds and practices of the Soltero family. Jeremy looked at when the report was due, as if it were one for school.

Three weeks. He sighed. It could have been worse. They could have wanted it day after tomorrow. If they were really suspicious, they would have wanted it day after tomorrow. Of course, if they were *really* suspicious, they would have torn the house apart for answers.

But answers they wanted, even if they were willing—for now—to ask instead of tear. The more Jeremy looked at the written request, the less happy he got. The bureaucrats of Agrippan Rome took pride in their attention to detail. They'd outdone themselves here. They wanted to know how every item Crosstime Traffic traders sold was made. If that information wasn't available, they wanted to know where the traders got each one. They wanted to know how much the traders paid for each. They wanted to find out about profit margins. They were curious about why the traders always wanted grain, not cash.

"This is a mistake." Jeremy pointed to that question. "We take silver. Ask Livia Plurabella if you don't believe me."

"Let me see." Lucio Claudio examined the paragraph. He scratched his chin. "Do you claim the error makes the official request invalid?"

"I could," Jeremy said. Gaio Fulvio's man had to know as much, too. Any mistake on an official document invalidated it. That could be true even in the home timeline. Here, it was as much an article of faith as the cult of the Emperor.

"If you do, I will return with a revised request," Lucio

Claudio said. "I do not know when I will return. I do know the date on which we want your official report will not change—unless it moves up."

The Romans also wanted to know where Jeremy and Amanda's folks had gone. He'd already explained that to Sesto Capurnio. If they were still asking, the city prefect didn't much like what he'd heard. At least he wasn't sending men to dig up the basement and see if Mom and Dad's bodies were there. That was something—a very small something.

"I won't make the claim," Jeremy said. Lucio Claudio looked smug. Jeremy added, "I am going to remind you there's a war on, though. If King Kuzmickas and the Lietuvans lay siege to Polisso, I don't know if I can get the official report in on time. Flying cannonballs make it hard to write." He didn't want Lucio Claudio thinking himself the only one who could be sarcastic.

"I suggest you get to work on the report now, then." Lucio Claudio sounded just like a teacher when a student complained about too much work. "The sooner you start, the sooner you'll finish."

Thanks a lot, Jeremy thought. He almost said that out loud. Just in time, he swallowed it instead. He already had enough problems here. Why make things worse by offending Lucio Claudio? Sitting there eating honey cakes and sipping wine with him made the next half hour the most uncomfortable time Jeremy had ever spent. It wasn't a year before the local finally left. It only seemed that way.

Amanda looked up from the official request to her brother. She said, "Well, I know the best thing we can hope for."

"What? The Lietuvans blow up Polisso?" he asked.

"No. Mom and Dad get back before we have to give the prefect the report."

"Oh." Jeremy thought about that. He nodded, but not as if his heart was in it. "We can hope, yeah, but I just don't know. Something's got really messed up in the home timeline. If it hadn't, we wouldn't have been stuck here by ourselves so long already."

It wasn't that he was wrong. He was right. He was, in fact, much too right. Amanda had done her best not to think about why no one had sent them any messages, why no transposition chamber had shown up in the subbasement—or, for that matter, in the cave a few kilometers away.

If the Lietuvans besieged Polisso, that cave wouldn't do the Crosstime Traffic people much good. They'd be on the outside looking in. Could they get through a whole army? Maybe, but Amanda didn't see how.

She had to look at staying here not just for a summer with her folks, but forever. Forever. She couldn't imagine a scarier word. Only one thing kept her from breaking down and crying in something as close to panic as made no difference. She didn't want Jeremy laughing at her for going to pieces like a girl.

It never occurred to her to wonder how close Jeremy was to going to pieces himself.

"Sooner or later, they're bound to come after us," he said. Was he talking to convince her, or to convince himself? "They can't just leave us here." If he'd stopped there, it would have been a pretty good pep talk. But he went on, "I wish I knew what happened at the other end."

"Maybe . . ." Amanda let her voice trail away.

"Maybe what?" Jeremy asked.

Amanda said the worst thing she could think of: "Maybe somebody . . . found Crosstime Traffic."

People from the home timeline had only been traveling to the alternates for about fifty years. They hadn't discovered all of them. The math said they probably couldn't discover all of them. They hadn't even scratched the surface of the infinite swarm of alternates that were out there. They sure hadn't discovered anyone else who could go from one timeline to another.

But just because they hadn't discovered anyone like that didn't mean there wasn't anyone. In a timeline that had branched off from theirs long, long ago, other people might have figured out how to go crosstime five hundred years ago, or five thousand. They might have their own trading zone—or their own crosstime empire. And if they did, and if they noticed newcomers . . . they might not be friendly. They might not be friendly at all. That could be very bad news indeed.

"Nice, cheerful thought, all right," Jeremy said. "But I don't believe it. Why now? Why not before?"

"I don't know," Amanda said. "But why not now? If you've got a good reason, I'd love to hear it."

She really hoped her brother would come up with something. Jeremy *was* smart. And he was a year older. Most of the time, that didn't matter. Every once in a while, it did. If he knew why crosstime travelers from a faraway alternate couldn't have found the home timeline, that would have been wonderful.

But he just said, "It doesn't seem likely, that's all."

"Getting stuck here doesn't seem likely, either!" Amanda burst out. "But we are! Why?"

"Something went wrong somewhere—that's got to be it," Jeremy said, which was true but wasn't reassuring. "It doesn't mean the home timeline's been invaded by one where Alexander the Great discovered transposition chambers."

"It could mean that. You know it could," Amanda said.

"It *could* mean all kinds of things. Bombs. Earthquakes. Who knows what?" Jeremy was trying very hard to be reasonable. "Why come up with something that's never happened before and probably isn't happening now?"

"Because I never got stuck in an alternate before," Amanda blazed. The more reasonable Jeremy tried to be, the less reasonable she wanted to be.

He went right on trying: "It has to be something natural, something *possible*, for heaven's sake."

"What's so impossible about somebody else discovering crosstime travel?" Amanda asked. "We did ourselves, and we worry about it on some of the timelines that aren't far from ours. Why not somebody else, a long time ago?"

"Well, if somebody else did do it, they're liable to come up from the subbasement and wipe us out in the next twenty minutes," Jeremy said. "What are we going to do about that?"

Amanda hadn't the faintest idea. She hadn't thought she could feel any worse than she did already. Now she discovered she was wrong. "Thanks a lot," she told her brother. "You just gave me something brand new to worry about."

He shook his head. "Nope. No point worrying about that, because we *can't* do anything about it. What we can do is worry about this lousy official report, and about selling as much as we can, and about doing whatever we can to make sure the Lietuvans don't take Polisso. Getting captured and sold into slavery can ruin your whole day."

"So can getting killed," Amanda pointed out.

"That, too," Jeremy said.

He was so grave, so earnest, so serious, that Amanda started to laugh. She couldn't help it. When Jeremy was being reasonable, she didn't want to think. When he was being serious, she wanted to act like a clown. What went through her mind was, *Anybody would think he's my big brother, or something.*

"I don't know what else we can do except wait and hope and keep trying our best as long as we're stuck here," he said now.

That was what she'd been thinking, too. She hadn't liked the idea. It was the best they could manage. No doubt of that. It still seemed grim. Or it *had* seemed grim, till he said it. Then, all of a sudden, it was the funniest thing in the world. That made no sense at all, which didn't stop it from being true. She giggled.

Jeremy gave her an odd look. "You're weird," he said.

"You only just noticed?" Amanda laughed harder than ever. It was probably no more than reaction to too much stress carried for too long. It felt awfully good anyhow.

Solemn as usual, Jeremy shook his head again. "No, I'd suspected it for a while now."

"Really? What gave you the clue, Sherlock?" *I'm punchy,* Amanda thought. *Well, who could blame me? I've earned the right.*

The market square was a busy place these days. Everybody who lived in Polisso was trying to get hold of enough food to last out a siege. The soldiers who'd come to reinforce the garrison were laying in food, too. They all reminded Jeremy of squirrels gathering nuts for the winter. But that was important business for the squirrels, and this was important business for the locals.

If you had grain to sell, you could pretty much name your price. Somebody would pay it. Jeremy knew how many modii of wheat were stored under the house. He didn't want to sell them, though, even if he could make a lot of silver on the deal. The local authorities already wondered about Amanda and him. They would ask why those sacks of wheat hadn't left the city, the way they thought the grain had. They would accuse him of profiteering if he sold now.

A soldier was arguing with a farmer. "You should take less," he said.

"How come?" the farmer said. "When am I going to get another chance to make this kind of money?"

"But you're cheating me," the soldier said.

"By the gods, I'm not," the farmer answered. He was a big, burly man, almost as tall as Jeremy and half again as wide through the shoulders. Next to him, the soldier was a skinny, yappy little terrier. The farmer went on, "If you don't want to pay what I ask, you don't have to. I'll find other customers."

"Not if the city prefect or the commandant sets a top price," the soldier said. "They can do that. All they have to do is declare danger of siege. Everybody knows that's real. Then fixing prices is as legal as buying and selling slaves."

"Oh, yes. It's legal. But prefects don't try it very often," the farmer said. "And do you know why? Because when they set a top price, they always set it too cursed low. Then nobody wants to sell *any* grain. It just disappears from the market, and people start going hungry."

"You— You—" The soldier looked as if he couldn't find anything bad enough to call the farmer. "To the crows with you!" he snarled at last, and stalked off. Disgust showed in every line of his body.

Laughing, the farmer turned to Jeremy and said, "I'd like to see him get a better deal from anybody else."

Jeremy nodded. The farmer thought the way a merchant had to think. But if your city was in danger, didn't you have to ease off on that approach? If you didn't, wouldn't you end up without a city to do business in? Who decided when you did that? How did whoever it was draw the line?

Those were all good questions. Jeremy didn't have good answers for any of them. He was scratching his head as he went on to the temple dedicated to the Emperor's spirit.

When he stopped in the narthex to get a pinch of incense to light on the altar, the clerk who took his three denari for it looked puzzled. "By the records, Ieremeo Soltero, you have already made the required offering. Why are you here?"

"To make another offering," Jeremy said. "Polisso may be in danger, after all."

"How . . . public-spirited of you," the clerk said.

Jeremy did his best to look modest. He felt more like a hypocrite than ever. But he wanted officials seeing him acting public-spirited. It might help take the heat off Amanda and him. Even if it didn't, it couldn't hurt. And what were three denari to him? Nothing but Monopoly money.

The clerk gave him his receipt and the incense. It smelled sweeter than the last pinch he'd got. Maybe they saved extra-cheap stuff for people making required offerings, and gave you something better if you were doing it because you really wanted to. Jeremy didn't know for sure. Up till now, he didn't think any trader had made offerings that weren't required.

He carried the incense into the temple proper. There they were, all the gods the Romans recognized, in statue or painting or mosaic form. They all seemed to be looking at him. He didn't believe in any of them except possibly Jesus, and the Jesus he knew wasn't the same as the one in this world. The effect was impressive even so.

Several pinches of incense already smoked on the altar. Either other people wanted to look public-spirited, or they were worried. *Well, I'm worried, too,* Jeremy thought. But he didn't believe lighting this incense would help make his worries go away.

He lit it anyhow, then stepped on the twig he'd used to make it start burning. The smoke from the incense definitely smelled better than it had the last time he sacrificed. The image of Honorio Prisco III stared blindly from behind the altar. Jeremy recited the prayer an Imperial Christian gave the Emperor's spirit. It still felt more like pledging allegiance to the flag than praying. But neither of the two men who stood near the altar to listen to prayers complained. He'd done what he needed to do, and he'd done it right.

And now he understood—a little better, anyhow—what his dad said about the uses of hypocrisy. He wondered if he'd ever have the chance to tell Dad so.

Even though Amanda's house had running water, she liked visiting the fountain. People of the female persuasion couldn't go as many places or do as many things in this world as men could. At the baths and at the public fountains, age and wealth and social class didn't matter so much. A woman could say what she pleased, and a lot of women did.

When Amanda went to the fountain on a warm, sticky summer afternoon, she found several women complaining about the soldiers quartered in their houses. "They eat like dragons," said a plump middle-aged woman in a saffron tunic. "And then they grumble about the cooking! Do they pay a sestertio for what they get? Do they? Not likely!"

Another woman, also plump, nodded. "They lie around snoring till all hours, too. And they don't bathe often enough— or at all." She held her nose. For good measure, she scratched as if she had fleas.

Amanda wondered how much she'd had to do with soldiers before. Her tunic was saffron yellow, too, which meant she had money. Saffron dye wasn't cheap here. And, in this world, you had to be rich to have enough food to get overweight.

A couple of lines of Kipling from English Lit also ran through Amanda's head.

> *For it's Tommy this, an' Tommy that, an' "Chuck 'im out,*
> *   the brute!"*
> *But it's "Savior of 'is country" when the guns begin to*
> *   shoot.*

They'd never heard of Kipling in Agrippan Rome. But he understood what made them tick, all right.

"The soldiers aren't so bad," the slave girl named Maria said in a low voice. "We have some in our house, too, and they don't do anything worse than pat me a little."

In the home timeline, that would have been bad enough. It struck Maria as a miracle of moderation here. Different worlds, different standards. Amanda had to work to make herself remember that. It wasn't always easy. Of course, next to Maria's being a slave to begin with, how big a deal was it that some soldiers let their hands roam more than they might have? Probably not very.

Maria asked, "How is your mother? I have not seen her for a while."

"She and Father, uh, left Polisso," Amanda said. "He took her to a healer in Carnuto who's supposed to be one of the best, this side of Rome or Athens."

"I hope he will help her," Maria said gravely. She didn't say anything about Dad and Mom leaving the two Solters children on their own here. By local standards, they were plenty old enough to take care of themselves.

"I got a letter from my father not long ago," Amanda said. "He says Mother is doing much better."

"She will do better away from Polisso. I think that's very likely," Maria said. With a sour smile, Amanda nodded. Maria let out a small, sad sigh. "Having your letters must be nice. You can talk back and forth with Carnuto, and I can't even make myself heard across the street sometimes."

I can talk back and forth a lot farther than that—or I could if we weren't cut off, Amanda thought. Out loud, she said, "If you want, I could teach you your letters. It isn't very hard. Then you'd be able to read and write, too, at least some. And it's like anything else. The more you do, the easier it gets."

Maria's jaw dropped. "Could you?" she whispered. "I don't think my owner would mind. I'd be worth more to him if I knew something like that. And"—her eyes widened—"and I'd be able to read the Bible for myself. What could be better than that?"

Not all the books in the New Testament here were the same as they were in the home timeline. The Gospel according to John didn't exist in Agrippan Rome. It was supposed to date from the first half of the second century. By then, history here was different enough from what had happened in Amanda's world that John either hadn't written or had never been born at all. The Acts of the Apostles had the same name, but didn't say all the same things. And some of Paul's epistles went to churches to which he hadn't written in the home timeline. Comparative Bible scholarship across timelines was a field that was just getting off the ground.

It was also a field Maria had never heard of. She never would, either. As far as she knew, hers was *the* Bible. Amanda said, "Yes, I think you should be able to." There were two or three translations into classical Latin (none by St. Jerome, who'd never lived here) and several more into neoLatin. Some of those were from the classical Latin, others from the original Hebrew and Aramaic and Greek. Imperial Christians had an official version. Other kinds of Christians had different favorites.

"The Bible. The word of God, in *my* mouth." Maria looked as if she'd just gone to heaven. "It would be a miracle."

"No, it wouldn't," Amanda said. "It's just something you learn how to do, like—like weaving, for instance."

"But everybody learns how to spin and weave," Maria said. "You have to, or you don't have any clothes. Reading isn't like that. Plenty of free women—plenty of rich women, even—can't read."

"It's not hard, honest," Amanda said. In the home timeline, the only people who could spin or weave were the ones who did it for a hobby and the ones who worked in living-history museums. Almost everybody could read, though. Across the timelines, people first learned what they most needed to know. Back home, that was reading. Here, it was weaving.

Livia Plurabella came up and said, "May I speak to you for a moment, Amanda Soltera?"

"Sure," Amanda said, and turned away from Maria. The slave dropped her eyes to the cobblestones. When free people spoke with each other, she had to show she knew her place. Amanda asked, "Is something wrong with the razor you bought, my lady?"

"No, no, no." Impatiently, the banker's wife shook her head. "I just wanted to put a flea in your ear."

"What do you mean?" Amanda understood the phrase. The older woman wanted to warn her about something. She didn't know what the banker's wife thought she needed warning about.

Livia Plurabella spelled it out: "It's all very well to be polite to a creature like that." She pointed toward Maria, who still made as if she were paying no attention to her social betters. "It's all very well to be polite, yes. We are by the fountain, after all. The usual rules do slip. If they didn't, we'd never hear anything juicy, would we?" She smiled, but only for a moment. "There is a difference, you know, between being polite and being *friendly*. That's a bit much, don't you think?"

The most annoying thing was, Livia Plurabella meant well. She was trying to save Amanda from showing bad manners. That meant Amanda couldn't get as angry as she wanted to. Smashing her water jug over the older woman's head would get her talked about, no matter how tempting it was. She said, "Oh, it's all right. I don't think the slave girl minds."

Livia Plurabella took a deep breath. "Whether she minds isn't the point, dear," she said sharply. Then she gave Amanda a suspicious look. "Are you making fun of me, young lady?"

"I wouldn't do that for the *world*," Amanda exclaimed.

"Hmm." The banker's wife didn't seem any happier. "On your head be it," she said, and stalked away.

On your head be it. No matter how Amanda usually aped the manners of this world, she wasn't really part of it. She didn't feel in her belly that being friendly with a slave was wrong, the way a free woman here would. Livia Plurabella's warning would have horrified a local merchant's daughter. It wouldn't have been necessary in the first place, because a local merchant's daughter would have played by the rules without needing to be warned. If Amanda felt like breaking the rules every once in a while, she would, and that was all there was to it.

She turned back to Maria. "Where were we? Talking about how easy reading is, weren't we?"

The slave girl said, "Don't get into trouble on my account, Mistress Amanda." She sounded worried. She looked worried, too.

Amanda snorted. "She can't do anything to me." Only after the words were out of her mouth did she wonder how true they were. A banker's wife was an important person in Polisso. Which people you knew, what connections you had, mattered more here than in Los Angeles. Connections mattered back home, but the laws and customs there assumed one person was just as good, just as important, as another. That wasn't true here.

Maria's expression showed how untrue it was. The slave said, "She's got clout."

"Well, if you think we don't . . ." Amanda let that trail away. The merchants from Crosstime Traffic had money. Nothing made a better start for connections. But money was only a start. Amanda wasn't from here. Livia Plurabella was local. And the authorities in Polisso were already curious—to say the least—about how the crosstime traders operated. *If you think we don't have clout . . . you may be right.*

She filled her jar at the fountain. Most of the women swung full jars up onto their heads and carried them home that way. A few, though, carried them on the hip full as well as empty. Even with a hand up to support the jar on her head, she couldn't have been smooth and graceful like the locals. She would have looked like a clodhopper, a country bumpkin—but country bumpkins carried water jugs on their heads, too.

She had just left the fountain when she heard a noise like distant thunder. It came from the north. But it wasn't thunder. Some clouds drifted across the sky, but there was no sign of rain. For a moment, she was puzzled. Then she knew what it had to be—gunfire. The Lietuvan army was on the way.

Eight

Jeremy didn't know whether climbing up on the city wall was a good idea. Amanda thought he was nuts. Maybe he was. But he wanted to see what was going on out beyond Polisso. He wasn't the only one, either. Lots of locals were up there, staring out at the advancing Lietuvan army.

Soldiers hurried back and forth on the top of the wall. If ordinary people got in their way, they pushed them aside. They didn't waste time being nice. Not far from Jeremy, a soldier knocked a man sprawling. When the local lurched to his feet, blood dripped down his face. He didn't say anything. If he had, the soldiers might have pitched him off the wall, and it was a long way down.

On came the Lietuvans. Their army was bigger than the Roman force that had come into Polisso. It flew banners of gold, green, and red—the colors of Lithuania in the home timeline. Lietuvan soldiers wore dull blue surcoats and tunics and breeches. That made them easy to tell apart from the Romans. Their helmets were simpler—more like iron pots plopped on their heads. Their weapons seemed almost identical, though. Horsemen had pistols or lances or bows and sabers. Foot soldiers carried pikes or muskets and straight swords.

They had cannon, too. You couldn't very well besiege a town without them. Slowly, the guns left the road and began taking up positions around the city. Cavalrymen went with them to protect them from any Roman attack.

But the Romans didn't seem interested in sallying from Polisso, not right then. Instead, they started shooting from the wall. Jeremy wished he had earplugs. Having a cannon go off close by was like getting smacked in the side of the head.

Flames belched from the gun's muzzle. So did a great cloud of dark gray smoke. The cannon and its four-wheeled carriage jerked back from the recoil. Ropes kept it from jerking back too far. At a sergeant's shouted orders, the gun crew yanked on the ropes and ran it forward again. A man with a dripping swab on the end of a long pole stuck it down the barrel to make sure no bits of powder or wadding still smoldered inside. The swab steamed when he brought it out again.

That smoke made Jeremy cough. It also smelled familiar. He wondered why for a couple of seconds. He'd never stood near a cannon going off before. Then he knew what the odor reminded him of. He'd smelled it at parks on the Fourth of July, when they set off fireworks. Gunpowder then, gunpowder now. Pretty flowers of flame in the night air then. A cannonball flying now.

Jeremy saw the divot it kicked up when it hit. It kept rolling after it struck the ground, too. The Lietuvans in its path dodged. Jeremy had read about a Civil War soldier who tried to stop a rolling cannonball with his foot. He'd ended up having the foot amputated.

The cannon crew were reloading as fast as they could. Another man used a tool called a worm—like a short corkscrew on the end of a long pole—to drag out any chunks of wadding the swab might have missed. As soon as he finished, still another man set a bag of powder in the muzzle of the gun. A soldier with a rammer shoved it down to the back of the cannon. In went the cannonball. It got rammed down, too. So did rags—the wadding—which made the cannonball fit tightly inside the barrel.

At the rear of the cannon, a soldier poked a sharp spike into the touch-hole. He punctured the powder bag so fire could reach the charge inside. To make sure it did, he sprinkled a little finely ground gunpowder in and around the touch-hole. "Ready!" he yelled to the sergeant. All the men on the gun crew jumped to one side, so the recoiling gun carriage wouldn't run over them.

"Fire!" the sergeant shouted. A soldier with a length of slowly burning fuse—they called it match here—on the end of a long stick, a linstock, brought the smoldering end to the touch-hole. Jeremy heard a brief fizz as the fine priming powder there caught. Then—*boom!*—the powder in the main charge caught and sent the cannonball hurtling toward the Lietuvans. The whole cycle started over.

Other cannon on the walls of Polisso were shooting, too. The din was unbelievable. And the Lietuvans started shooting back. Not all of their guns could reach the wall. Every so often, though, the wall would shudder under Jeremy's feet when a ball thudded home.

And Lietuvan foot soldiers marched forward so they could shoot their muskets at the Romans on the wall. They didn't break up and spread out, the way modern soldiers in the home timeline would have. Instead, they stayed in neat formation. A cannonball plowed through one block of men. Half a dozen

Lietuvans went down one after the next, dead or maimed. The rest closed ranks and kept coming.

How did you train a man so he wouldn't run away when the fellow next to him got torn to pieces? This wasn't video-game blood. It was real. It would splatter you, all hot and wet. You could smell it. And you had to know it could have been *your* blood, it could be *your* blood next. But the Lietuvans advanced anyhow.

A gate opened—not one of the main city gates but a postern gate, a little one. Out thundered some of the heavy cavalry Jeremy had followed into the city not long before. The lancers roared toward a block of Lietuvan infantrymen.

Bang! Bang! Bang! Some of the matchlocks the Lietuvans carried went off. Two or three Roman horsemen and horses fell. The rest pitched into the Lietuvans, first with their lances, then with swords.

"Ha!" said a man near Jeremy. "We caught 'em by surprise. They didn't post pikemen out in front of their musketeers. Our lancers would've had a harder time then."

He might have been talking about a football team not blitzing the quarterback on the other side. He wasn't a soldier. His tunic might have been twin to Jeremy's. But he spoke with a serious fan's serious knowledge. Civilians here knew how the game of war was played. Wars came along often enough to let the rules be known. They didn't change much from one to the next.

Out on the battlefield, more Lietuvan soldiers came up to help the men under attack. The Roman horsemen broke off the fight and galloped back toward the city. Behind them, Lietuvan muskets banged. Another couple of Romans slid out of the saddle. One of them thrashed and writhed on the grass. The other lay very still.

The rest of the cavalry got back into Polisso. The spectators and some of the soldiers on the walls cheered. Jeremy found himself yelling and clapping his hands along with everybody else. He wondered if he *had* lost his mind. This wasn't a football game. People were dying, really and truly dying, out there. How could you cheer?

Were the Romans better than the Lietuvans? Was Emperor Honorio Prisco III a finer fellow than King Kuzmickas? Not so you'd notice. But the Lietuvans were trying to break into Polisso and do horrible things to the people inside. Jeremy was one of those people, Amanda another. The Roman horsemen were fighting to keep the Lietuvans out. Wasn't that a reason to cheer for them? The locals thought so, and Jeremy had a hard time believing they were wrong.

After a pause, the Lietuvans moved forward again. This time, they did what the man by Jeremy had said they should. They put a double line of pikemen in front of the musketeers. If horsemen came out again, the long pikes would help keep them away.

Cannon kept booming from the wall. Every so often, a cannonball would knock people over like a bowling ball knocking down pins. But bowling pins didn't keep moving after they were hit. They didn't scream, either. Through the guns' thunder, Jeremy heard the shrieks of wounded men.

Again, though, the Lietuvans who weren't wounded kept right on coming. When they got close enough, the musketeers touched the smoldering ends of their matches to the vents of their guns. *Bang! Bang! Bang!* Flame shot from the muzzles of all the muskets. A fogbank of smoke swallowed up the Lietuvan soldiers.

Bullets cracked past overhead. A couple of them didn't crack past, but struck home with wet, meaty thunks. Blood poured from a Roman artilleryman's face. It was amazingly red. He let out dreadful gobbling cries of pain. One of his pals led him off to a surgeon. What could the locals do for a shattered jaw, though? That wound would have been bad in the home timeline.

And the man standing next to Jeremy clutched at himself and fell over. One minute, he was handicapping the war. The next, it reached out and grabbed him. He looked more astonished than hurt. He tried to say something, but blood poured from his mouth and nose instead. It poured from the wound in his chest, too. Jeremy gulped. He hadn't realized how much blood a man held. He had to step back in a hurry, or it would have soaked his shoes. After four or five minutes, the man on the flagstones stopped moving. He just lay there, staring up at nothing with eyes that would never close again.

More bullets whistled by. The civilians on the wall decided that wasn't a good place to stay. They went down inside Polisso in a disorderly stream. Jeremy gaped at the corpse that had been a happy, living, breathing man only minutes before. *That could have been me,* he thought. *If the Lietuvans had aimed a little more to the left, that could have been me.*

Death had never seemed real to him. At his age, it hardly ever did. But the sight—and the smell, for the man's bowels had let go—of that body made him believe in it, at least for a little while. So did the snap of another bullet, right past his ear. He didn't have to be here. He'd come up to see what war looked like. He'd found out more than he wanted to know.

Roman musketeers were shooting back at the Lietuvans as Jeremy went down the stone stairs and back into the city. He was nearer the end of the stream of civilians than the beginning. He took some small pride in that. As he walked back toward the house where he and Amanda were staying, he wondered why.

From the inside, Polisso hardly seemed a city under siege, not at first. Amanda's day-to-day life changed very little. The smoke and the smell of gunpowder were always in the air. Jeremy was right. It did smell like the Fourth of July.

Every so often, a cannonball would crash down inside the city. But that hardly seemed important, not at first. It wasn't as if Amanda could see the damage for herself while she stayed at home. No news crews put it on TV. No reporters interviewed bloodied survivors. It might have been happening in another country. But it wasn't.

Before too long, the bombardment got worse. The Lietuvans dug trenches and pits so they could move their cannon forward without getting hammered by Polisso's guns. As soon as each cannon came into range, it started blasting away at the city.

Amanda thought business would go down the drain during the siege. People wouldn't want to leave their homes, would they? They wouldn't want to spend money on luxury goods, either, would they? After all, they might need that money for food later on.

They came in droves. The people who could afford what

Crosstime Traffic sold had enough money that they didn't need to worry about saving it to buy grain. As long as there *was* grain, they would be able to afford it.

Livia Plurabella came back to the house to buy a watch. She and Amanda were in the courtyard talking when a cannonball smacked home two or three houses away. The banker's wife took it in stride. "That was close, wasn't it?" she said, and went back to talking about which pocket watch she would rather have.

"You were afraid of a sack before, my lady," Amanda said. "Aren't you worried about one now?"

Livia Plurabella blinked. "I was. I remember talking about it with you, now that you remind me," she said. "But now . . . Now life has to go on, doesn't it? We'll do the best we can to hold out the barbarians. And if we can't—then that will be the time to be afraid. Till then, no."

She made good sense. "Fair enough," Amanda said. Another cannonball hit something not too far away with a rending crash. Amanda managed a shaky laugh. "Sometimes not being afraid is pretty hard, though."

"Well, yes." Livia Plurabella's laugh was a long way from carefree, too. "But we have to try. The men expect it from us. They say they want us all quivering so they can protect us, but they go to pieces if we really act like that. Haven't you noticed the same thing?"

Amanda didn't know everything there was to know about how things worked in Agrippan Rome. She thought back to the home timeline. Things weren't so openly sexist there, but all the same . . . She found herself nodding. "I think you have a point, my lady."

"Of course I do." The banker's wife took her own rightness

for granted. "Now show me these hour-reckoners again, if you'd be so kind."

"Sure." Amanda held them up, one after the other. "These are the three most popular ladies' styles." One was metal-flake green, one was eye-searing orange, and one was hot pink. Like the men's pocket watches, they all had gilded reliefs on the back. Amanda had never decided which one was the most tasteless. She wouldn't have been caught dead with any of them.

But Livia Plurabella sighed. "They're all beautiful." Amanda only smiled and nodded. If her drama teacher at Canoga Park High had seen her face just then, he would have known she could act. "Which one costs what?" the local woman asked.

"This one is two hundred denari." Amanda pointed to the green monstrosity. "This one is two hundred ten." She pointed to the orange catastrophe. "And this one is two hundred twenty-five." She pointed to the pink abomination.

As she often did with customers, she guessed which one Livia Plurabella would choose. She turned out to be right again, too. The banker's wife picked up the pocket watch with the hot-pink case. "This is so elegant, I just can't say no to it. Two hundred fifteen, did you say, dear?"

"Two twenty-five," Amanda answered. Again, what she was thinking didn't show on her face. Livia Plurabella wasn't the sort of person to make slips by accident. She'd wanted to see if Amanda would call her on it. Knowing that, Amanda enjoyed calling her on it twice as much.

"Two twenty-five." Livia Plurabella's voice drooped. But she nodded anyhow. "Well, all right. We can do that. Draw up the contract."

The cannon kept booming as Amanda wrote out the classical Latin. She hardly looked up from what she was doing. Life went on, sure enough. She couldn't do anything about the Lietuvans outside. Since she couldn't, she tried to pretend they weren't there.

"Here you are," she said, and handed the contract to Livia Plurabella. The matron read it, then signed both copies.

She gave one back to Amanda and kept the other. "I'll send a slave with the payment," she said, as she had before. "And if a cannonball doesn't squash him to jelly coming or going, I'll have a fine new hour-reckoner." She laughed. "One thing—with the Lietuvans outside the city, I don't have to worry that he'll run off with the money."

"Er—no," Amanda said uncomfortably.

Livia Plurabella wagged a finger at her. "That's right. You're the one who doesn't approve of slaves. Well, my dear, if you like working like a slave yourself, that's your affair. But believe you me, the better sort of people don't." She got to her feet and swept out of the house. All by herself, she made a parade.

"The better sort of people." Amanda spat out the words. Then she spat for real, on the dirt in the courtyard herb garden. The idea of slavery disgusted her. Having to put up with it here disgusted her more.

If she were a slave and her mistress gave her that much money to buy something, what would she do? *I'd be gone so fast, her head would spin,* she thought. But it wasn't that simple. Agrippan Rome had slavecatchers, just like the American South before the Civil War. Whenever you went into a town, you had to show who you were and what your business was.

The records would go into a file. That made things easier for anyone who came after you.

You couldn't even run across the border to Lietuva, not in peacetime. The Lietuvans gave back runaway slaves from the Roman Empire. That way, the Romans gave back runaway slaves from Lietuva. You scratch my back, I'll scratch yours. And the poor slaves who wanted nothing but the chance to live their own lives? Too bad for them.

There were bandits in the mountains. Some of them were runaways. But that was no life, not really. Few lasted long at it. Army patrols did their best to keep banditry down. And crucifixion had never gone out of style in Agrippan Rome. Amanda shivered. It was an ugly way to die.

Another cannonball crashed into Polisso. Somebody shrieked. Amanda shivered again. Were there any ways to die that weren't ugly? She didn't think so.

Bang! Bang! Bang! Before the siege of Polisso started, Jeremy would have said the big iron knocker on the front door made noises like gunshots. He knew better now. The only thing that sounded like a gunshot was another gunshot.

He went to the door and opened it. The man standing there wasn't someone he knew. "Yes?" he said. "May I help you?"

"You are Ieremeo Soltero, called Alto?" The stranger was somewhere in his thirties. He was lean and dapper, and had a sly look that said he knew all sorts of strange things. By the way one dark eyebrow kept jumping, some of the things he knew were either funny or none of his business.

"Yes, that's me," Jeremy answered. "Who are you?"

"Iulio Balbo, called Pavo," he said. He didn't look like a peacock, but he might be proud as one. He went on, "I have the honor to be one of Sesto Capurnio's secretaries. The most illustrious city prefect sent me here to remind you that your official report is due in two days' time."

"Did he?" Jeremy said tonelessly.

"He certainly did." The secretary smirked. He enjoyed seeing other people in trouble.

"Doesn't the city prefect have more important things to worry about right now?" Jeremy asked. "Will he read the official report while the Lietuvans knock down the walls and break into the city? Will he take it with him when they drag him away to the slave market?"

That wiped the smirk off Iulio Balbo's face. "If you are trying to be funny, Ieremeo Soltero—"

"Funny?" Jeremy broke in. "I'm not trying to be funny. I'm only trying to find out whether the city prefect cares more about keeping Polisso safe or about making sure all the forms get filled out at the right time." There was a lot of bureaucratic foolishness in the home timeline. He'd seen that. No one who went to a public school could help seeing it. But here in Agrippan Rome bureaucracy wasn't just foolish. It was downright idiotic. And the people who ran things didn't seem to notice.

Iulio Balbo's eyebrows rose. No matter how sly he was, he was a gear in this ponderous bureaucratic machine. He wasn't likely to see any humor in it, and he didn't. In a voice like winter, he said, "The report is due. It is expected. It is required. If you do not submit it on or before the due date, you will suffer the penalties the laws on the subject lay down. Do you understand this formal notice?"

"Oh, yes, I understand it," Jeremy answered. "Do you understand you're liable to go off to the Lietuvan slave market along with the most illustrious city prefect?"

"Defeatism is a crime," Iulio Balbo said. "Defeatism in time of declared war is a worse crime. Defeatism while besieged is a still worse crime." As usual, the locals had precise distinctions between one degree of what they thought crime and another.

Jeremy was too angry to care. "I am not being defeatist. The city prefect is. He is paying attention to these things that are not important when he ought to be doing nothing but defending the city. If you asked the garrison commandant about it, what would he say?"

Maybe Annio Basso and Sesto Capurnio were working well in harness. If they were, Iulio Balbo would just laugh at that crack. But he didn't laugh. He scowled and turned red. "Do not try to stir up quarrels between the prefect and the commandant," he warned. "That is also an offense."

What isn't an offense here? Jeremy wondered. "I'm not trying to stir up anything," he said. "I asked a reasonable question, and you didn't give me an answer. Or maybe you did."

"You may be as clever as you please. You may quibble with words however you please. The official report is still due in two days. Remember that. Obey the law." Iulio Balbo's bow was a small masterpiece of sarcasm. He stalked away like a cat with ruffled fur.

Muttering, Jeremy closed the door. He was the sort who usually put schoolwork off till the last minute. Without a deadline, he couldn't get interested in what he was supposed to do. Well, he had a deadline now. This was work of a different kind from what he got in school. There, he had to show off how much he knew. Here, he would have to disguise most of what he knew.

He sat down with pen and ink and paper and got to work. He set out to make the report as confusing as he could. To do that, he started by writing it in classical Latin, not neoLatin. The old language was made for bending back on itself until someone reading it wasn't quite sure exactly what it said. Maybe that hadn't been true when classical Latin was the Roman Empire's usual spoken language. Jeremy wouldn't even have bet on that. Now, though, one of the things officials here used it for was confusing one another. Jeremy intended to use it the same way.

He tried to make his answers to the questions the locals had asked him contradict one another. He had to be careful with that. If he was too obvious about it, he would get himself in trouble. But if he made his classical Latin fancy enough, nothing was obvious.

As soon as he figured that out, the official report stopped being a nuisance. It stopped being something he *had* to do. It turned into something that was fun to do. When he'd finished the first few sections, he showed Amanda what he'd written. "What do you think?" he asked.

She started working her way through it. She hadn't got very far before she looked up and crossed her eyes. "What are you talking about here?" she said. "It sounds like it ought to mean something, but I don't think it does."

"Oh, good," he said. "That's what I was trying to do."

"Will the city prefect let you get away with it?" she asked.

"I hope so," Jeremy answered. "The first thing he'll do is make sure we did turn in an official report by the due date.

That's how I figure it, anyhow. When he sees we did, he may not even have anybody read it right away. He's got other things to worry about, after all—yeah, just a few. And if he does have somebody read it and they decide they don't like it, what can he do? Have us write another one, right? This will buy us time, anyhow."

Amanda nodded. She didn't seem to want to meet his eyes, though. That was all right. He didn't want to meet hers, either. They both had to be wondering whether buying time mattered. It certainly did, if the home timeline could get in touch with them fairly soon. But every passing day made that seem less likely. If they really were stuck here . . .

Jeremy shook his head. He wouldn't think that. He refused to believe it. Amanda said, "Before you give this report to the locals, scan it into the computer. That way, everyone will know just what you've told them." She wouldn't believe they were permanently cut off any more than he would.

"I'll do that," he promised. "I just wanted you to see what I was up to."

"I like it," his sister said. "You've got nerve." She pointed to him. "When you turn it in, make sure you get a receipt from the clerk who takes it. Don't give the locals any excuse to say we didn't follow the rules."

That was also good advice. "I'll take care of it," Jeremy said. "Now I have to finish writing the silly thing."

The more of it he wrote, the sillier it got, too. It also occurred to him that telling the exact truth would have been sure to convince officials here that he was out of his mind. Tempting—but no. The secret of crosstime travel had to stay hidden.

When he carried the official report to the prefect's palace, he saw a few buildings with holes in them. A handful of others had been knocked flat. But the siege, so far, hadn't done all that much damage. Jeremy knew Polisso had been lucky. If a fire started on a windy day and began to spread . . . That was one more thing he didn't want to think about.

He gave the report to one of Sesto Capurnio's secretaries—a junior man, not Iulio Balbo. The fellow took it and stuck it in a pigeonhole without giving it more than a quick glance. He seemed surprised when Jeremy asked for a receipt, but gave him one without making a fuss.

As Jeremy started back toward his house, he thought, *Maybe this is one of those stupid assignments where they don't even look at it once you turn it in.* Somehow, though, he had trouble believing it.

There was an ancient stone plaque by the fountain near the traders' house. In classical Latin full of abbreviations, it told how a man named Quintus Ninnius Hasta had given the money to set up the fountain. That plaque had been standing there for two thousand years, more or less. Amanda wondered if anyone inside Polisso knew anything else about Quintus Ninnius Hasta. She also wondered if anyone outside of Polisso had ever heard of him at all.

When she carried a water jar to the fountain early one muggy morning, she stared in surprise and dismay. A cannonball had smashed the marble plaque—and most of the brick wall in which it was set. Chunks of shattered stone and brick lay in the street. Women kicked through them on the way to get water.

"Well, so what?" one of those women said when Amanda exclaimed about the loss. "Plenty of other old stuff in this town, sweetie, believe me."

She wasn't wrong. A little talk showed that most of the other women had the same point of view. Amanda didn't, and couldn't. In the part of Los Angeles where she'd lived all her life, nothing dated back earlier than the middle of the twentieth century. The first European settlement in California wasn't much more than three hundred years old. To her, things that had stood for two thousand years were precious antiques. They weren't routine landmarks or, worse, old junk.

"If you worry about all the old things," a woman said, "how are you ever going to put up anything new?" Again, most of the heads around the fountain bobbed up and down in agreement.

That wasn't a question with an easy answer, either. If you lived where other people had been living for a couple of thousand years, you didn't get excited about remains of the distant past. You took them for granted. And if, say, you needed building stone, you were liable to knock down something old and reuse what had gone into it. That was often easier and cheaper than hauling in new stone from somewhere else. And if that old building had been standing there for a thousand years, or fifteen hundred—so what?

Try as she would, Amanda couldn't think, *So what?* To her, it was worth keeping around just because it was old. The local women laughed at her. "If a place like that's falling down around your ears, what good is it?" one of them asked.

"Better to get rid of it," another woman agreed.

"But . . . But . . ." Amanda tried to put her feelings into words. After some struggle, she did: "But you could learn so much about the way things were long ago if you studied old things."

All the women around the fountain laughed at her. "Who cares, except for a few old fools with more money than sense?" said a squat woman with a burn scar on her cheek.

"Things weren't so different, anyway," a gray-haired woman added.

By the standards of the home timeline, she wasn't wrong. Things in Agrippan Rome had changed much less in the twenty-one hundred years since Augustus' day than they had in the home timeline. And people here weren't much aware of the changes that had happened. When modern painters showed ancient scenes, they dressed people in modern clothes. They didn't remember that styles had changed. They had ancient Roman legionaries wearing modern armor, too. They did—usually—remember soldiers in the old days hadn't known about muskets. But that was about as far as it went.

A cannonball howled through the air overhead and smashed into something made of brick or stone. "There goes some more old junk!" The woman with the scar sounded gleeful. To her, it might have been a joke.

The gray-haired woman nodded. "Somebody'll need a new house or a new shop," she said. "I hope it's somebody rich."

"Because they can afford it better?" Amanda asked.

"No, by Jupiter!" The gray-haired woman kicked at the cobblestones. "Because poor folks like me always get it in the neck. Let the rich fools find out what it's like to do without."

Several of the other women waiting their turn at the fountain nodded or spoke up in favor of that. But then one of them said, "If the Lietuvans pounded the walls the way they're pounding the city, we'd have more to worry about."

"Maybe they want to scare us into surrendering," the gray-haired woman said.

"Good luck!" Three women said it at the same time. The one with the burn scar added, "You have to be crazy to surrender to the barbarians."

"Crazy or starving!" another woman put in.

"Even if you're starving, you have to be crazy," the scarred woman said.

"What do the Lietuvans say about us?" Amanda asked.

Like her remark about saving old buildings, that one got less understanding than she would have wanted. The women around the fountain didn't know what the Lietuvans said. Not only that, they didn't care. King Kuzmickas' subjects were the enemy, and that was that. "I hope they come down with smallpox," one said.

"*I* hope they come down with the plague," another said, overtrumping.

Everyone shuddered at that. This world had never known a plague outbreak as bad as the Black Death of the fourteenth century. It had seen several smaller ones over the years, though—plenty to make people afraid of the disease. Amanda and Jeremy had antibiotics to protect them if plague ever came to Polisso. The locals weren't so lucky.

Cannon on the wall boomed. They were trying to knock out the guns the Lietuvans were using. It wasn't easy, though. The trenches the Lietuvans dug so they could get their cannon closer and closer to Polisso didn't come right toward the city. If they had, cannonballs shot from the walls could have bounced along them and wrecked guns moving forward.

Instead, they approached at an angle. That way, the guns were harder to hit, even if they took longer to get really close. At each stop on the way, the Lietuvans parked them in pits protected by mounds of earth. The Roman cannon had trouble getting at them.

And the Lietuvans kept on shooting, too. Every few minutes, a cannonball would smack down somewhere inside Polisso. The woman with the scar on her cheek had filled her water jar, but she didn't leave. The company at the fountain was probably better than back at her house. When another crash resounded from not very far away, she said, "Gods be praised we haven't had any bad fires."

Jeremy had thought of that, too. Here, it produced the same sort of shudder as mention of the plague had. In a city without fire engines, a big blaze was a deadly danger. The scarred woman rubbed at her cheek. Amanda wondered how she'd got burned. Even without a fire blazing out of control, Polisso had countless open flames. Lamps, candles, torches, fireplaces, cookfires, bonfires every now and then to get rid of garbage . . . So many things that could go wrong.

Another cannonball screamed in. In the heartbeat before it struck, Amanda thought, *It sounds like it's coming straight at me.* And it was. It slammed off the cobbles only two or three meters from where she was standing, banged against the side of the fountain, crashed into two walls, and clattered about on the road till it finally stopped.

Those first few crashes kicked up stone fragments of all sizes, some as deadly as bullets. Amanda yelped in sudden surprise and pain. A tiny chunk of flying stone had drawn a bloody line across the back of her hand. And she was lucky.

When she looked up from her own little wound, she found out just how lucky she was.

On one of its bounces, the iron ball had hit the scarred woman. It smashed her skull like a rock dropping on an egg. She lay facedown in the street. Her blood and the water from the jar she'd dropped puddled together. She'd never known what hit her. Another woman was down, clutching at her leg and screaming. Blood gushed from that wound, too. Which of the two women was luckier? Amanda couldn't have said.

Other women were also hurt by the cannonball and by the fragments. Their cries dinned in her ears. This was ten times worse than any traffic accident she'd ever seen. She wanted to throw up. She wanted to run away, too. Instead, she ran forward. She did what she could for the wounded women. That wasn't much past putting on bandages, making the more badly injured ones lie down, and telling them they'd be all right. Some of the time, she knew she was lying.

She wasn't the only one helping. Several other women who weren't hurt did the same. Screams brought men running, too. One of them was a doctor. He made bandages. He set broken bones. And he had opium against the pain. That wasn't much, but it was better than nothing. When Amanda had done all she could, she went home. She didn't realize she was sobbing till she was almost there.

Nine

Jeremy wouldn't have thought he could sleep with muskets and cannon going off within a hundred meters of the house—to say nothing of the ones the Lietuvans were shooting at Polisso. But he didn't have a whole lot of trouble. When he was tired enough, he *did* sleep. Amanda had complained the first few days after the shooting started. She hadn't since, or not about the noise. She'd come home splashed with blood and green around the gills when the cannonball smashed down by the fountain. Jeremy hadn't said a word to her about that. He'd known the same horror when he came down off the wall. In person, war was even uglier than books and movies made it out to be.

And yet the Romans and the Lietuvans took it in stride. So did the people in the other gunpowder empires in this world. He'd wondered about that even before this round of fighting broke out. Now, lying on his lumpy bed, looking at the ceiling it was too dark to see, he thought he'd found an answer. He didn't know if it was *the* answer, but it was *an* answer.

In his world, almost everybody lived to grow old. Pain-killing drugs that really worked cushioned the end when it came at last. Before the end, most people went through most of their lives without a whole lot of pain. Few cared to risk their comforts by shooting at their neighbors. If your life was likely to be long and pretty comfortable, why would you take the chance of throwing it away?

But that was in the home timeline. Things were different here. They'd been different in his world too, before anesthetics and antibiotics and dentists who knew what they were doing. Here, babies and toddlers died all the time from diarrhea and typhoid fever and whooping cough and diphtheria. One child in three didn't live to be five years old. Here, toothaches went on and on—unless teeth got pulled while the sufferer was awake. Here, infections and boils and blood poisoning and food poisoning happened every day. Here, there were no tetanus shots. People died from smallpox and the plague and tuberculosis. If they got cancer, they died from that, too—died slowly and in agony, a centimeter at a time.

In this kind of world, war looked different. You weren't likely to live a long, healthy, pain-free life no matter what you did. If you died in battle, that was liable to be a faster, more merciful death than you would get if you weren't a soldier. With all those things being so, why not take up a sword or a pike or a musket and try to do unto the other fellow before he did unto you?

Jeremy didn't think soldiers paused and reasoned that out. They didn't have to. In Agrippan Rome—and in Lietuva, too—songs and poems and statues celebrated generals who'd won glory and soldiers who'd been heroes. If a young man didn't want to stay on the farm, what was he likely to do? Join the army. That was the best chance to change his lot he was likely to have.

The other difference was, wars here weren't overwhelmingly destructive. In the home timeline, two dozen countries could blow up the world if they ever thought they had a reason to. Here, most of Agrippan Rome wouldn't feel this war at all. Neither would most of Lietuva.

And so, people seemed to think, why not fight? So what if we fought twenty years before, and fifty years before, and seventy, and a hundred ten? This time, we might win, or at least get even.

All that made some sense when looked at from a distance. When seen close up, it could have been the mad logic of beings from another planet. Jeremy still had nightmares about the man with most of his jaw shot away and his gobbling cries of pain. He didn't know everything that went into Amanda's nightmares, but he knew she had them. She'd scared him awake crying out in the night more than once.

Outside of Polisso, a Lietuvan cannon barked. A couple of seconds later, inside Polisso, the cannonball crashed home. What did it hit? Whom did it maim? Jeremy didn't know. Wherever it came down, it was too far away for him to hear the shrieks of the wounded.

He yawned. He shifted his weight again on the lumpy mattress. The wooden bed frame creaked. He closed his eyes. It seemed no darker with them closed than it had with them open. He yawned again. Another cannon fired, and another. No doubt more of them went off all through the night, but he never heard them.

He woke up with light leaking in through the slats of the shutter. Sitting up in bed, he scratched his chin. His beard was on the scraggly side. It would probably stay that way for another couple of years. He didn't care. Better a scraggly beard than shaving with a straight razor with nothing but olive oil to use instead of shaving gel.

Yawning some more, shaking his head to get the cobwebs

out, he walked down the hall to the kitchen. He was almost there before he consciously noticed the gunfire. He shook his head again, this time in surprise. This was how you got used to being stuck in the middle of a war. Till a cannonball tore a hole in *your* house, you just went on about your business.

Amanda was already in the kitchen, eating bread and honey and drinking watered wine. "Good day," she said.

"Good day," Jeremy answered. He tore his own piece of bread from the loaf. No one here had ever heard of sliced bread. That annoyed him. It wasn't the biggest thing that did, though. He said, "Don't you get sick and tired of speaking this language?"

"Oh, yes. *Oh,* yes." His sister nodded. "But what choice have we got? If the locals hear us using English, what will they think? They'll think it's Lietuvan. That's the only foreign language anyone's likely to hear around here. And if they think it's Lietuvan, they'll think we're spies. So—neoLatin."

"NeoLatin," Jeremy agreed dully. He bit into the bread. It tasted good, but it was gritty. Was this how it would be for the rest of his life? A language that wasn't his, food that wore down his teeth, an empire that had forgotten freedom and never heard of so many other things?

Another cannonball smashed something to smithereens. If the gunner had turned his cannon a little to the left . . . In that case, Jeremy might not have had to worry about the rest of his life.

Amanda didn't want to go back to the water fountain, not after what had happened there. She didn't think she was more likely to get hurt there. That wasn't it. She could get hurt anywhere, and she knew it. But she didn't want to be reminded of where the other women had got hurt.

The locals hadn't done much to clean things up, either. Broken stone and bricks still lay where they had fallen. For that matter, the cannonball still lay there, too. It wasn't all that much bigger than her closed fist. Strange to think something so small could have done so much harm.

As no one had cleaned up the rubble, so no one had cleaned up the bloodstains. They were brownish-black now, and dry, not wet, gleaming scarlet. But she still knew what they meant. They meant anguish for people who hadn't done anything to deserve any. How many husbands were without wives, how many children without mothers, because of that round lump of iron?

Most of the women at the fountain this morning hadn't been there when the cannonball struck home. Amanda thought she could tell which ones had. They were the ones who flinched whenever another cannonball smacked into Polisso. Amanda flinched, too. After seeing what she'd seen, she didn't know how anyone could keep from flinching.

The slave girl named Maria came out of her house with a water jar on her hip. "Good morning, Mistress Amanda," she said. "God bless you."

"God bless you," Amanda answered automatically. But, in this place, that didn't seem adequate. She waved with her free hand. "Do you think God blessed what happened here?"

Maria only shrugged. "I am sorry, truly sorry, people were hurt. But I am less than a mote in the eye of God. I cannot know His purposes. Neither can any other mere mortal."

"You really mean that," Amanda said in slow wonder.

"You really doubt it." Maria sounded every bit as amazed.

They both stared, neither understanding the other in the least. Maria said, "I thought even an Imperial Christian would have more faith in the Lord."

Amanda said, "I thought even a strong Christian would be able to think for herself a little bit."

And then, at the same time, they both said, "How can you be so blind?"

That might have killed the strange, delicate friendship that had grown up between them. Friendship between slave and free wasn't easy in Agrippan Rome. Neither was friendship between a native of Agrippan Rome and someone from the home timeline. Pile the one on top of the other and this friendship should have been impossible to begin with. But Amanda and Maria really did like each other.

Maria's eyes twinkled. Amanda's eyes sparkled. They both started to laugh. Maria wagged a finger at Amanda. "You are impossible!" she said.

"Well, you are pretty difficult yourself," Amanda retorted. They laughed some more.

"You are more than half a heathen," Maria said. By the standards of strong Christians in Agrippan Rome, that was true and more than true.

"You're drunk on God," Amanda said. By the standards of ordinary Americans in the home timeline, that was also true and more than true. Maria had very little but her God. No wonder she clung to Him so tightly. After a moment, Amanda added, "You're nice anyway, though."

"So are you," Maria said. They put down the jars and hugged each other.

Another cannonball crashed into a building. A rumbling roar followed the first sharp impact. A wall—or maybe the whole building—had fallen down. "I hope nobody was inside," Amanda said.

"Me, too," Maria said. They hugged again, clutching each other for whatever reassurance they could find. Then, with a sigh, Maria picked up her water jar. "Amanda—" She broke off.

"What is it?" Amanda asked.

"I've prayed *so* hard." Maria's voice was soft and shaky, her thin face pinched with worry. "I've prayed and prayed and prayed, and the Lietuvans are still out there. They're still smashing things up. They're still killing people. I know it's God's will—but I have so much trouble seeing *why*." She sounded on the edge of tears.

"And you're asking me?" Amanda said in dismay. "That kind of question makes me feel like Atlas, holding up the heavens on my shoulders."

Maria nodded. If she was offended, she kept it to herself. Lots of people here used figures of speech from the Greek myths even if they didn't believe in them. People did the same thing in the home timeline, though not so much. The slave girl said, "You think about these things, anyhow. A lot of people never do."

"Maybe I do, but I haven't got any real answers," Amanda said. "Either things happen because God makes them happen, or they happen because they just happen—you know what I mean?"

"Oh, yes," Maria said. "Some people call Fortune a god. I don't believe that." She set her chin and looked stubborn.

"Well . . ." Amanda paused. "If things happen because God make them happen, then you need to figure out why *bad* things happen."

"Satan," Maria said. "It has to be Satan."

"But if God's all-powerful, why does He let Satan do things like that?" Amanda asked. Maria's face was the picture of hard, serious thought. After close to half a minute, she gave Amanda a sad little shrug. Amanda also shrugged. She said, "I don't know, either. And if things just happen because they happen, what can you do about it? Nothing I can see."

"You sound like a philosopher," Maria said wistfully.

Amanda laughed. "Not likely! Philosophers are supposed to have answers, aren't they? All I've got are questions."

"Maybe even questions help," Maria said. "All I had before were things to worry about." She still had those, of course. But they didn't seem to worry her quite so much.

Water poured out of the fountain. Amanda filled her jug. Maria filled hers. She put it on her head when she was through. As usual, Amanda put hers on her hip again. Maria looked tall, erect, and graceful carrying her jar the way she did. Amanda knew she would have looked like a clumsy fool trying to do the same. Enough women carried full jars the way she did to keep her from standing out. That was all she cared about.

"See you soon," Maria said.

"Take care of yourself," Amanda answered. "Do you have enough to eat?"

"Yes. My owner hasn't changed what he gives me at all," Maria said. *My owner.* There it was, ugly as a slap in the face. Just hearing the words made Amanda want to be sick, or to lash out and hit something. But Maria took them in stride, if not for granted. Real worry in her voice, she asked, "What about you, Amanda? Are you and your brother all right?"

"We're fine, so far," Amanda said. She and Jeremy were a

good deal better off than that, but she didn't want to sound as if she were bragging. She didn't think Maria would do anything to betray her trust, but you never could tell who might be listening.

"That's good," Maria said, and then, wistfully, "You've got money. If you've got money, you can always get food, as long as there's any food to get."

Again, she didn't make anything special out of it. It was just the way this world worked. It was probably the way any world worked. But hunger was a much more common guest here than in Los Angeles in the home timeline.

Maria went into her owner's house. Amanda turned away and started back toward the house where she and Jeremy lived. Those words again—*her owner*. Words, and the ideas behind them, had enormous power.

But what can I do? Amanda thought unhappily. Even if she bought Amanda, set her free, and found her work where she could make a living—not always easy to do for a freedwoman—then what? How many slaves just like her would remain in Polisso afterwards? Up into the thousands, surely. How many in all of this Roman Empire? In Lietuva? In Persia? In the gunpowder empires in India? In China? Millions all told, without a doubt.

And Crosstime Traffic had only a few outposts in this whole world. Some problems were just too big to solve with what was available to tackle them. Amanda hated that, which didn't make it any less true.

Jeremy was sitting in the courtyard reading a poem when a cannonball crashed into the kitchen. The poem had kept him interested all the way through. It was in neoLatin, about a girl on a trading ship who'd been captured by Scandinavian pirates but escaped, and about her adventures getting back to the Empire. It wasn't great literature. It was more like this world's closest approach to reality TV. But it wasn't dull, not even slightly.

All the same, he dropped the scroll and jumped to his feet when half a dozen roof tiles exploded into red dust. A magpie that had been sitting on the roof flew away as fast as it could, screeching in alarm.

From her room, Amanda let out a startled squawk: "What was *that*?"

"We just got hit," Jeremy answered. "I'm going to see how bad."

There was a hole in the roof in the kitchen, and another one in the far wall. But the planks under the roof tiles weren't smoldering. The cannonball hadn't smashed any weight-bearing beams. No big cracks ran out from the whole in the wall. The stonework still seemed sound.

Amanda came into the kitchen behind Jeremy. As he had, she looked around. "We're lucky," she said after a few seconds.

"I was thinking the same thing," he said. "I can put boards over the hole in the roof to keep the rain out till somebody really repairs it. And some plaster will take care of the one in the wall."

"I suppose so." Amanda hesitated. "Do you think we'll ever get back?"

In a way, the question came out of the blue. In another way, Jeremy had trouble thinking about anything else. How surprising was it that his sister felt the same way? Not very. He shrugged. "I have to think so. Whatever's gone wrong, it can't stay messed up forever." *Why not?* he wondered. *It shouldn't have got messed up in the first place. Since it has, who knows how long it can stay that way?*

He wondered whether Amanda would point that out. She didn't, not in so many words. Instead, she asked, "Do you think you could stand it if we had to stay here forever?"

"I wouldn't like it, that's for sure," Jeremy answered. "Stand it? I don't know. What other choice would I have?"

"It would be horrible," Amanda said.

He couldn't very well argue with that. They still had enough merchandise from the home timeline to make a lot of money, probably enough to keep them wealthy for the rest of their lives. But even the richest people in Polisso did without so many things anyone from the home timeline took for granted. It would seem a bare, empty life. They might as well be shipwrecked among savages. As a matter of fact, they were. "We just have to go on," Jeremy said. "I don't know what else to tell you."

His sister nodded. "It's what I keep telling myself," she said. "Sometimes it lets me get through the day—most of the time, in fact. But when they go and knock a hole in the house—two holes in the house—even going on doesn't seem very easy."

"Yeah. I know." Jeremy cocked his head to one side. There was a new breeze in the kitchen because of those two holes. "I go down to the basement, and I try to send a message back home from the PowerBook, and it doesn't let me. . . ."

"I go down there, too," Amanda said. "Sometimes I don't even try to send a message. But the door opens when you touch the palm lock. The electric lights come on. The furniture looks like it comes from Home Depot or WalMart—and it does. There *is* a computer. I see all that stuff, and I remember we *did* come from the home timeline. It's not just something I dreamt or made up inside my head."

Jeremy made himself grin. "If it is, we're both nuts the same way." He spoke in a low voice—and in English. Making himself use his own language instead of neoLatin took a real effort.

And hearing English made Amanda blink. "That's right," she said in the same tongue. "Will we ever be able to speak our own language to anybody but each other?"

"I don't know." For safety's sake, Jeremy fell back into neoLatin. "I just don't know."

Another cannonball screeched by overhead. It slammed into a house or shop not too far away. Jeremy and Amanda looked at each other. If the Lietuvans broke into Polisso or starved it into surrender, nothing they'd talked about would matter very much. They wouldn't have to complain about how empty even the richest person's life here was. They wouldn't be rich. They'd be slaves—or they'd be dead.

Amanda was sewing up a tunic seam when someone rapped on the door. She wanted company just then about as much as she wanted another head. But Jeremy was at the market square, and it might be business. With a mutter of regret, she put down the tunic. She walked out of the courtyard and up the entry hall. The door was barred. She took the bar out of its brackets, set it aside, and opened the door.

There stood Lucio Claudio, called Fusco. "Good day," Amanda said, meaning anything but. "What can I do for you?"

"I am looking for Ieremeo Soltero," answered Gaio Fulvio's man of affairs.

"He's not here right now," Amanda said. "Can I help you?"

"I doubt it," Lucio Claudio said. Amanda glanced over at the iron bar she'd just put down. *No, you can't hit him over the head with it,* she told herself. *People would talk.* It seemed a great pity. The local, who didn't know she was contemplating his sudden departure from this world, went on, "It has to do with the official report he submitted."

"Oh. Then I can help you." Amanda stepped aside and gestured politely. "Won't you come in? Would you care for some wine?"

"It is written in the classical language. How could you—?" But Lucio Claudio caught himself. He'd already done business with Amanda. "No. Wait. You have already proved that you are familiar with it."

"That's right. I have. And I am." Amanda's smile was anything but sweet. She repeated, "Won't you come in?"

Lucio Claudio's face said mere females had no business knowing classical Latin. It also said mere merchants had no business knowing the old language. And if the merchant happened to be a girl, or the girl happened to be a merchant . . . "Very well." He didn't sound any happier about being there than Amanda was to have him there.

When she took him back to the courtyard, she pointed to the hole in the kitchen roof. Jeremy had put boards over it, but the roofer hadn't replaced the shattered tiles. As she pointed, a cannonball thudded home somewhere not far away. She said, "At a time like this, don't you have more important things to worry about than official reports? We submitted it on time. It's accurate. Isn't that enough to satisfy you?"

The local's swarthy skin darkened further, probably with annoyance. He said, "What could be more important than keeping complete and thorough records?"

"You're joking," Amanda said. Then she realized he wasn't. In Agrippan Rome, records were at least as important as people. Another cannonball landed somewhere a little farther away. She asked, "Don't you think you ought to be worrying about keeping the Lietuvans out of Polisso? Shouldn't everything else wait on that?"

"Certainly not," he answered. She might have suggested that he ate with his fingers—except the locals did eat with their fingers, and had a complex set of manners for doing so. "Though besieged, we are still Roman. Life must go on as normally as possible."

That could have sounded brave and noble. To Amanda, it sounded infuriating. But she didn't let her anger show. She would have to keep on dealing with Lucio Claudio and with people like him. Or, if she didn't, other crosstime traders would. *If there still are other crosstime traders,* she thought. *If they ever come back to Agrippan Rome.* She shivered. She doubted more and more that they ever would.

All she said, then, was, "Let me get you your wine, in that case, and you can go ahead."

She poured a cup for herself, too. If she hadn't, Lucio Claudio might have thought she was trying to poison him. He spilled some on the paving stones and murmured a prayer to Dionysus. Amanda spilled some, too. She prayed for the Emperor's spirit, not to any of the gods. An Imperial Christian could go that far and no further.

Lucio Claudio's sneer said he didn't think it was far enough. But it was legal. He didn't complain, not out loud. Instead, he took out the official report Jeremy had written. "Some of this is not as clear as it ought to be," he said.

Amanda knew her brother had written the report so it wouldn't be clear. She couldn't very well tell that to Lucio Claudio, though. "You must be mistaken," she said.

He shook his head. "No, I am not," he insisted. "Look here, where the report speaks of your sources for these remarkable trade goods you have. . . ."

"May I see it, please?" she asked. Reluctantly, Lucio Claudio handed it to her. People were careful with papers here. This was the only copy of the official report. The only way to get another one would be to have a secretary copy it all out. She read the passage he pointed at, then said, "It seems plain enough to me."

"Nonsense," Lucio Claudio said.

"It is not nonsense," Amanda said. "Don't they teach anyone in Polisso what an ablative absolute is and how to use it?" If she could argue about classical Latin grammar and how it worked, she wouldn't have to argue about what was and wasn't in the official report.

And she'd flicked Lucio Claudio on his pride. He took a big, angry gulp of wine. "We may be near the frontier here, but we have good schools," he insisted. "We have excellent schools, in fact. Why, three hundred years ago the poet Settimo Destro, called Sinistro, had his verses quoted from one end of the Empire to the other. And where did he come from? Right here in Polisso!"

Amanda was happier arguing town pride than the official report, too. "Three hundred years is a long time," she said.

"What have you done since your left-handed poet lived?" *Sinistro* meant *left-handed*. "Not much, if you don't understand what this means."

"Suppose you explain it," Lucio Claudio said.

"I don't need to explain it. It's as plain as the nose on your face. Let me read it to you, so you can see for yourself." Read it she did, in classical Latin: "'They having secured the required articles from their suppliers, who, having taken all precautions to produce them with the maximum practicable degree of quality and artistic excellence, conveyed the aforementioned goods to those who would distribute them for retail distribution, they delivered these aforesaid articles of commerce to the famous metropolis for final distribution to and among its most excellent citizens.' There! Isn't that obvious?"

Lucio Claudio fumed. He'd wanted to talk about the official report in neoLatin. But if Amanda stuck to the old language, he had to do the same. If he didn't, he would lose face. He would sooner have been blown to bits by a Lietuvan cannonball than admit that a merchant's daughter knew more about classical Latin than he did.

Instead of admitting it, he snatched the official report away from her. He went through it till he found another passage he didn't like. Triumph in his voice, he said, "What about this? It does not explain why you have these remarkable goods and no one else does. That, after all, was the whole point of requiring an official report from you in the first place."

"So you could steal our trade secrets, you mean," Amanda said. That made Lucio Claudio look as if he'd bitten into a lemon. Everybody was touchy about trade secrets in Agrippan

Rome. With no patents or copyrights to protect knowledge, people had to be. Not even the government could poke at them too hard, not without risking trouble. Amanda held out her hand. "Let me see it, if you please. How can I answer when you keep taking things away from me?"

"Here," Lucio Claudio said. "And no quibbles over ablative absolutes this time, if you please. The sentences are very straightforward."

Even you understand them, you mean? It was on the tip of Amanda's tongue, but she didn't say it. A bureaucrat who was doing his job, going through the motions, was one thing. A bureaucrat with a personal grudge was something else again, and something much more dangerous. She read Jeremy's answer and nodded. "You're right. This is very straightforward. It says we get our goods from the finest suppliers in the Roman Empire. That's the truth. The quality of what we sell proves it."

"But who are these suppliers?" Lucio Claudio demanded. "Why can't anyone else find them and deal with them?"

"That *is* our trade secret," Amanda said. "If everyone knew where to get these goods, where would our living be?" She smiled. "Would you like some more wine?"

They went round and round for the next hour. Jeremy had done a good job of writing the report so that it sounded impressive but didn't say anything. Finally, Lucio Claudio gave up and went away. Amanda would have liked that better if she hadn't been pretty sure he would come back.

People in Polisso had stopped carrying food out in the open. That was an invitation to get knocked over the head and have it stolen. After almost four weeks, the Lietuvan siege was starting to pinch the city. When shoppers brought grain or olives home from the market square, they put them in leather sacks that could have held anything. They tried not to go alone, too. Having friends along made thieves try someone else.

Jeremy bought wheat and barley in the market square every so often. He wanted people to see him doing it. That way, nobody would start wondering if he and Amanda were hoarding.

He, too, had a plain leather sack for carrying home the grain. He headed back to his house by himself, but he wasn't worried. He was young and big and looked strong. No one had bothered him yet.

He was only a couple of blocks from the house when three punks stepped out of a shadowed doorway. "Oh, it's you," the biggest one said—they'd met before. "What have you got?"

Before Jeremy could answer, a cannonball smashed through a door about a hundred meters away. One punk flinched, then tried to pretend he hadn't. Jeremy said, "I've got barley." He felt fairly safe admitting it. Plenty of people were going back and forth. If the three toughs tried robbing him, they'd get jumped on. People here were more likely to do that than they were in Los Angeles in the home timeline. Punks often carried knives here, but so did ordinary men. You didn't run the risk of going up against an assault rifle with your bare hands.

And the leader of this little gang shook his head. "No, that's not what I meant," he said. No doubt he sounded much more innocent than he was. He could see this wasn't a good spot for a robbery as well as Jeremy could—better, probably.

He gave Jeremy a mocking little half-bow. "What *jokes* have you got?"

"Oh, jokes." Jeremy tried not to show how relieved he was. "Let me think." He'd looked at *The Laughter-Lover* a long time ago. "Well, there was the cheapskate who named himself as heir in his own will."

The punks groaned, which was about what that one deserved. "You can do better," their leader said. *You'd better do better*, his tone warned. If they started thumping Jeremy for telling lousy jokes, ordinary people might not stop them—might join in, as a matter of fact.

He tried again: "There was a halfwit who bought a house and went around carrying one stone from it so he could show people what it was like."

They groaned again. They didn't seem quite so disgusted this time, though. "What else have you got?" the biggest one asked.

"There was another halfwit—this one wanted to cross a river," Jeremy said. "When he rode onto the ferryboat and didn't get down from his horse, somebody asked him why not. He said, 'I can't! I'm in a hurry!'"

"That's not too bad," the leader said after looking at his two buddies to see what they thought. "But try to have some better ones next time we run into you." He swaggered on up the street.

Jeremy stood there staring after him till a bad-tempered man in a tunic full of fancy embroidery shouted for him to get out of the way. That tunic shouted, too, and what it said was, *I'm important! Don't mess with me, or you'll be sorry!* In Los Angeles, that kind of display would have provoked Jeremy to ignore the bad-tempered man. People here paid more attention to status. With a twinge of regret, Jeremy moved.

He got the barley back to the house without any more trouble. Amanda said, "We have a new hole in the roof to fix." She pointed. Sure enough, another cannonball had hit the kitchen, about two meters to the left of the first hole.

Jeremy said something about what the Lietuvans did for fun that he couldn't possibly have known for sure. Then he asked, "Are you all right? Is the house all right?"

"It scared me out of a year's growth, but it didn't hurt me," his sister answered. "It seemed worse than the last one, because it didn't go out through the wall. It banged around inside the kitchen till it finally stopped. I was here in the courtyard. It smashed some jars. Some grain got spilled, but it missed the big amphora full of olive oil, thank goodness."

"That would have been a mess," Jeremy agreed.

"It sure would," Amanda said. "But do you know what? I wasn't even thinking about the mess. I was thinking how bad it would be to lose the whole amphora of oil when we're under siege and it would cost an arm and a leg to buy another one." She looked at him. "I'm starting to think the way the locals do. That scares me worse than the cannonball in the kitchen."

"I don't blame you," Jeremy said. If they really were stuck in Agrippan Rome forever, they would have to make that adjustment sooner or later. They couldn't live here the way they would have back in the home timeline. Polisso was a different place—such a different place!—from Los Angeles. They couldn't look at the world here the same way and hope to survive.

Will I end up buying slaves, then? Jeremy shuddered and shook his head. Nothing could make him do that. Better to be dead than to do that, even if it was as ordinary for someone rich here as owning a fancy car was back in L.A.

"I know what you're thinking," Amanda whispered. The horror in her eyes matched the horror Jeremy felt. "We can't. No matter what else we do, we can't."

"No. We won't," Jeremy said. "Not ever. No matter what." He did his best to laugh. It sounded pretty ghastly. "This is all dumb, anyhow. Before too long, we'll be back in touch with the home timeline. Mom and Dad will come up from the transposition chamber in the subbasement, and everything will be fine."

"Sure." Amanda nodded. But she wouldn't look at him. A cannonball screeched through the air and thudded home fifty meters away. Somebody screamed. That was all real. The home timeline? The home timeline seemed like a dream, and a fading dream at that.

Ten

If I can't go back to the home timeline, what do I have to do to make this one as bearable as I can? The longer Amanda stayed in Polisso, the more she asked herself that question. Asking it was easy. Finding any kind of answer wasn't.

The only thing she could come up with was, *Get rich. Stay rich.* If she had money, she wouldn't go hungry. The food she did eat would be a little better. Her clothes would be warmer in the winter, and not quite so scratchy. Her bed would be a little softer. She would be able to buy books to help pass the time. If she got sick or hurt herself, she would be able to buy poppy juice—opium—to ease the pain.

And that was about all. So much of what she'd taken for granted would be gone forever. If her teeth gave her trouble, she could either get them pulled without anesthetic or suffer. If she got sick with something that the medicines she and Jeremy had wouldn't cure, she would either get well or die on her own. No doctors worth the name. No hospitals.

She ground wheat into flour in a stone quern. The repeated motion made her shoulder ache. If she did it for years, it would give her arthritis. If she didn't do it, she wouldn't have any bread to eat. The work was boring. It would have gone by faster if she could have gabbed with friends or listened to music or watched TV while she did it. No phone. No CD player. No TV.

"No nothing," she muttered. Grind, grind, grind. When she baked at home, she'd taken flour for granted, too. Machines made it. It came out of a sack. When you had to make it yourself, you didn't take it for granted. Why couldn't she get more than this pathetic little bit with each turn of the quern? Grind, grind, grind.

Jeremy walked into the kitchen. "How's it going?" he asked cheerfully. Why shouldn't he be cheerful? *He* wasn't grinding flour. Amanda screamed at him. He jumped half a meter in the air. "Well, excuse me for breathing," he said when his feet thumped back onto the ground. "What did I say that was wrong?"

Part of Amanda was ashamed at losing her cool. "Nothing, really," she mumbled. But the rest of her was angry, and she decided she wouldn't sweep it under the rug after all. There weren't any rugs here to sweep it under, anyhow. She shook her head. "No, not nothing. I don't see you in the kitchen. I don't see you with a sore shoulder. I just see you eating bread."

"I'm making money for us," he answered.

That was true. And if they were stuck here for good, they would need all the money they could get their hands on. Amanda had just been thinking about that. But even so . . . "I could do that just as well as you could," she said.

"You could do it pretty well, yeah," her brother said. "Just as well? I don't know. Some of the locals get weird about dealing with a girl."

"That's 'cause they're a bunch of sexist yahoos," said Amanda, who'd gone all the way through *Gulliver's Travels* not long before. The parts of the book everybody knew, where he went to Lilliput and then to Brobdingnag, were only the icing on the cake. The real essence came later.

"Sure they are," Jeremy said. "But just because an attitude is stupid, that doesn't mean it's not real."

Again, he wasn't wrong. That didn't mean Amanda liked his being right. "If I could only get out of this kitchen more, I'd show you what I can do," she said.

He didn't say, *How are you going to do that?* If he had, she wouldn't just have screamed. She would have thrown something at him. Then again, he didn't need to ask the question out loud. It hung in the air whether he asked it or not.

The scary part was, *How are you going to do that?* had an answer. The answer was, *Buy a slave to do the work for me.* That was what the locals—the prosperous locals, anyhow—did. They didn't have food processors or kneading machines or automatic dishwashers or vacuum cleaners or washing machines or any of a zillion other gadgets. They had people. They had them, and they used them. That let the ones who weren't slaves take care of *their* business—and also think about things like literature and what passed for science here.

Seeing slavery was dreadful enough for somebody from late twenty-first–century Los Angeles. Beginning to understand how and why it worked was a hundred times worse. "They'd better find us and get us out of here," Amanda whispered.

"Yeah," Jeremy said. Both of them had forgotten the quarrel. As Amanda had followed his thoughts not long before, he hadn't had any trouble knowing what she was thinking. It disgusted him as much as it did her. Yes, this was why the locals kept slaves. Worse, this was why, from their point of view, it made sense.

Amanda shook her head. No matter how much sense it made, it was still awful. "They'd better get us out," she repeated.

"That's right," Jeremy said. "If they don't get us out of here, we can sue them."

"Wait a minute," Amanda said. Her brother looked back at her, bland as unsalted butter. Amanda made a horrible face at him. It was so horrible, it made him—just barely—crack a smile. She aimed her index finger as if it were a gun. "You're being ridiculous on purpose."

"What about it?" Jeremy retorted. "It's better than being ridiculous by accident, don't you think?"

She didn't have a good answer for that. As cannon roared and muskets barked, as walls fell down with a crash, she wondered if there were good answers for anything—not just in this world but in any. "I wish we were back in the home timeline," she said, which wasn't an answer but was the truth.

"So do I," her brother said. "And that and some silver will buy me wine in a tavern. If they fix whatever's wrong—if they *can* fix whatever's wrong—they'll bring us home. If they don't, or if it isn't, we figure out how to make the best of things here." He strode forward. "You want me to grind flour for a while?"

"Sure!" Amanda said.

Jeremy was awkward rotating the central stone in the quern. She had to remind him to keep feeding wheat in at the top. Otherwise, he would have happily ground away at nothing. He worked steadily for about ten minutes. Then he started grumbling and rubbing his shoulder. After another five minutes, he stepped away from the counter with a proud smile on his face. "There!"

Amanda clapped her hands—once, twice, three times. She couldn't have been more sarcastic if she'd tried for a week. "Wow! Congratulations! Yippee!" she said. "That's about enough flour for a muffin—a small muffin. Don't stop. You're just getting the hang of it."

He looked as if she'd stabbed him in the back. "I was trying to help," he said.

"I know you were," she said. "You were starting to do it, too—and then you went and stopped. Where do you think your bread comes from every day? Let me give you a hint: it's not a miracle. It's me standing there turning that miserable quern till my shoulder really starts hurting, and then turning it some more. If I don't make flour, we don't eat bread. It's that simple—or it would be, except you can make flour, too. Go ahead. You were doing fine."

"And what will you do while I'm taking care of that?" Jeremy asked suspiciously.

"Me? I'll stand here fanning myself with peacock feathers for a while," Amanda answered. "Then I'll peel myself some grapes: a whole bowlful, I think. And then I'll drop them into my mouth one at a time. I'll make sure I do all this stuff while you're watching, too, so it drives you especially wild."

He gaped at her. She wondered if she'd gone too far with that, far enough to make him angry. But then he started to laugh. Even better, he started to grind more wheat into flour. Amanda wished she really did have some grapes to peel, to help keep him going.

Jeremy already knew most women worked harder than most men in Polisso. That stint at the quern drove the lesson home. So did the way his shoulder ached the next day. He'd been doing work his body wasn't used to, and it told him it wasn't happy.

Amanda spent more time than that at the quern just about every day. How did her shoulder feel when she got up every morning? How would it feel twenty years from now, if she ground grain just about every day between now and then? People's bodies wore out faster in this world than they did in the home timeline. The work here was a lot harder. And, except for wine and opium, nothing here could make pain go away. No one here had ever heard of aspirins, for instance.

Down in the secret part of the basement, Jeremy tried to send a message to the home timeline. As usual, no such luck. He wondered why he went on bothering. Every time he failed, he felt terrible. *But if I ever do get through, that'll make up for all the times I don't!*

Besides, if he didn't keep trying, what would that be? A sign that he'd given up hope. He might be stuck in Agrippan Rome. Resigning himself to getting stuck here was a whole different story.

The siege went on. The Lietuvans pounded away at Polisso. The gunners on the walls shot back at them. Little by little, King Kuzmickas' cannoneers wrecked the Roman guns. No doubt they lost some of their own, too. The question was who could hold out longer, the besiegers or the besieged?

That was one of the questions, anyhow. Another was how long would the Romans farther south in the province of

Dacia need to send an army up to Polisso and try to drive the Lietuvans back into their own kingdom? Jeremy had no idea what the answer to that was, but it was on his mind. It had to be on the mind of everybody trapped inside Polisso.

It had to be on Kuzmickas' mind, too, and on the minds of his soldiers. They wouldn't want to be stuck between an advancing Roman army and the garrison of a town that still defied them. If they could take Polisso soon, it would be in their interest to do so. Getting their guns closer to the walls and shooting at all hours of the day and night made good sense for them.

Jeremy didn't think trying to storm Polisso made good sense for the Lietuvans. Annio Basso, the commandant of the city, would surely have agreed with him. So would all of Annio Basso's colonels and captains. When everybody on one side thinks the other side couldn't be dumb enough to try something—well, what better time to try it?

No one in Polisso looked for an all-out assault on the walls. Jeremy certainly didn't. Unlike some other men in Polisso, he didn't claim afterwards that he did, either. Like just about everyone else in town, he was asleep when the attack started.

King Kuzmickas' men chose the middle of a dark, moon-less night. Like anything else, that had both advantages and disadvantages. The inky blackness of nights without electric lights let them get close to the wall before the Romans saw them. On the other hand, that same inky blackness made them stumble and trip over their own feet and think they were closer to the wall than they really were. Taking everything into account, a little moonlight might have helped the attack.

When the first horn calls and shouts of alarm rang out

from the wall, Jeremy slept through them. He'd had trouble falling asleep, because the Lietuvans were shooting more than usual. Later, he realized they were hiding the racket their advancing soldiers made. But that was later. At the time, all he thought was that there was a devil of a lot of noise.

Along with the gunfire, he heard shouts from the direction of the wall. At first, he couldn't tell through the din what people were shouting. That they were yelling anything at all surprised him. Except for the cannon going off every now and then, he hadn't heard much at night. He'd learned to ignore the cannon. How was he supposed to ignore people yelling like madmen?

Then he made out what the soldiers were yelling: "Ladders!"

He knew little about warfare. He didn't want to learn anything more. But one thing seemed plain enough. When some people started shouting, "Ladders!" it was because other people were trying to climb them. The only people who could trying to climb ladders here were King Kuzmickas' Lietuvans.

For a little while, Jeremy thought Kuzmickas had gone out of his mind. Assaulting Polisso couldn't possibly work— could it? Then he heard more shouts on the wall, and not all of them sounded as if they were in neoLatin. If the Lietuvans had got men up on the walls, that could mean only one thing.

Trouble. Big trouble.

Those shouts on the wall raised shouts inside Polisso. More and more people woke up and discovered their city was under attack. By the cries and screams Jeremy heard, a lot of the locals believed Polisso was as good as lost.

At first, he thought they were idiots. Then he realized they might know more about what was going on than he did. He wished that hadn't occurred to him. He would have been a lot happier if he hadn't. *Ignorance is bliss,* ran through his mind.

"Jeremy?" That was Amanda, out in the hall. "You awake?"

"No, I'm still sound asleep." He got out of bed. Sleeping in the clothes you also wore during the day had one advantage: you didn't need to get dressed. He opened the door. "How are you?"

"Not so good," she answered. "What are we going to *do*?"

Before Jeremy could answer, a herald up the street shouted, "Citizens of Polisso, stay in your homes! Do not give way to fear! Soldiers will keep the invaders out of the city!"

"That's what we'll do," Jeremy said. "We'll sit tight—for now, anyway."

"Do you really think the soldiers can drive back the Lietuvans?" Amanda asked. "What do we do if they *don't*?"

"Well, we can't run, because there's nowhere to run to," he said. "We can surrender and be slaves—if they don't kill us for the fun of it—or we can fight. I don't see much else. Do you?"

"The basement," she said. "The subbasement."

He shook his head. "They aren't set up to live in. Maybe they ought to be, but they aren't. If we were hiding for a few hours from people who would go away, that'd be different. But if the Lietuvans win, they're here to stay. Before too long, we'd have to come out, and they'd have us."

Soldiers ran by the house, their chainmail clanking. They shouted in neoLatin. They were Romans, then. Jeremy didn't know what he would have done if they'd been shouting in Lietuvan. Panicked, probably.

"I wish we had Dad's pistol," Amanda said.

"Wish for the moon while you're at it," Jeremy said. "Can you imagine trying to explain *that* to the city prefect?"

Amanda only shrugged. "I don't care. I'd rather be alive and free and explaining with a bunch of lies than killed or sold in a slave market somewhere in Lietuva. If Polisso falls, it doesn't matter whether the link with the home timeline comes back afterwards. Nobody would find us."

Jeremy hadn't thought of that. His sister was right. He wished she weren't. He said, "No guarantee the pistol would save us. If Polisso falls, we couldn't shoot enough Lietuvans to make much difference." He wasn't sure he could shoot anybody. But if the choice was between killing and dying or being enslaved, he thought he could pull the trigger—not that there was any trigger to pull.

He turned away, hurrying out into the courtyard and then across it. "Where are you going?" Amanda called after him.

"To the storeroom and the kitchen."

"What for?"

He didn't answer. He was trying not to break his neck in the darkness. When he got into the storeroom, he had to feel around to find what he wanted. It was pitch black in there, and he hadn't brought a lamp. Even in the dark, though, he didn't need long. And he knew where things were in the kitchen even without any light.

"What on earth—?" Amanda said as he went past her and out toward the front door. "What *are* you doing with the sword and those knives?"

"Putting them where we can grab them in a hurry if we have to," Jeremy said. "We haven't got a pistol. The sword is the best we can do. And a couple of those carving knives have blades that are almost as long. They're better than nothing."

He hadn't been sure he could shoot anybody. He was even less sure he could stab somebody. And using a sword or a knife took more skill and practice than using a firearm. He had next to none of those, Amanda even less. In an emergency, though, you did what you could with what you had and hoped for the best. If this didn't count as an emergency, he'd never seen one.

Amanda didn't argue with him. He'd been afraid she would. Instead, she went up the hall herself. She came back with one of the knives, looked at it, started to put it down, and then hung on instead. "Just in case," she said.

She didn't say in case of what. Jeremy didn't need her to draw him a picture. Women and girls had reasons not to want to be taken as slaves that most men didn't need to worry about. Who could say how much those would matter till the moment came?

Maybe it wouldn't. Jeremy hoped not. Outside, more men in chainmail ran past. Like the last lot of soldiers, these yelled back and forth in neoLatin. With luck, that meant the Romans were getting the upper hand in the fight on the wall.

With luck . . . "We ought to make a thanks-offering at the temple if the Lietuvans don't get in," Jeremy said, and Amanda nodded.

Somewhere not far away, a horn blared out a call. Both Jeremy and Amanda's heads whipped toward those notes. Jeremy had heard lots of Roman military horn calls. This didn't sound like any of them. It was wilder and fiercer. And if it wasn't a Roman horn call, it could only be . . .

"The Lietuvans!" someone down the block cried—a sort of a despairing wail. "The Lietuvans are in the city!"

A volley of musket fire that seemed to come from right up

the street proved the man was right. More shouts rang out from most of the houses close by. Those were as full of dread as the first.

And there were fresh shouts, shouts of "Kuzmickas!" and "Perkunas!" and other things Jeremy couldn't understand. They were all in an oddly musical language, one full of rising and falling syllables. Lietuvan in this world wasn't quite the same as Lithuanian in the home timeline, but it wasn't very far away.

Amanda's lips were squeezed tight together. She looked as if she was clamping down hard on a scream. Jeremy didn't blame her. He was clamping down pretty hard himself. She whispered, "What are we going to do?"

"Sit tight as long as we can," Jeremy answered. "If it looks like the city's going to fall. . . . If it looks like that, maybe our best chance is to try to get away. But we don't know how many Lietuvans got in, or how the fight's going. Everything still may turn out all right."

She nodded, even though her eyes called him a liar. Another volley of musketry rang out, this one even closer to the house. Men shouted the Roman Emperor's name and some ripe insults in neoLatin. The Roman legionaries hadn't given up this fight, then.

Neither had the Lietuvans. They yelled back. More guns banged. Boots thudded on cobblestones. Soldiers ran back and forth right in front of the house. A wounded man shrieked. Jeremy couldn't tell if he was a Roman or a Lietuvan. When people were healthy, they all sounded different. When they were badly hurt, they all sounded the same.

Metal clashed on metal. Matchlock muskets were slow and clumsy to reload any time. In the middle of the night, the job had to be next to impossible. You could reverse them and use them for clubs—or you could throw them down and use swords instead.

It sounded as if the whole battle for Polisso were being fought there outside the house. That couldn't have been true. But it still seemed that way. Every shot and groan and sword clanging off sword or spearhead came to Jeremy's ears from what felt no more than five meters away. He could only have made sure of that by going out in the street and seeing for himself. Except for jumping off a cliff, he couldn't have found a better way to kill himself. He stayed inside.

"Come on!" Amanda said whenever the Romans rallied—or whenever they wavered. "Come on—you can do it!" She suddenly stopped and looked amazed. "I'm rooting for people to kill other people. That's so sick!"

"Tell me about it," Jeremy answered. "I'm doing the same thing."

People were killing other people out there in the street. If more Romans killed Lietuvans than the other way round, Polisso would stay—what? Free? Polisso hadn't been free before the Lietuvans broke in. It wouldn't be free if they all packed up and marched away as soon as the sun came up. But it would be . . . unsacked. Jeremy didn't even know if that was a word. He didn't care, either. It was what he wanted, more than anything else in the world.

He heard, or thought he heard, more shouts in neoLatin than in Lietuvan. The Romans sounded excited. The Lietuvans sounded scared. Or did they? Was he hearing it that way because that was what he wanted to hear? How could he tell? How could he know? By waiting to see what happened—no other way.

Someone pounded on the front door.

Jeremy froze. Amanda gasped. Someone pounded again—not with the knocker, but with a heavy fist on the oak timbers. Whoever was out there shouted something. The shout wasn't in neoLatin.

"What are we going to do?" Amanda said. Jeremy started for the door. She grabbed his arm. "Don't let them in!"

"Let them in? Are you nuts?" he said. "I'm going to pile furniture and stuff behind the door so they have a harder time breaking it down."

"Oh," she said, and then, "I'll help."

They carried tables and chests of drawers in from the parlor and the bedrooms. The Lietuvans weren't pounding with fists any more. They'd found something big and heavy. By the way it thudded against the door, Jeremy would have guessed it was a telephone pole, except they didn't have telephone poles here. They didn't have many in Los Angeles any more, either, but some were still left. The door and the iron bar across it seemed to be doing all right. But the brackets that held the bar in place were starting to tear out of the door frame.

"Why did they have to pick *our* house?" Amanda groaned.

"Because we're lucky," Jeremy answered, which jerked a startled laugh out of her. He clenched his fingers around the hilt of the sword till his knuckles whitened. He didn't know how much good it would do, but it wouldn't do any if he didn't have it. "Where are the Roman soldiers when we really need them?"

One of the brackets came loose with a tortured crunch of splintering wood. The door sagged back as if someone had punched it in the stomach. Jeremy and Amanda pushed against the pile of furniture to try to hold it closed. No good. More people were pushing from the other side. A Lietuvan's scowling, blood-streaked face appeared in the doorway. Sword in hand, he started scrambling over the obstacles toward Jeremy and Amanda.

"Get back!" Jeremy shouted to his sister.

She shook her head. "I'll help!" She had her kitchen knife out and ready, too.

The Lietuvan thrust at Jeremy, who jerked back just in time to keep from getting spitted like a corn dog. With a mocking laugh, the soldier scrambled forward—till a little table broke under his weight. His laugh turned into a howl of dismay as he went down *splat!* on all fours.

Jeremy jumped forward and stabbed him in the arm. The Lietuvan screamed. The sword grated on bone. Blood spurted out. Jeremy could smell it, like hot iron. The Lietuvan jerked away and ran back the way he'd come. The sword pulled free. Jeremy brandished the bloodstained blade.

Later, he realized what an idiot he was. He'd been lucky with the one soldier. If the Lietuvan's pals had come after him, how could he have held them off? But just then a swarm of Romans shouting Honorio Prisco's name charged up the street. Instead of breaking into the house—had they intended to use it for a strongpoint?—the Lietuvans fell back.

Jeremy stared at the bloody sword. He had blood on his hand, too, and on his arm, and splashed on the front of his tunic. He didn't know whether to be proud or be sick.

Amanda said, "Let's prop the door closed. Maybe we can at least halfway fix that bracket, so it'll stay shut by itself. Then we won't be an easy target for every burglar in town."

"Burglars!" Jeremy dropped the sword—he almost dropped

it on his toes, which wouldn't have been so good. "Right now, I don't . . . care at all about burglars." He'd almost said something much juicier than that. "We've got . . . worse things to worry about than burglars." That was also understated, and also true.

"I know." But Amanda cocked her head to one side, listening. "I think this new push really is driving the Lietuvans back. The noise does sound like it's farther from here and closer to the wall than it has been for a while."

"I hope so," Jeremy said after cocking his head to one side and listening. He meant every word of that. In wondering tones, he went on, "I don't know whether to hope that Lietuvan bleeds to death or gets better."

His sister shrugged. "I don't much care one way or the other. All I care about is that you're all right." She paused and seemed to be listening to herself in almost the same way as she'd just listened to the street fighting. "Did I really say that?" Slowly, she nodded. "I really did. And you know what else? I meant it, too."

"Good." Jeremy picked up a leg from the table that had broken under the Lietuvan. He smacked it into his palm. "Maybe I can use this to hammer the bracket into place. If I could go get a couple of tools from Home Depot, fixing it would probably take about ten minutes. But if I could do that . . ." He let his voice trail away and got to work making what repairs he could.

Going to the water fountain two days later reminded Amanda of what a close call Polisso had had. Bloodstains were everywhere. She'd never seen so much blood. Here and there, where it had pooled between cobblestones, flies gathered in buzzing clouds. They flew up as she walked past. One of them lit on her and crawled along her arm. She made a disgusted noise and shook it away.

No bodies lay in the street. They'd already been dragged away, Romans and Lietuvans alike. They'd probably been plundered first: of weapons, of money, of armor, of food, of everything down to their shoes and their drawers. She wondered if scavengers in Polisso had quietly made sure some of the soldiers were dead. She wouldn't have been surprised.

Bullet scars marked the brick and stone ground floors of houses and shops. Bullet holes peppered the timber upper stories. In one way, though, the damage would have been worse in the home timeline. Here, neither side had been able to shoot out any glass windows. As far as Amanda knew, Polisso had none.

Several women were already at the fountain when she got there. "Everything all right with you, dearie?" one of them called.

"I'm still here. I'm still in one piece," Amanda answered. "The town's still here, too. It's . . . not in as many pieces as it might be."

The local woman laughed. "Ain't it the truth?" she said. "When those barbarians got inside, I didn't know whether to go up on the roof and throw tiles down on their noggins or hide under my bed."

"That's how Pyrrhus of Epirus got it," another woman said. "Roof tiles, I mean, not hiding under the bed."

Amanda had heard of Pyrrhus of Epirus. He was the king who'd given his name to the Pyrrhic victory. He'd fought the Romans, beaten them thanks to war elephants, but almost ruined his army doing it. Afterwards, looking things over, he'd said, "One more victory like this and we're ruined!"

That was where her knowledge stopped. And she would have bet knowing even that much put her ahead of nine out of ten—maybe ninety-nine out of a hundred—people in Los Angeles in the home timeline. But this housewife on the edge of the Roman Empire knew how he'd died, even though he'd been dead for more than 2,300 years.

At first, that astonished Amanda. After a little while, though, it didn't any more. Pyrrhus was part of the locals' history in a way he wasn't back home. These Romans nowadays thought of themselves as—were—descended from the ones who'd battled and finally beaten Pyrrhus. They knew who he was the same way most Americans knew who Cornwallis was. He was almost a favorite enemy. He'd been tough, he'd been clever, he'd been dangerous—and he'd lost. What more could you ask for in a foe?

Some of the women who'd been at the fountain the morning before started going on about what they'd seen. They were amazingly calm about mutilated bodies. Amanda gulped. The woman who'd mentioned Pyrrhus noticed she was green and said, "Sweetie, if those Lietuvan so-and-sos had whipped our boys, *we'd* look like that now."

She was right. That didn't make Amanda like it any more or make it any better. And when Roman legionaries took a town in Lietuva or Persia, they acted the same way. Soldiers played by tough rules in this world.

Come to that, soldiers played by tough rules in any world. The home timeline didn't have much to be proud of. The main difference was, they tried to cover up the worst of what they did in the home timeline. Here, they were likely to boast about their atrocities. They thought such horrors made other people afraid of them.

A cannonball howled through the air. The Romans had driven the Lietuvans out of Polisso, but King Kuzmickas hadn't given up and gone home. He was still out there, and so were his soldiers. If they couldn't storm the city, they still might starve it into surrendering.

You're full of cheerful thoughts today, aren't you? Amanda said to herself.

And then, all at once, she did feel better. Here came Maria. The slave girl smiled and waved to her. "Good to see you're safe," she said.

"Same to you," Amanda answered.

"I was worried," Maria said. "You never can tell what will happen when the enemy gets into a city."

Amanda knew more about that now than she'd ever wanted to. "I'll say! The Lietuvans broke into our house. Ieremeo drove them off with his sword."

"Bravely done!" Maria said.

"It was, wasn't it?" Amanda knew she sounded surprised. Bravery wasn't something people thought about much in the home timeline. How often did anyone there have the chance to be brave? How often did anyone there *want* the chance to be brave? Didn't the chance to be brave mean the chance to get killed, or at least badly hurt? Measuring yourself against a chance like that was what made bravery.

"I should say it was," Maria answered. "Your brother with just a sword against trained soldiers with mailshirts and helmets and everything . . . He couldn't have frightened them off all by himself, could he?" She suddenly looked frightened. "I mean no disrespect to him, of course, none at all."

What's that all about? But Amanda needed only a couple of seconds to realize what it was about. Maria had remembered she was a slave. She might have offended a freewoman. If she did offend, she could pay for it. Painfully.

"It's all right," Amanda said quickly. "What's that proverb? 'Even Hercules can't fight two,' that's it. We would have been in a lot of trouble if the legionaries hadn't come up the street just then. The Lietuvans went off to fight them, and they never came back."

Now what was the matter? Maria was looking at her as if she'd picked her nose in public. Voice stiff with disapproval, the slave girl said, "I wouldn't have thought even an Imperial Christian would believe in Hercules."

"Who said I believe in him?" Amanda answered. "It's just a proverb."

Maria wouldn't see it. The more Amanda tried to explain, the more stubborn the slave got. As far as she was concerned, the word was the thing. "You've talked of pagan gods twice now in the last couple of weeks," she said sadly. "Either one thinks they have power, or one tells lies on purpose, knowing they are lies. And lies come straight from Satan."

"You don't understand," Maria told her. "I wanted you to know I wasn't mad because you said my brother couldn't fight off a bunch of Lietuvans by himself. I already knew he couldn't, and I was trying to find a fast way to say I knew it. That's all I was doing, honest."

"It is not honest to treat pagan things as if they are real," Maria said. "If you believe they are real, how can you believe in the one true God?"

"But I don't believe they are. I told you that, and it's the truth," Amanda said.

Even more sadly, Maria shook her head. "I will pray for you," she said, and turned away.

She didn't feel like being friendly any more. She couldn't have made it any plainer if she'd slapped Amanda in the face. Amanda had broken a rule nobody she approved of would break, and so she didn't approve of Amanda any more. No doubt she meant it when she said she would pray. In the here-and-now, though, that did Amanda no good at all.

I don't belong here. This isn't my world. Of course I'm going to make mistakes in it every once in a while, Amanda thought miserably. If things were the way they were supposed to be, that wouldn't have mattered so much. She could have got away whenever she needed to. But not now. Whether this was her world or not, she couldn't get away from it—and she'd just lost the only real friend she had.

Eleven

Jeremy saw more piles of rubble in Polisso than he had the last time he went to the market square. Amanda said, "If this siege goes on, how much of the city will be left?"

"Beats me," he answered. "We're just lucky we haven't had a bad fire." Polisso had nothing better to fight fires than a big wooden tub with a hand pump and a leather hose. They called it a siphon. Any blaze that got well started had no trouble staying ahead of it. Fire was a nightmare here, especially fire with a strong breeze to fan it.

A gang of municipal slaves with shovels and hods cleared bricks from the street. The skinny, weary-looking men worked as slowly as they could get away with. Every once in a while, the overseer—who was much better fed than the work gang—would growl at them. They'd speed up for a little while after that, then ease back down to the usual pace again.

The overseer didn't growl too often. He knew when he could push them. They knew when they could slack off, and by how much. If he didn't get that minimum amount of work out of them, he *would* let them hear about it. They didn't want that, so they gave him what he needed—and not a copper's worth more. Little by little, the work got done. If it wasn't finished today—and it wouldn't be—they'd come back tomorrow. What difference did a day make, one way or the other? That was how the slaves seemed to feel about it, and the overseer as well.

When Jeremy and Amanda got to the market square, he saw that the city prefect's palace had had several chunks bitten out of it. He had that odd feeling you get when something bad happens to someone you don't like. He didn't like Sesto Capurnio one bit, but he hoped—he supposed he hoped—none of those cannonballs had mashed the prefect.

Next door to the palace, the temple stood undamaged. "Look at that," said a man who displayed some well-made wooden bowls and platters. "Only goes to show, the gods look out for their own."

"Oh, garbage," the coppersmith beside him said. "It could be fool luck just as easy as not."

Plainly, they'd been going through all the variations in that argument for a while now, in almost the same way as the slaves moved wreckage up the street. They weren't in any hurry about it. The more they stretched it out, the longer it could amuse both of them. In Polisso, entertainment was where you found it.

Jeremy and Amanda went on to the temple. As usual, they had to wait in line in the narthex to buy incense for their thanks-offering. Today, though, the clerk who sold it to them and took down their names didn't act snooty. He said, "I've already made my offering. When the barbarians got in, I thought we were all done for. I've never been so glad in all my life."

"I know what you mean," Jeremy answered. "They broke into our house. If the legionaries hadn't driven them back . . ."

He didn't say anything about stabbing the Lietuvan soldier. He wasn't proud of that. He knew he'd had to do it—the man would have killed him without a second thought—but he still wished he hadn't. He decided he did hope the Lietuvan would get better—after he went home.

"No wonder you're here to make a thanks-offering, then," the clerk said. In memory of the hard time just past, he was acting much more like a human being, much less like nothing but a gear in the Roman imperial machine.

"We're here." Jeremy meant here, as in alive—not *here*, as in the temple narthex. "That's why we're making the thanks-offering."

And the clerk—yes, amazingly lifelike—smiled and nodded. He understood what Jeremy had in mind. Who would have thought it? Clerks didn't get paid to understand, and so they mostly didn't bother. "Here is your incense," this one said. "May your god and the spirit of the Emperor look kindly on the offering."

"Thank you," Jeremy said. After a disaster, people pulled together for a while. Mom and Dad had talked about how things were like that after the last big quake in L.A., and they always mentioned that. Sure enough, almost getting the city sacked counted for a disaster.

He and Amanda each had a little pinch of cheap incense in an even cheaper earthenware bowl. They walked into the temple's main hall side by side. There in the paintings, the mosaics, the statues in niches, were all the gods the locals believed in and Jeremy didn't. It was almost a WalMart of religion. Dionysus? Aisle 17. Mithras? Aisle 22. Isis? She's way over there by the checkout stands.

He whispered to Amanda. She smiled. But then, all at once, it didn't seem quite so funny. Maybe because he too was feeling the aftereffects of disaster, he suddenly saw the swarm of gods here as something more than superstition mixed with bureaucracy. Whether he really believed in them or not, the gods meant reassurance to a lot of people. And everybody needed reassurance every now and then, especially after a brush with catastrophe.

He went up to the altar in front of the Roman Emperor's bust. Even the line around the neck that showed where one head could replace another didn't bother him today. Wasn't it a symbol of how the Empire went on no matter what the Emperor looked like? It was if you looked at it the right way.

The altartop had been polished to begin with. The touch of lots of bowls with pinches of incense in them had worn it smoother still. The marble was cool and slick under Jeremy's fingers as he set down his bowl. He reached for a twig, lit it at the waiting flame, touched it to the stuff in the bowl, and then stamped it out.

Smoke curled up from the pinch of incense. It smelled more greasy than sweet. It had to have next to no myrrh or frankincense in it. None could have come into Polisso since the siege started. Here, now, that hardly seemed to matter. The thought counted more than the actual physical stuff that went into it.

Beside him, her face serious, Amanda was lighting her thanks-offering. He wondered what she was thinking. He couldn't ask, not here. Locals were coming up to make offerings of their own. He and his sister stood with their heads bent in front of the altar for a little while, then withdrew.

When they got outside, Amanda said, "That's funny. I really do feel better."

"I was thinking the same thing!" Jeremy exclaimed. "It meant something today. Even if we don't exactly believe, we weren't just going through the motions."

His sister nodded. "That's right. I was thankful I *could* make the offering."

"There you go!" Jeremy said. "I was looking for that, but you found it."

"I wish I could find some other things that matter more," Amanda said. "A way home would be nice."

"I know," Jeremy said, and then, "I don't know. I just don't know any more." Lost hope? He shook his head. It wasn't that. He would never lose hope. But he'd lost optimism. Whatever had happened back in the home timeline, it was—it had to be—a lot worse than he'd thought when the connection between there and here first broke.

A cannonball sailed through the air. When you were out in the open, you could really watch them fly. They didn't move too fast for the eye to follow, even if their paths did seem to blur. This one smashed into the roof of a leather worker's shop. Red tiles—they really were a lot like the ones on the roofs of Spanish-style houses back in Los Angeles—crumbled into red dust and smoke. A woman—the leather worker's wife, or maybe a daughter—let out a scream. He was down below, putting the finishing touches on a saddle. He threw it down and ran upstairs, cursing.

"I know how he feels," Jeremy said.

"I know how *she* feels," Amanda said.

Jeremy thought about that. Then he said, "He can't hit back at the Lietuvans any more than she can." He waited to see what Amanda would say. It was her turn to do some thinking. In the end, she didn't say anything. But she did nod. Jeremy felt as if he'd passed an odd sort of test.

———

Rap, rap, rap. Pause. *Rap, rap, rap.* Amanda raised a pot of porridge several chain links higher above the fire so it wouldn't scorch while she went to see who was at the door. *Rap, rap, rap.* Whoever it was wanted to make sure she and Jeremy knew he was there. *Rap, rap, rap.* She wondered if the knocker would come off or if the door would fall down. They'd had it fixed, but . . .

She almost ran into her brother in the front hall. "Want me to take care of it?" Jeremy asked.

She knew what he meant. The locals would expect to deal with somebody male. She stuck out her chin. She didn't much care what the locals expected. "It's all right," she said. "They can talk to me. Or they can—" She used a gesture common in Polisso, but not commonly used by girls.

A local would have been horrified. Jeremy laughed. He bowed as if she were the city prefect. "All yours, then."

Jeremy behind her, she unbarred the door and opened it. Just in the nick of time, too. The man standing there was reaching for the knocker again. "Good day," Amanda said pleasantly. "No need to do that any more. We knew you were here."

He blinked and then frowned. By the way one eyebrow went up even as his mouth turned down, he recognized sarcasm when he heard it. That was almost as rare in Polisso as it was in Los Angeles. He said, "You are requested to come to the city prefect's palace at once."

NeoLatin had separate words and separate verb forms for the singular and plural of *you*. He'd used the plural, including her and Jeremy. "Who requests that?" she asked.

"Why, the most illustrious city prefect himself, of course," the man replied. He would be one of Sesto Capurnio's chief secretaries, or maybe his steward. He wore a tunic of very fine wool with very little embroidery on it. That meant he had a good deal of money without much status. Did it mean he was a slave? It might well. Slaves here could have money of their own. They could even, though rarely, own other slaves. Amanda sometimes wondered how well anyone from the home timeline understood all the complications to society in Agrippan Rome. She knew she didn't.

She did know the request wasn't really a request. It was an order. But the fact that the city prefect hadn't phrased it as an order meant she and Jeremy had gained status. It didn't mean she could say no. She said yes the nicest way she knew how: "My brother and I are honored to accept the most illustrious city prefect's kind invitation."

"We certainly are," Jeremy agreed.

The secretary or steward or whatever he was looked relieved to hear him speak up. *You sexist donkey,* Amanda thought. But this whole world was full of sexist donkeys. She couldn't change it all by herself, no matter how much she wished she could. The man said, "Come with me, then, both of you."

Amanda moved the porridge higher above the fire and made it smaller so the food wouldn't burn. And then go they did, back through the battered streets of Polisso. The gang of slaves they'd seen on their trip to the temple a few days before—or maybe a different gang—worked at its usual unhurried pace to clear away another ruined wall. When they got to the square, Amanda saw that a cannonball had hit the temple. Jeremy caught her eye. She knew what he was thinking. *So much for miracles.* She nodded.

But she really *had* felt better coming out of the temple after the thanks-offering. That wasn't a miracle. She knew it wasn't. It still counted for something, though.

Sesto Capurnio's flunky led the two crosstime traders into the city prefect's office. The prefect himself sat behind his desk. The painted busts of several recent Emperors stared out at Amanda and Jeremy from in back of him. Amanda found that slightly eerie, or more than slightly.

When Sesto Capurnio spoke, she half expected the lips on all the busts to start moving in time with his mouth. They didn't, of course. Only he said, "Good day."

"Good day, most illustrious prefect," Amanda and Jeremy replied in chorus. He bowed. She curtsied. Still together, they went on, "How may we serve you?"

Sesto Capurnio shook his head. "I did not call you here on official business," he said. "This is a . . . a private conversation. Yes, that's it, a private conversation." He looked pleased at finding the phrase.

Amanda glanced at Jeremy, just for a moment. His eyes met hers. Past that, their faces showed no expression. That was something they'd had to learn. But, even though Jeremy's face stayed blank, she was sure he was thinking right along with her again. When an important person told you something was a private conversation, did you believe him? Not on your life!

Did you let him know you didn't believe him? Not on your life!

"What can we do for you, then, your Excellency?" Amanda still sounded respectful, but she didn't curtsy this time.

The city prefect said, "If King Kuzmickas receives, uh, certain presents from the great and glorious metropolis of Polisso, there is a chance that he will accept those as a symbol of the city and withdraw without troubling us any further."

Would the King of Lietuva do something like that, or was Sesto Capurnio having pipe dreams? Amanda didn't know.

She didn't think anyone from the home timeline could have answered a question like that. People from the home timeline didn't know enough about this one.

Jeremy asked, "A symbol of the city, you say? Do you mean a symbol of surrender, your Excellency, even if you don't really give up Polisso?"

"No! By the gods, no!" Sesto Capurnio shook his head. His jowls wobbled back and forth. Watching them made Amanda queasy. Far fewer people were heavy here than in the home timeline. The city prefect was one of them, though. He went on, "What would my career be worth if I gave the King of Lietuva such a token? The Emperor would think I had acted unwisely, and he would be right."

When the prefect talked like that, Amanda believed him. If he was starved into giving up, that was one thing. But if he acted too friendly toward Kuzmickas while Honorio Prisco III could still get his hands on him, that would be something else again. Amanda asked, "Well, what do you want from us, your Excellency?"

"You have some of the richest, most unusual gifts anyone in Polisso could give the King," Sesto Capurnio answered. "Your razors, your mirrors, your knives with many tools, your hour-reckoners most of all . . ."

"So you want us to give you some of our goods so you can give them to Kuzmickas?" Amanda asked. "I think we can do that, as long as you pay us back for them." If the prefect insisted the watches and such were for the good of the city, she was ready to hand them over without getting paid. But she wanted to get the protest on the record.

"The city will pay you for what you give—and I will accept your official report." Sesto Capurnio not only agreed, he sweetened the deal. He really had to want them to go out to the fearsome King of Lietuva. He went on, "If I make the presents to Kuzmickas, though, I would have to do it as city prefect. It would be an official act by the government. That is what we cannot have, as I explained before. If private citizens give Kuzmickas presents, that is unofficial. Do you see the difference? That is why this is a private conversation, too."

Amanda and Jeremy looked at each other again. Amanda gave a small nod. Her brother gave an even smaller shrug. "I think we see, your Excellency," Amanda said cautiously.

"Good." Sesto Capurnio beamed at them. "Then I will send the two of you out to the King as Polisso's unofficial—very unofficial—ambassadors."

In an odd way, Jeremy almost admired Sesto Capurnio. The city prefect had solved a lot of his problems at one fell swoop. He was giving King Kuzmickas rich presents. If the King of Lietuva decided to act like a barbarian and break his truce, he would have Jeremy and Amanda, but nobody who actually lived in Polisso all the time. And if Kuzmickas did seize them, Jeremy would have bet Sesto Capurnio would find or invent some legal excuse to get his hands on the trade goods. Yes, a pretty slick move all the way around.

Except for us, Jeremy thought.

A soldier at the postern gate nodded to him and Amanda. The Roman smelled of sweat and garlic. "Ready?" he asked them.

"We'd better be," Jeremy said. Amanda nodded.

"Good fortune go with you, then." The soldier opened the gate. Rusty hinges squeaked. Postern gates almost always stayed closed. They had nothing to do with the ordinary traffic that went into and out of a city. They were for letting soldiers out to make a surprise attack against invaders who were assailing one of the main gates, and for other small, often secret, things like that.

This mission was small, but it wasn't secret. It couldn't be, not with the guns on both sides silent and with soldiers watching from the walls. Jeremy carried a staff with a spray of dried olive leaves attached to the top. In this world, the Romans and Lietuvans and Persians all used that as a sign of truce.

A Lietuvan carrying a similar staff came out of King Kuzmickas' camp. Polisso had grown out of a Roman legionary encampment. Roman soldiers on campaign still camped with everything just so, with each unit in its assigned place, with the camp streets at right angles to one another, and so on. Lietuva had imitated the Roman Empire in a lot of ways. Making camp wasn't one of them.

Tents of every size, style, and color fabric sprawled here, there, and everywhere, all higgledy-piggledy. If there were any real camp streets, Jeremy couldn't make them out. The closer to the encampment he got, the more he noticed that here was a place that smelled even worse than Polisso. He hadn't dreamt that was possible. It nearly made him want to congratulate the Lietuvans.

The big blond man with the staff of truce called, "Good day," in neoLatin. In the same language, he went on, "Do you speak Lietuvan?"

"I am sorry, your Excellency, but we do not," Jeremy answered. "Will we need an interpreter to speak to his Majesty?" The city prefect hadn't said anything about that.

To his relief, the blond man shook his head. "No, the King

knows your tongue. Things would have been easier in ours, but he will get along. Come with me, if you please."

They came. The Lietuvan led them through the camp toward the biggest, fanciest tent in it. Jeremy supposed that made sense. Who else but the King would have that kind of tent? Soldiers stared at them. Those stares didn't seem mean or fierce, just curious.

Guards stood outside the King's tent. One of them spoke in Lietuvan. The guide answered in the same strangely musical language. He turned back to Jeremy. "Before you see his Majesty, you will have to be searched. We do not want you Romans trying to steal a victory by murdering the King."

Jeremy looked at the guards. He looked at Amanda, who rolled her eyes. "Those big lugs aren't going to search my sister," he said.

"Oh." To his surprise, the guide turned red. He spoke to the guard chief in Lietuvan. They went back and forth. At last, the guide said, "The King's women will search your sister." Surprising Jeremy again, he added, "We meant no offense."

Now Amanda nodded. "All right," Jeremy said.

"You come here," a guard told Jeremy in slow, heavily accented neoLatin. He patted Jeremy down and searched the bag he had with him. Since the bag had Swiss army knives and straight razors in it, Jeremy wondered if he would get upset about them. A security man in the home timeline would have. This fellow seemed to understand they were meant as presents, not murder weapons. He nodded. "All good. You wait for sister now."

Two of King Kuzmickas' women brought Amanda out of a little tent a few minutes later. Like Lietuvan men, they wore breeches tucked into high boots, which made them scandalous to the Romans. They glittered with gold: belts, rings, bracelets, necklaces, big hoops in their ears. Their fair hair hung straight and free. The style was closer to what Jeremy would have seen at Canoga Park High than the fancy curls Roman women wore. The Lietuvans wore more makeup than either Romans or high-school girls.

One of them spoke to the guard chief. By the way he nodded, she'd given Amanda a clean bill of health. The other Lietuvan woman eyed Jeremy. She might have been sizing up a horse or a dog. She said something. She and her friend both laughed. So did a couple of the guards.

Jeremy stood there stolidly. He did his best to pretend the women didn't exist. They thought that was funny, too.

"I will take you to the King," said the Lietuvan who'd brought Jeremy and Amanda to the royal pavilion. One of the guards held the tent flap so they could duck their way inside.

King Kuzmickas sat in what looked like a folding wooden patio chair covered in gold paint. *A portable throne,* Jeremy realized. Guards with drawn swords stood on either side of it. The King's red-gold beard was streaked with white. A gold circlet shone in his greasy hair. He would have been very handsome if he'd lost twenty kilos. The fur robe he wore had to be valuable, even if it did make Jeremy a little sick. He'd been doused with rosewater, and had bad breath.

"Your Majesty!" Jeremy bowed low. Amanda curtsied, as she had for Sesto Capurnio.

"Good day, both of you," Kuzmickas said. He had a light, true tenor voice. His neoLatin was very good, almost perfect, with only a vanishing trace of the Lietuvan accent that made him sound as if he were singing ordinary speech. He looked the two crosstime traders over. "I did not think you would be so young."

"We are old enough to bring you presents from Polisso, your Majesty," Jeremy said.

"Oh, no doubt." Kuzmickas pointed at him. The King's nails were perfectly shaped but dirty. "You have some of those fancy things that are all the talk of the border the past few years?"

"Yes, your Majesty," Jeremy said.

"Good. I have seen some of these. I would like to see more. I would like to have more for myself." King Kuzmickas was nothing if not direct.

Amanda spoke up: "Polisso would like to have peace."

"Oh, yes. I know." Kuzmickas sounded amused. "Some of us are likelier to get what we want than others."

"You've already seen our city isn't easy to take," Jeremy said.

"And so? Not many things that are worthwhile are easy. Just because something is hard does not mean it cannot be done." The Lietuvan King sounded like one of those boring lessons on how to get ahead in life. Those lessons might be boring. That didn't make them any less true, which worried Jeremy.

But he wasn't there to argue with Kuzmickas. He was there to try to make him happy. "Here is one of our gifts for you, your Majesty," he said, and gave the King a straight razor in a mother-of-pearl sheath that doubled as a handle.

He had to show Kuzmickas how to free the blade with his thumbnail. Kuzmickas tested the edge on the ball of his thumb. He raised an eyebrow in surprise. "Yes, this is very fine," he said. "A good tool for smoothing a throat—or for cutting one." He did not sound as if he was joking.

Amanda said, "Here is a mirror for you, your Majesty."

She gave him one of the biggest ones they had, in a frame set with sea shells.

Kuzmickas stared into it. He muttered a few words in Lietuvan. By the smile on his face, they meant something like, *I sure am a handsome fellow.* "I like this," he said in neoLatin. "It is better than the mirrors we make. I will not try to tell you any different."

"And here, your Majesty . . ." Jeremy gave the King a Swiss army knife.

Kuzmickas had learned his lesson with the razor. He started using his thumbnail to free blade after blade, tool after tool. Each new one made the smile on his face get wider. "Yes," he said. "This is a wonderful toy, and useful, too. I would like to meet the knifesmith who made it, to tell him how clever he is."

There was no smith, of course. Somewhere, someone sitting at a computer had designed the knife. After that, machines had done the rest. Just for a moment, Jeremy felt a twinge of regret about that. People here really got their hands on what they made in a way they seldom did in the home timeline. But machines could do things with so much less labor, it made the trade worthwhile.

"And finally, your Majesty . . ." Amanda pulled out a blue-plate special. She showed King Kuzmickas what the big, shiny pocket watch was for, how to wind it, and how to read the hands.

"Better than a sundial. I can take it anywhere. And I can tell the hour at night. And it is beautiful." Kuzmickas was good at figuring out the advantages of what was new technology to him. His taste might have been a different question. He went on, "But what if I forget to wind it? What happens if it stops?"

He was clever, sure enough. Few people here ever wondered about that. Amanda answered, "Wait till noon, your Majesty, noon on a sundial, and set it to six o'clock." Like the Romans, the Lietuvans started the day at sunrise, not at midnight.

"And if I don't have a sundial handy, I can figure out when noon is on any sunny day—close enough, anyhow," Kuzmickas said, nodding. "That is fine. Thank you." People here didn't worry about time to the minute. Time to the half hour—or at most to the quarter hour—was close enough for them. Maybe watches would change that. It hadn't happened yet.

"We hope your presents please you, your Majesty," Jeremy said.

"If you had brought me Polisso's surrender, that would have pleased me more," Kuzmickas answered. "But wait. Fair is fair, and never let it be said I take without giving in return. I have presents for you as well."

He called out in Lietuvan. The man who hurried up and bowed to him was small and dark. He looked more like a Roman than a Lietuvan. *A slave?* Jeremy wondered. He realized he would never know. The King pointed to him and Amanda in turn and spoke as if giving orders. The little dark man bowed again, nodding over and over. He raced away as fast as he had come.

When he came back, he carried a jacket of some thick, brown, lustrous fur and a necklace. "This marten jacket is for you, Ieremeo Soltero," King Kuzmickas said. "It will keep you warm no matter what the weather. Try it. You are large. I hope it will fit you."

"Thank you very much, your Majesty." That was the biggest lie Jeremy had ever told. Putting on the jacket felt like the hardest thing he'd ever done. In his world, in his time, only a few perverts wore fur. He knew that hadn't been true for his ancestors, but they'd had all sorts of other nasty habits that he didn't want to imitate, too. He could smell the animal hides that made up the jacket. It *was* warm, but not all the sweat that sprang out on his forehead rose because it was. He managed to hold his voice steady as he said, "It fits well, your Majesty. Thank you again."

"You are welcome." Kuzmickas waved indulgently. "You will not offend me by taking it off. I know it is too much for today's weather."

"Yes." Jeremy got out of it in a hurry. He could still feel the weight of it on his shoulders, though. He fought not to be sick.

Kuzmickas turned to Amanda. "This necklace is of fine Lietuvan amber. When you wear it, think of me." He beckoned her forward and put it on her.

"Thank you very much, your Majesty. It's beautiful," she said. Jeremy was jealous of her. She could sound grateful and mean it. The home timeline had nothing against amber.

"And I give you one other gift," Kuzmickas said. "You will have paint or whitewash in your home?" He waited till Jeremy and Amanda gave him puzzled nods, then went on, "If Polisso falls to us, paint a white X on your door. You will not be harmed or enslaved. You will come under my protection. This gift is for you alone. If we see many white X's when we break in, we will ignore them all. Do you understand?"

"Yes, your Majesty." Jeremy wasn't sure he ought to thank King Kuzmickas for that. He wasn't sure he and Amanda ought to use the gift if Polisso fell, either. It didn't seem fair. But he wasn't sure they wouldn't use it, either. He'd heard too many horror stories about things that could happen in the sack of a town. Instead of saying thank you, he bowed.

That seemed to satisfy the King. "Go back to Polisso," he said. "Before the summer ends, we will see whose gods are stronger. Yours may be more clever, but mine—mine can fight."

Jeremy had to pick up the marten-fur jacket. Touching it was as bad as wearing it. *I can't be sick till I get someplace where nobody can see me,* he told himself again and again as he walked back to Polisso. And he wasn't, quite, though afterwards he never knew why not.

Whatever the city prefect thought, Amanda and Jeremy's visit to King Kuzmickas didn't change anything much. Amanda hadn't expected that it would. The King of Lietuva politely went on with the truce till the two crosstime travelers got back inside the walls of Polisso. Then the Lietuvans started shooting again. They fired one cannon to let the Romans know the truce was over. The Romans shot back with one gun to show they understood. After that, both sides returned to banging away with everything they had.

Amanda liked her amber necklace. She knew what her brother had to be thinking about getting a fur jacket. She would have felt the same way herself. And Jeremy had to keep holding on to it as the Roman officials questioned him about the meeting with King Kuzmickas. It seemed like forever before they finally got back inside their own house.

As soon as they did, Jeremy dropped the jacket. He disappeared into the bathroom at a dead run. Amanda's own stomach heaved as she listened to the sounds of retching.

When Jeremy came out, his face was pale as parchment.

"Are you all right?" Amanda asked.

"I'll tell you, I'm a lot better," he answered. "And as soon as I drink some wine and get this horrible taste out of my mouth, I'll be better yet."

"I'll get it for you," said Amanda, who wasn't sure he could walk to the kitchen without falling over.

"Thanks," he said when she handed him the cup. He sipped carefully. "Don't want to drink too fast, or I'm liable to throw up again. That miserable, horrible thing!" He wouldn't even look toward the jacket. "I could *smell* it."

"What are you going to do with it?" Amanda didn't want to look at the fur, either. She wasn't sure she could smell it, but she imagined she could. That was just about as bad.

"What *can* I do with it?" Jeremy answered. "Even if we weren't stuck here, we couldn't take it back to the home time-line. I can't sell it inside Polisso as long as the siege is going on. Word might get back to Kuzmickas. That wouldn't be good if the Lietuvans take the town. We just have to hang on to it."

"I'll put it in a cabinet," Amanda said. "You've had enough to do with it. I'll shove it along with a broom handle or something, so maybe I won't have to touch it."

"Would you?" Jeremy looked happier. Maybe it was the wine. Maybe it was the thought of not having to deal with the fur any more. It was the fur, all right, for he said, "Thanks, Sis. I don't think anybody's ever done anything nicer for me. When I had to pretend I liked it . . ." He started turning green again.

"Cut that out," Amanda said sternly. "I told you I'd take care of it, and I will. Just remember, the acting you did there will make you a better bargainer from now on."

Her brother nodded. "Yeah, that's true. But you can pay too high a price for some things, you know what I mean?"

"Oh, yes." Amanda nodded. "I'll deal with it. You don't have to worry about it any more." She went out to the kitchen. Instead of a broom, she found a mop. That would do well enough. She pushed the fur jacket ahead of her on the floor, as if she were herding along an animal that didn't want to cooperate. The poor martens whose furs went into the jacket hadn't wanted to cooperate. They hadn't had a choice.

There was a chest that held mostly rags. Amanda opened it. She needed two or three tries to pick up the jacket with the end of the mop handle. It was heavier than she'd thought. She could have just stooped and gathered it in her hands, but that never occurred to her. She didn't want to touch it any more than Jeremy had. At last, she managed to get it into the chest. Down came the lid—thud! For good measure, Amanda closed the latch.

She nodded, pleased with herself. The jacket was gone. It might as well never have existed. *Out of sight, out of mind,* she thought. She shouldered the mop as if it were a legionary's matchlock musket and marched back to the courtyard. "There," she said.

Her brother let out a long sigh, almost an old man's sigh. "Good. Thanks again. I owe you one." He laughed. "I don't know where I can find one that big to pay you back with, though."

"Don't worry about it," Amanda answered. "This is what family is for."

"I knew it was for something," Jeremy said. Amanda stuck out her tongue at him. Almost forgotten by both of them, the siege of Polisso ground on.

Twelve

Jeremy and Amanda both ate meat. Jeremy had never wondered why that didn't bother him when wearing fur did. If he had wondered, he would have said people needed protein, but they could keep warm without killing animals. And that would have been true, but it wouldn't have been the whole truth, though he might not have realized it wouldn't. The whole truth was that he was as much a part of his culture as the people of Agrippan Rome were of theirs. He noticed their quirks. His own were water to a fish.

Since he ate meat, he had to buy it in the market square. With Polisso besieged, there wasn't much to buy: pork every now and then, from people who kept pigs, and what the sellers claimed to be rabbit. Jeremy didn't buy any of that. His bet was that it would meow if you sliced it.

When he brought back pork, Amanda cooked it till it was gray. Back in the home timeline, people didn't worry about trichinosis any more. Here, the danger was as real as a kick in the teeth. All sorts of things you didn't need to worry about in the home timeline could make you sick here.

Even when he'd stopped buying very often, he kept going back to the market square. Women gossiped at the fountains. The square was for men. One drizzly morning, he heard a rumor he'd been hoping for: someone said the Roman Emperor, or at least an imperial army, was on its way north to fight the Lietuvans.

"How do you know it's true?" he asked the man who'd passed the news to him—one of the people who were selling what had to be roof rabbit.

"Well, my brother-in-law told me, and he's pretty sharp," the fellow answered.

That did not strike Jeremy as recommendation enough. "How does he know?" he asked. "Who told him?"

"You think my brother-in-law would make something up?" The man with the mystery meat sounded indignant. Jeremy only shrugged, as if to say, *How should I know?* The other man thought it over. Then he shrugged, too. "Well, maybe he would."

"Terrific," Jeremy said.

"You want to buy some rabbit?" the man asked him. "If you've got any prunes or anything like that, you can make a nice, tasty sauce for it."

"No, thanks," Jeremy answered. "If I had mice, I'd get some of it from you. They'd all run away."

"Funny," the local said. "Ha, ha, ha, ha. There. You hear me laughing?"

"No," Jeremy told him. "I didn't hear me joking, either." The local sent him a gesture that meant something nasty. The one Jeremy gave back meant something just as nasty. They parted on terms of perfect mutual loathing.

Jeremy headed back to the house without any meat. On his way there, though, he heard two men who looked like blacksmiths talking about the army coming up from the south. That left him scratching his head.

He told Amanda about them. "What do you think?" he asked. "Were they listening to the other guy's brother-in-law?"

"Who knows?" she answered. "We'll just have to wait and see, that's all. Maybe everybody's saying, 'Yes, there's an army coming,' because we're all sick of being cooped up here. But maybe there really is an army. We won't know till it starts shooting at the Lietuvans. If it ever does."

"Schrödinger's army," Jeremy said, thinking of cats. Amanda made a face at him. He made one right back. She was his sister, after all. He couldn't let her get away with something like that. But he hadn't been joking with her, either. If you couldn't tell whether an army was real till it showed up—or didn't show up—how much good did it do you?

The only thing an army that *might* be real did was to pump up hope. That could help for a little while, maybe. But if more time went by and the army didn't show up, wouldn't hope sink lower than it would have if it hadn't been lifted in the first place?

He wondered if the city prefect or the garrison commander had got worried about morale in Polisso. Even if the rumors about an approaching Roman army weren't true, they might think it was in their interest to start them. Or people who were in danger of losing hope on their own might have started the rumors, to make themselves feel better. Or . . .

Jeremy gave up. He couldn't tell. He just didn't know, and he didn't have any real evidence one way or the other. Sooner or later, he'd find out. Till then . . .

Till then, I'll worry. That's what I'll do, he thought.

Amanda set her palm on the proper spot in the basement wall. The concealed door slid aside and let her into the chamber the locals weren't supposed to discover. The electric lights in there came on. Seeing them made tears sting her eyes. Some small part of the tears came because the lights were bright after the gloom of the basement. But most of them sprang from the lights' being electric. They were things from the home timeline. Every time she came down here, not being able to go back there ate at her more.

It's home, she thought as the door silently slid shut behind her. *How can anybody blame me because I want to go home, because I don't want to stay here?* People from Polisso would find Los Angeles endlessly marvelous, endlessly exciting. But they might well want to come back to the timeline of Agrippan Rome once they'd seen what there was to see. And Los Angeles was a richer place where you could do more things—do more kinds of things—than you could in Polisso. If it wasn't home, even that wouldn't matter. When it was . . .

The lights weren't all that reminded her of home. The sheet-metal cabinets, the table with the plywood top, the blue plastic chair with the slotted back—they were ordinary things, but they were things from her world. In the home timeline, you didn't have to be somebody important to sit in a chair with a back instead of on a stool. That wasn't a big difference between the two worlds, but it was a difference. Differences gnawed at her spirit like acid now.

And the computer. The difference there was what the PowerBook could—or rather, couldn't—do now. It was supposed to connect her to the home timeline, to the world that knew how to move between worlds, how to talk between worlds. It was supposed to, but it didn't. It was like a friend who'd let her down. It *was* a friend who'd let her down.

Amanda had to make herself walk to the blue plastic chair. She had to make herself pull it out, had to make herself sit down in it. And it took everything she had in her to make herself look at the laptop's monitor. Her brother said the same thing. She and Jeremy had been disappointed so many times.

Is anybody there?

Three little words. She'd heard that *I love you* was supposed to hit you like that when the right person said those three little words. These three? Nobody talked about these three. But *I love you,* even when she heard it from the right person, was going to have to do some pretty fancy work to top them.

She blinked. *Is anybody there?* stayed on the screen. She wasn't imagining it. If King Kuzmickas had taken Polisso without getting one single soldier scratched, he might have let out a whoop with one tenth the joy of the one that burst from Amanda's lips. She sprang out of the chair. She jumped up and down. She did the wildest, whirlingest dance the world had ever seen.

And then she did something a lot harder than that. Instead of answering right away, she turned her back on the beautiful monitor. She left the secret basement. The door closed behind her again, shutting her out. She went upstairs to primitive, smelly, besieged Polisso.

Jeremy was watering the herbs in the herb garden. A few spices, like pepper and cinnamon, were expensive, imported luxuries here. As for the rest, the ordinary ones like basil and thyme, you grew your own if you wanted them. Otherwise you did without.

"There's something I think you ought to see," Amanda said.

She tried to sound calm, to hold the excitement out of her voice. She tried, but it didn't work. Jeremy's head came up as if he were a wolf scenting meat. "Is it—?" He stopped, as if he didn't want to go on for fear of hearing no.

But Amanda said, "Yes!"

Her brother whooped even louder than she had. He was out in the open, not in a soundproof basement. He didn't care at all, and neither did Amanda. Somebody next door exclaimed in surprise. They didn't care about that, either. Jeremy set down the water jug. It was a wonder he hadn't dropped it and smashed it. He grabbed Amanda's hands. They did sort of a two-person version of the crazy dance she'd done by herself down below.

They were both laughing and panting when they finally stopped. "What does it say?" Jeremy demanded. "Tell me what it says!"

"Come see for yourself," Amanda told him. But then, as they both hurried to the stairs, she added, "It's just asking if we're here. I haven't even answered it yet."

"Well, we'd better!" Jeremy said.

"You bet." Fear filled Amanda as she set her palm on the patch of wall where it was supposed to go. The door slid aside, opening the secret part of the basement. She and Jeremy hurried in. They both ran to the PowerBook on the table. Her fear grew. Would the message still show on the screen? Had she imagined she saw it because she wanted to see it so badly?

Is anybody there?

The words were real. Seeing them there again, seeing Jeremy see them, made Amanda as happy as she had been when she saw them the first time. She would have been glad to go back to the temple to make one more thanks-offering.

Those three words made her more grateful than anything else she'd ever known.

"Wow," Jeremy said, his eyes wide and shining. Amanda nodded. Jeremy shook his head, as if fighting to believe it. Amanda understood that, all right. Her brother started to say something, then stopped and shook his head again. He turned to her and almost bowed. "You found it. You do the talking."

"Okay." With that, she switched from neoLatin to English. "Answer." That was an oral command the computer recognized. She paused to think for a moment, then just spoke simply: "This is Amanda. Jeremy and I are both here. We're all right, but the Lietuvans have Polisso under siege. What went wrong back there?"

That summed up what the home timeline needed to know, and what she and Jeremy most wanted to find out. She had another frightened moment when she sent the message. Would the laptop tell her it couldn't go through, the way the machine had so many times before?

It didn't. From everything she could tell, the message went crosstime just the way it was supposed to. Softly, she clapped her hands. Beside her, Jeremy said, "Yeah."

Then they had to wait. That hadn't occurred to her. Back in Porolissum in the home timeline, wouldn't somebody be watching the monitor every single minute? She'd thought somebody would. Maybe she was wrong.

Five minutes went by. Ten. Fifteen. She wanted to kick something. She also wanted to scream. *Had* the message made it back to the home timeline?

And then the screen showed new words. Even before she read them, she and Jeremy both cheered again. Why not?

They weren't cut off any more. Only now, as the isolation ended, did Amanda realize how bad it had been.

She leaned forward to get a better look at the monitor. *This is Dad,* the new message began. She grinned at Jeremy, who was grinning back. *Gladder than I can tell you that you're okay. We're starting to get things sorted out here, too.*

"What happened?" Amanda asked again.

This time, the answer came back right away. *Terrorists. Nationalist terrorists,* Dad said. *They bombed a lot of crosstime sites here in Romania, all on the same day. It was a nice piece of work, if you like that kind of thing.*

"Terrific," Jeremy said.

"Hush," Amanda told him. "There's more."

And there was. Their father went on, *That would have been bad enough by itself, but they also planted tailored viruses at some of the blast sites. Guess what? Both of the ones that connect to Polisso in Agrippan Rome got lucky. They've finally managed to decontaminate enough to set up computers here, but I'm wearing a spacesuit to talk to you guys.*

"Urk," Jeremy said. This time, Amanda didn't hush him. She felt like going urk herself. Making real viruses these days was almost as easy as making computer viruses had been at the start of the twenty-first century. And real viruses could do as much damage in the real world as computer viruses had in the virtual world. They could, if you were ruthless enough to turn them loose. Nagorno-Karabakh and a big chunk of Azerbaijan next door were still uninhabitable. Armenians blamed Azerbaijanis; Azerbaijanis blamed Armenians. No one was ever likely to know who'd really used that Ebola variant. It was so hot, it had probably killed off whoever started it. That was poetic justice of a sort.

Fighting tailored viruses was dangerous enough in the home timeline. If one of them got loose in an alternate like Agrippan Rome, it might take out a third of the population or more. Natural epidemics had done that in the past. Unnatural epidemics . . . Amanda didn't even want to think about it.

"How's Mom?" Jeremy asked.

She's fine. She sends her love, Dad answered. Amanda breathed a sudden sigh of relief. If Mom's appendix had waited a little longer to act up, she would have got stuck here. That could have been very bad. Amanda couldn't think of anything much worse, in fact.

She asked, "How long before you're able to come and get us?"

Crosstime Traffic and the Ministry for the Environment here both have to decide it's safe, Dad said. *A week or two, probably. But you said there was a war going on there?*

"That's right," Amanda said. She and Jeremy took turns telling what had happened since they got cut off. "We've had to sell for money instead of wheat and barley," she put in at one point. "We didn't have any place to put the produce, and then we didn't want the locals calling us hoarders."

Don't worry about that, Dad said. *No one will complain that you went against the grain.*

For a second, Amanda just accepted that. She opened her mouth to start to answer it. Then she saw the revolted look on her brother's face. She read the message again. She made a horrible face, too. "Well, that's Dad for sure," she said.

"You better believe it," Jeremy said. "Nobody else in the world makes puns that bad." From revolted, his expression suddenly went crafty. "Except maybe me." He spoke to the PowerBook: "Answer. Wheat like to tell you to clean up that last message. We could barley understand it. It seemed pretty corny. Send."

"Ow!" Amanda exclaimed. "Where's something I can hit you with?" Jeremy looked proud of himself, which wasn't what she'd had in mind.

There was a pause at the other end. Amanda hoped Dad wasn't running out and throwing up. That could be awkward in an antivirus spacesuit. At last, he answered, *Your sense of humor is as rye as I remember.* He must have typed that in instead of dictating it. If he'd spoken into the computer, it would have written *wry*, which was right, and not *rye*, which was wrong, to say nothing of ghastly. For good measure, he added, *But I don't want to be on the oats with you.*

"That's rice," Amanda said. Jeremy groaned, not quite in praise. It wasn't the best comeback, but they were running out of grains.

Dad got back to business. *Just hang on till we finish decontaminating here,* he said. *That's all you need to do now. Like I told you, it won't be too long.*

"As long as the Lietuvans don't get into Polisso again, we'll be fine," Jeremy said. Amanda thought he'd put in one word too many, but it was too late to stop him.

Sure as houses, Dad wrote back, *Again?*

"They got some men in at night," Amanda said. "Not too many, though, and Polisso is crawling with Roman soldiers. We had to pay the prefect a sort of a bribe to keep from having any quartered on us. They drove the Lietuvans out again."

Are you all right? Is the house all right?

"We're fine," Jeremy said quickly. "And the house is okay. A couple of cannonballs hit the roof and smashed some tiles, but that's it."

He didn't say anything about the broken-down front door. It was just about as good as new, so Amanda could understand that. And he didn't say anything about the Lietuvan soldier who'd stumbled when the table broke under him. He didn't say anything about stabbing the Lietuvan, either. Amanda supposed she could also understand that. Jeremy didn't want to think about it, and it was all over with anyhow, and it would only worry Dad. *We're fine* was an awful lot simpler—and it was the truth.

Maybe one of these days I'll get the whole story out of you, Dad wrote. Even when he couldn't see faces and hear voices, he wasn't so easy to fool. But he went on, *For now, I'm just glad you are fine. I hope I'll see you soon. I've got to go get out of this suit and clean up now. I love you, and so does your mom.*

" 'Bye," Amanda and Jeremy said together. They didn't get an answer. Amanda wished they would have, but Dad had already said he was going. "They found us again!" she said. She couldn't imagine a more wonderful sentence.

"Yeah." By the glow in Jeremy's eyes, neither could he.

But then Amanda found one: "We're not going to have to stay here."

"Yeah!" Jeremy said again. "That would have been— pretty bad. I kept trying not to worry about it, but . . ." His voice trailed away. "Sometimes you can't help it."

"No. You can't." Amanda had thought about living out the rest of her life here, and wondered how long it would be. It would certainly have seemed long, with hard work filling so much of it. She wouldn't have had the whole world and lots of alternates at her fingertips, the way she had back home. Anything outside of Polisso would have faded to a whisper, almost to a dream.

She would have had to live with stench and dirt the rest of her life. Sooner or later, the drugs they had here would have run out or got too old to do any good. Doctors in Agrippan Rome didn't know anything, and mostly didn't know they didn't know anything. Dentists were even worse. If her wisdom teeth gave her trouble when they came in, what could she do? Take poppy juice and hope for the best.

But none of that was the worst. If she and Jeremy were stuck in Polisso, they would have had to become part of the city in a way they weren't now. They would have had to make real friends, good friends, here. If they didn't, they wouldn't have any. How were you supposed to live your life without friends?

When you made friends, though, you went out with them and you did what they did. If they wanted to go to the arena to watch beasts fight or gladiators go at each other, how could you say no all the time? They thought that was good, clean fun. If you didn't, how could you stay friends?

It got worse, too. She and Jeremy were both young. If they had to stay in Polisso, they might—they probably would—end up getting married. Marriages here were usually business arrangements, not love matches like the ones in the home timeline. Even so, how could you live with somebody when you couldn't tell that person what you really were?

And here, if she and Jeremy did marry, they would be bound to marry somebody with money. In Polisso, if you had money, you had slaves. That would have put them nose to nose with something they fought to keep at arm's length. Amanda didn't see any way she could persuade a Roman husband slavery was wrong. Since she couldn't . . . Could she be a good mistress? Maybe. If she were, would it make her feel any less unclean? She doubted that. She doubted it very much.

She also had one worry that Jeremy didn't. What would having a baby be like in this world without hospitals? Women did it all the time. Polisso wouldn't have had any people if they didn't. But mothers died here from childbed fever. Babies died, too. More than a third of the babies born in Agrippan Rome didn't live to be five years old. How could you love a child if you knew you might lose it the next minute? How could you not love it if it was yours? She didn't see an answer to either question.

Now she wouldn't have to look for one. "Let's go upstairs," she said.

"Okay." Jeremy's voice came from far away. Had he been thinking about all the reasons he was glad not to be trapped here? Amanda wouldn't have been surprised.

The door slid shut after she and Jeremy left the secret part of the basement. There they were, back in Agrippan Rome. Amanda sighed. Staying here for another week or two was going to be hard. But staying forever would have been a lot harder.

Jeremy was playing catch in the street with Fabio Lentulo and trying not to get smashed when he heard somebody say, "They're going!" He didn't have much chance to worry about who was going. The apprentice had thrown the ball so that he had to catch it without banging into either a mule or the soldier who was leading it.

"Watch yourself, kid," the soldier growled with the sour disapproval so many grownups had for anybody younger than they were.

"Sure," Jeremy said. Even if the soldier's whiskers were turning gray, he could probably whale the stuffing out of somebody who didn't fight for a living. Besides, Jeremy had just made a great catch. He wasn't going to be fussy with anybody about anything.

He tossed the ball high in the air, so that Fabio Lentulo would have time to run under it—if he ran right into the middle of another bunch of soldiers. He didn't. One of the soldiers picked up the ball and flipped it to him. "Thanks," he said—the legionary could have kept it just as easily.

When he threw it back, though, he tried to take Jeremy's head off with it. Jeremy had won a point in the game, and he didn't like it. Jeremy won another point—or at least kept from losing one—when he snatched the ball out of the air. Fabio Lentulo sent him a gesture that was anything but complimentary.

"Same to you, with olive oil on it," Jeremy said. They both laughed. Buddies could insult each other as much as they pleased. But if Jeremy had aimed his gibe at Fabio Lentulo's mother instead of the apprentice, he would have had a fight on his hands. In some ways, Polisso and Los Angeles weren't so different.

Two men came up the street toward Jeremy and Fabio Lentulo. One of them said, "Are you sure they're pulling out?"

"By the gods, you can go up on the wall and see for yourself if you don't believe me," the other man replied.

"They haven't got the nerve to stay and fight it out," the first man said.

His friend shrugged. "I don't know about that. If you ask me, they're going off to fight the relieving army when it's still too far from Polisso for the garrison here to pitch into 'em from behind."

They walked on, still arguing in a good-natured way. "Well?" Fabio Lentulo said. "You going to throw me the ball or not?"

"Here." Jeremy tossed it to him, soft enough for a six-year-old to catch. "Did you hear what they said? Sounds like the Lietuvans are leaving."

"To the crows with the Lietuvans." Fabio Lentulo threw the ball so that Jeremy would have to splash through a puddle to go after it.

But he didn't go after it. He just let it fall with a thump. It didn't have much bounce to it. He said, "If they let me, I'm going up onto the wall. I don't know about you, but I want to see King Kuzmickas leave."

"Why? So you can wave bye-bye?" Fabio Lentulo knew Jeremy and Amanda had gone out to give the King of Lietuva presents.

Jeremy sent back the gesture the apprentice had given him. "No, so I can be sure he's gone. Or didn't you worry about a cannonball coming down on your head or getting sold into slavery?"

"Me, I kept hoping a cannonball would come down on my boss's head. He already treats me like a slave," Fabio Lentulo answered. He probably wasn't kidding, or not very much. An employer could order an apprentice around much as a master could order a slave. The difference was, an apprentice became his own man once he was trained. A slave was never his own man; he always belonged to somebody else. Fabio Lentulo went on. "Besides, none of that stuff happened to him. His place didn't get hit even once." He spread his hands, as if to say, *What can you do?*

"All right. I still want to see Kuzmickas leave, so I'm going up on the wall," Jeremy said. "Are you coming?"

"Oh, I'll come," Fabio Lentulo said. "You're not going to be able to go around town telling people I'm yellow." Jeremy's challenge would have got a lot of young men in Los Angeles to go with him. Here in Polisso, any of them would have risen to it as automatically as a trout rising to strike at a fly. People here did behave in a more macho way than they did in the home timeline. They thought that was what they were supposed to do, and they did it.

In school, Jeremy had learned nothing could travel faster than light. He didn't think his teachers had heard about the speed with which rumor could spread. He and Fabio Lentulo were part of a line going up the stone stairs to the top of the wall. Grumbling soldiers herded the civilian gawkers along like so many sheep. "Yes, the barbarians are pulling out," they said. "You can take your gander, if it makes you happy. Mind you don't get your stupid heads shot off. The Lietuvans haven't quit fighting, and they aren't gone yet."

Jeremy discovered how true that was a moment later. A Lietuvan soldier popped up out of a trench, aimed a matchlock in his general direction, and pulled the trigger to bring the burning match down on the priming powder. The priming powder caught and set off the main charge. The musket went off. A great cloud of gray smoke made the musketeer vanish. The bang of the gun reached Jeremy half a second later— about the same time as the bullet whined past his head. He ducked. He couldn't help it.

When he looked behind him, he saw that Fabio Lentulo

had ducked, too. That made him feel better. Now his friend couldn't tease him for being a coward, either. And why did such teasing matter to him? Maybe he had more macho in himself than he wanted to admit.

But even though some of the Lietuvans were still shooting at Polisso, the rest did seem to be leaving. Tents around the city were coming down. Wagons drawn by horses or mules or oxen were rolling away. Companies of musketeers like the man who'd shot at Jeremy were marching off to the south. Distantly, the breeze brought commands in musical Lietuvan to Jeremy's ears.

"They *are* going," he said.

"Looks that way," Fabio Lentulo agreed. Then he yelled something truly vile at King Kuzmickas. He followed it with a gesture much nastier than the one he and Jeremy had aimed at each other.

He wasn't the only one doing such things, either. Half the men seemed to be swearing at the Lietuvans or sending them obscene gestures or doing both at once. The big blond soldiers shouted back in their language. They sent the Romans gestures different but no less foul.

And some of them kept on shooting at Polisso. The legionaries on the wall shot back at them. About ten meters in front of Jeremy, a civilian fell down, clutching at his leg. His howl of pain pierced the jeers like a sword piercing flesh.

When Jeremy and Fabio Lentulo walked by where he'd been wounded, the crosstime trader didn't look at the scarlet puddle of blood on the stone. He didn't need to look to know it was there. He could smell the hot-metal scent, as he had when he stabbed the Lietuvan soldier.

By contrast, the apprentice stared and stared at the gore.

"Got him good," he remarked. "Did you hear him yell?"

"A deaf man would have heard him yell," Jeremy answered.

Fabio Lentulo thought that was funny, and laughed out loud. Jeremy hadn't meant it for a joke. There was a lot more raw agony in this alternate than in the home timeline. Bad things happened to people more often in Polisso than in Los Angeles. People here could do much less about them, too.

Joys, on the other hand . . . The Lietuvan soldiers were going away. With luck, they wouldn't be able to come back. That would do for joy till something better came along. Jeremy shook his fist at the withdrawing soldiers. He never wanted to see them again, or King Kuzmickas, either.

As soon as the Lietuvans were gone, the defenders of Polisso opened the gates. People poured out of the city. Some—the scavengers—made for the Lietuvan camp, to bring back and sell whatever the enemy had left behind. Others just wanted to get away from their houses, to get away from their neighbors, for a little while. Amanda was one of those.

She couldn't go by herself. That wasn't done. It wasn't safe, either. But she and Jeremy went out together. He didn't feel the need to get away as much as she did. But he did see— she made him see—she would be impossible unless she got out for a little while. Out they went.

As far as guns would reach from the wall, the ground was cratered, the grass torn to shreds. She'd seen that when she and her brother went to call on King Kuzmickas. When the wind swung, it brought the stink of the Lietuvan encampment to her nose. The Lietuvans had been even more careless of filth and dirt and sewage than the Romans were. That they could have still surprised her.

"They probably would have had to leave pretty soon even if there weren't a Roman army coming up from the south," Jeremy said. "In an alternate like this, sickness kills more soldiers than bullets ever do."

Amanda knew he was right. That didn't mean she felt like listening. She didn't answer. She just kept walking till the wind swung again and the stench went away. Then she stepped off the road. She lay down on her back in the grass. It tickled her ankles and her arms and her cheeks. She looked up and saw nothing but blue sky.

"Ahhh!" she said.

For a wonder, Jeremy didn't spoil the moment. He stayed out of her way and let her do what she wanted—what she needed—to do. When she sat up again, she brushed grass out of her hair with both hands. She looked forward to using real shampoo once more, too. Her brother stood by the side of the road, sword on his hip, watching for Lietuvan stragglers and any other strangers who might be dangerous. He'd plucked a long grass stem and put it between his teeth.

"Except for the sword, you look like a hick farmer on an ancient sitcom," Amanda told him.

"Is that a fact?" he said, doing a bad half-Southern, half-Midwestern accent. Then he went back to neoLatin: "All the backwoods farmers on all those stupid programs were as modern as next week next to the peasants in this alternate."

"Well, sure," Amanda said. Peasants here were cut off from the wider world around them in a way nobody in America had been since the invention of the telegraph. They might have been more cut off from the wider world than peasants in

Europe since the invention of the printing press. That went back a long way, but only a third of the distance to the breakpoint between the home timeline and Agrippan Rome.

A cool breeze blew down from the mountains to the north. It didn't say winter was coming, not yet, but it did say summer wouldn't last forever. The harvest was on the way—and it would come even sooner in chilly Lietuva than here. There was another reason King Kuzmickas' army would have had trouble besieging Polisso much longer.

Jeremy spread his arms. The breeze made the wide sleeves of his tunic flap. He said, "Everything's so peaceful, so quiet. I'd almost forgotten what quiet is all about."

"Cannon and muskets going off and cannonballs smashing into things are even noisier than traffic back home," Amanda agreed. "They may be more dangerous, too."

"Heh," Jeremy said, and then, "It all seems so stupid. Is owning Polisso worth killing so many people? I can't see it."

"Neither can I," Amanda said. "But could you explain the Software War so it made sense to the city prefect here?"

"You can't explain anything so it makes sense to Sesto Capurnio. I ought to know," Jeremy said. Amanda made a face at him. He made one right back at her. Then he went on, "All right. I know what you mean. But copy protection is something *worth* fighting over."

"We think so. Would the Romans? Would the Lietuvans? Or would they figure it wasn't worth getting excited about, the way we do when it comes to owning one of these little cities?"

"Who knows?" her brother said. "I'll tell you something else, though—I don't much care just now."

Amanda didn't care very much, either. She didn't feel like squabbling with Jeremy right this minute. The fresh breeze teasing her hair, the clean smell of the meadow, the calm after so much chaos, and the knowledge that she'd be going back to the home timeline before long . . . all of them joined together to make her as contented as she'd ever been. When she looked to her right, she saw a hawk flying by. The locals would have called that a good omen. She was willing to do the same.

Thirteen

Having the Lietuvans gone didn't mean Polisso came back to normal right away. The city usually had farmers bringing in produce and eggs and sometimes livestock to sell in the market. Here, now, the farmers didn't have much to sell to the people in the city. Kuzmickas' soldiers had lived off the countryside as much as they could. Locusts might have stripped it barer. Then again, they might not have.

As they left, the Lietuvans had ruined as many grainfields as they could, too. Polisso and the surrounding farms could look forward to a lean harvest. Jeremy would have worried more about that if he'd expected to stay in town through the winter.

Being back in touch with the home timeline changed his whole way of looking at things. For better or worse—mostly for worse—he'd started to think of Polisso as home. Now he felt like a visitor, a tourist, again. Things that happened here happened to other people. They weren't likely to affect him much.

He was in touch with Michael Fujikawa again, too. His friend was back from his summer in alternate North China—and back to school at Canoga Park High. *You're lucky*, Michael wrote. *You don't have to worry about history homework and Boolean operators.*

Lucky, my left one. Jeremy answered. *For one thing, I was scared Amanda and I would be stuck here for good—except it wouldn't be very good. And besides, think of all the work I'll have to make up when I do get back.*

Poor baby. Here's the world's smallest violin playing "Hearts and Flowers" for you, Michael sent. Jeremy laughed. His grandfather had said that, and run his forefinger over the top of his thumb when he did to show the violin. The joke had to be ancient. Jeremy had never heard it from anybody but Grandpa. He wondered where on earth Michael had picked it up.

His friend went on, *I am glad you two are okay, though. I knew something was wrong when we got cut off. Terrorists, I heard. That's no fun. Lucky they didn't have nukes.*

"Gurk!" Jeremy said when that showed up on the Power-Book's monitor. Ordinary explosives and tailored viruses were bad enough. Nukes . . . Terrorists didn't have an easy time getting them, but bad things happened when they did. And how would anybody have rebuilt the transposition chambers if even vest-pocket nukes had gone off in them?

One thing happened after the Lietuvans went away— Jeremy and Amanda started selling pocket watches and mirrors and razors and Swiss army knives hand over fist. That wasn't just because they'd given them to King Kuzmickas, either. Their goods had always had snob appeal. But now Polisso's rich seemed to realize they wouldn't need to spend their last denari on grain. And so they started spending their money on luxuries instead.

After Amanda sold a blue-plate special, Jeremy said, "Shame we can't start taking payment in grain again, not in silver. But they'd still come down on us for hoarding if we tried."

"Anybody who comes here from now on will have a hard time insisting on grain," Amanda said. "I wish that hadn't happened." She found more things to worry about than Jeremy did.

Shrugging, he said, "I don't know what else we could have done. We didn't have any place to put more grain once the transposition chambers stopped coming. Even if we did, people would have stopped giving it to us after the siege started. They didn't worry so much about money."

"I suppose," Amanda said, in a tone of voice that meant she was still worrying about it.

Jeremy didn't have the patience to straighten his sister out. (He also never wondered about how much patience she needed to get along with him.) He left the house and went over to the market square to see what sort of gossip he could pick up. (He thought of it as news.)

When he got there, he saw workmen busily repairing the city prefect's palace. Sesto Capurnio wouldn't have to worry about drafts or a leaky roof for very long. Ordinary people? What was the point of being rich and powerful if you couldn't get your roof fixed ahead of ordinary people? Masons patched holes with cement. Carpenters' hammers banged.

"Good thing the temple next door didn't get hurt too bad," said a man in the market square. "The gods would have to wait their turn, too."

"The gods can take care of themselves," another man answered. "That's probably why nothing much happened to the temple. But what about the poor so-and-sos who got their shacks knocked flat? What are they going to do?"

"Same as always," the first man said. "They'll get it in the neck." By the way he spoke and dressed, he wasn't a rich man himself. When he talked about what happened to the poor, it was from bitter experience.

"I don't suppose the city prefect would have got hungry if the siege had gone on, either," the second man said.

The first man laughed. "Not likely! City prefects don't go hungry. That isn't in the rules. If you don't believe me, just ask Sesto Capurnio."

"I'll tell you what I believe," his pal said. "I believe you're going to get in trouble if you don't stick a sandal in your big, flapping mouth." For a wonder, the first man did shut up.

Jeremy bought a handful of pickled green olives from a vender with a crock of them that he wore tied around his neck with a leather strap so that it bounced against his belly. Jeremy savored what salt and vinegar could do for olives. He spat the pits onto the cobbles of the market square. He wouldn't have done that back in the home timeline, but things were different here.

What would I have been like, if I'd got stuck here for twenty years and then gone home? he wondered. *Would I have done things like that without thinking about them, because everybody did them here? I bet I would.*

Somebody came into the square at a run. People looked up. That was out of the ordinary, which meant it might be important. And sure enough, the man yelled, "News at the gate! Our army beat the lousy Lietuvans! They're on their way home, fast as they can go!"

People in the square didn't all jump up and start cheering. They nodded to one another, as if to say they'd expected as much. Had they? Maybe some of them had. But others wouldn't want to show that they'd thought anything else was possible. And one man said, "Why didn't our army come six weeks ago? Then we wouldn't have had to go through so much trouble."

Another merchant said, "We're lucky they didn't wait till next spring, or till five years from now."

He laughed to show he meant it for a joke. The men who heard him laughed, too, to show they knew it was one. Jeremy wasn't so sure. They might all have been kidding on the square. Agrippan Rome was so bound up in rules and regulations, all its wheels turned slowly. The army had to be less sluggish than most parts of the government. And it *had* done its job here, even if it hadn't done it very fast.

Would the Romans know what to do with freedom if they got it? They'd done without it for a long, long time.

Jeremy shrugged. It wasn't his worry, not any more. Sure enough, he was and felt like a visitor here once more, not somebody who might have to put down deep roots. And that suited him just fine. Not living in Polisso for the rest of his life, even if that meant going back to high school and catching up on everything he'd missed, seemed pretty good.

Everything is clean now, in both transposition chamber areas, Mom wrote. *They're running a last few checks, and then we'll be able to come through.*

Amanda raised an eyebrow when she read that. If everything were clean now, her folks should have been able to come straight through now. The technicians wouldn't be running more checks. She sighed. She could understand why they didn't want to risk letting a tailored virus loose in Agrippan Rome. Doctors here couldn't do anything about natural germs, let alone genetically engineered ones.

She said, "Answer. We'll see you when we see you, that's all. We miss you. It's already been too long. Send."

The words—minus the opening and ending commands— appeared on the PowerBook's screen. They would also appear on the monitor Mom was looking at back home. When Mom and Dad came into Polisso again, word would be bound to get back to the city prefect. Amanda knew that Sesto Capurnio still half suspected she and Jeremy had knocked their parents over the head and buried them somewhere out of the way.

Well, I don't have to worry about what Sesto Capurnio suspects, not now, Amanda thought. She was just a tourist again, and she wouldn't even be that for very long. Burgers. Fries. Milkshakes. Sushi. Lamb vindaloo. Spit flooded into her mouth. She was tired of barley porridge and gritty brown bread.

It's been much too long, Mom agreed. *You don't know how much we've missed you and worried about you. Well, it won't be much longer. I've got to go. See you soon.*

"See you," Amanda said. She'd done plenty of worrying about herself, too. Nice to know somebody else was also doing it for her. That was a big part of what parents were for.

She didn't want to leave the cellar. Going back into the world of Agrippan Rome, the world of stinks, the world with slavery and without electricity, reminded her of everything she'd left behind. She'd get it back again, though. And she and Jeremy would get Mom and Dad back, too. It was like living in a fairy tale when you got three wishes.

But the three wishes hadn't happened yet. She just had the promise that they would. What to do in the meantime? The only thing she could see, was to get on with her life. She felt like Cinderella, back with her stepmother and nasty stepsisters before the Prince came along with the glass slipper.

The next morning, she put a water jar on her hip and went to the fountain. She would never be able to go there without thinking of the Lietuvan cannonball ricocheting through the crowd of women that one dreadful morning. She noticed local women also looking at the scars it had left behind on the stonework. The real damage it had done, though, had nothing to do with stonework.

Maria was at the fountain. She and a couple of free women were talking about the victory the Romans had won against King Kuzmickas. People in Polisso hoped it meant the Lietuvans wouldn't invade again any time soon. Past that, they didn't much seem to care.

One of the free women waved to Amanda. "What do you think?" the local asked. "You went out there and gave the King presents. Will he try again soon?"

"How can I know that?" Amanda said reasonably. "I just met him for a little while. I don't know how badly the legions beat him, either. If they really smashed up his army, maybe he'll stay in his own country for a while. If they didn't, though, he might think he'd have better luck next time and try again."

"Sounds sensible." The local woman seemed surprised. Maybe she wasn't used to logically thinking things through. Even back in the home timeline, a lot of people weren't. That never failed to startle Amanda when she bumped into it, which probably wasn't sensible on her part.

Maria smiled at her. Amanda cautiously smiled back. The slave girl seemed willing to be friendly, at least to a certain degree, no matter what she believed. Maybe that meant Maria wasn't quite so strict herself as Amanda had thought. More likely, it just meant the slave couldn't help being a friendly person even if her beliefs were strict. Maria said, "You seem happy."

Amanda nodded. "I *am* happy. I just got a message from my mother and father." She didn't have to say the message had crossed timelines to get here. "They ought to be back in Polisso in a few days."

"Oh, that is good news." Maria set down her water jar and gave Amanda a hug. Yes, she was a friendly person, all right. "I know you and your brother have been worried about them."

"A little." Amanda didn't want to say how much. She couldn't say all the reasons why she and Jeremy had been worried, either.

"They will have worried about you even more, what with the two of you under siege here. I'm sure they will reward the messenger when he tells them you are all right," Maria said. "I prayed that everything would turn out well for you and for them. I'm glad my prayers were answered."

Amanda didn't quite know how to take that. "Thank you," seemed the right thing to say. Stammering a little, she added, "Don't you, uh, pray for yourself, too? For your freedom?"

"Oh, yes," Maria answered calmly. "But God hasn't chosen to hear that prayer yet. In His own good time, He will. Or, if it pleases Him, He will leave me as I am. His will be done."

She means it, Amanda realized. Understanding that, believing it, was a bigger jolt than seeing how some people wouldn't think logically. Maria *believed,* no matter how friendly she was. Believing helped her accept her place. Accepting a low place wasn't something Americans were used to. Instead, they went out and tried to make it better. People in Agrippan Rome usually didn't. They couldn't.

"How do you stand it?" Amanda blurted.

"What can I do about it?" Maria still sounded calm and reasonable. "Nothing, not by myself." After echoing Amanda's thoughts, she went on, "Since I can't do anything, what's the point of getting upset? It would only make life harder, and life is hard enough as is. I'm more ready to be free than I used to be, I think. Now that you showed me how the alphabet works, I can read more and more, though it's still not easy for me. I go on from day to day, and I pray, and I hope."

"Would you like enough silver to buy yourself free?" Amanda asked impulsively. "I have it, you know."

Maria smiled again and shook her head. "I would rather be your friend than your debtor. It would take me years to pay back that kind of money, if I ever could."

"I didn't mean as a loan," Amanda said. "If you want to be free, I'd gladly pay your owner what you're worth." She couldn't change the whole Roman Empire here. But she could help a friend. If she got in trouble for that with Crosstime Traffic, too bad. She and Jeremy had piled up an awful lot of silver. Freeing Maria counted for more with her than buying grain. She'd had second thoughts about it before. Now that she was leaving . . . Yes, things seemed different somehow.

The slave girl's eyes went big and round when she realized Amanda meant it. "You would do that for me?" she said. Amanda nodded. Maria hugged her again. But then, worry in her voice, she asked, "What would I do if I were free?"

"You could go on working for your master, but as a freedwoman," Amanda answered. "You know his business. Wouldn't he be glad to have you? You'd be your own person, though. You wouldn't be his."

Even that wasn't a hundred percent true. Freedmen and freedwomen had obligations to the people who'd once owned them. But they couldn't be sold or mistreated, the way slaves could. And their children would be wholly free.

"I hardly believe my own ears," Maria said.

"Well, you'd better," Amanda told her. "I meant it. Take the water back, and I'll do the same. Then I'll meet you at Pulio Carvilio's shop."

Maria's owner, a cobbler, was a short, stocky man with a broad face, hairy ears, and scarred hands. "What's this I hear?" he said in a gruff, raspy voice when Amanda came in. He pushed the sandal he was repairing off to one side and set the awl he held down on the table. "You want to buy Maria from me?"

Amanda shook her head. "No. I want to buy her freedom."

Pulio Carvilio stuck out his chin, which made his jowls wobble. "She's a good worker. It'll cost you. She's worth five pounds of silver if she's worth a copper."

"Five pounds!" Amanda exclaimed. "That's robbery!" The haggle that followed was the strangest one she'd ever known. She was dickering over the price of another human being. When she let herself think about that, it made her sick,

I don't want her for myself, she thought. *I want her to be able to have herself.*

She got Pulio Carvilio down to four pounds of silver, but no further. He had the advantage in the bargain. The only reason she haggled at all was that he would have been shocked if she hadn't. If he wanted to think he'd skinned her in the deal, she didn't mind a bit.

Once they'd agreed, she and the cobbler and Maria had to go to the city prefect's palace to make everything official. It turned out to be more complicated than Amanda had expected. Almost everything in Agrippan Rome turned out to be more complicated than people from the home timeline expected. There were endless forms to fill out, most of them in triplicate. Pulio Carvilio couldn't read or write. That meant the clerk at the palace had to read everything to him, which made the whole business take twice as long as it should have. (Maria could hardly read, either, but the clerk didn't care about that. Till all the paperwork got filled out, she was just a piece of property with legs.) The clerk and Amanda both had to witness Pulio Carvilio's mark again and again and again.

And the clerk kept sniffing. "This is irregular," he said several times. "That a female should make such a purchase . . . Most irregular."

"Is it illegal?" asked Amanda, who knew it wasn't.

He was honest, or honest enough. He shook his head. "No. But it is irregular."

"Never mind that," Amanda told him. "Just think of the tax the Empire's getting." She had to pay him ten percent of what she was paying Maria's master. The government said that kept people from freeing slaves on a whim. Maybe it did. But Amanda thought the main purpose of the law was to make the government money.

Finally, all three copies of all the forms were filled out. The clerk nodded to Maria and said, "Congratulations, Maria Carvilia. You are free." As a freedwoman, she took the family name of her former owner. That was another sign freedwomen and freedmen weren't so very free after all. Amanda swallowed a sigh. She'd hoped for something better.

And then she got it. The clerk slid off his stool. He opened a drawer in a cabinet behind him. Amanda expected him to pull out one more document. Instead, he held what looked to her like nothing more than a funny hat. But Maria knew what it was. She clapped her hands together. "A Phrygian cap!"

"A Phrygian cap," the clerk agreed gravely. "The sign of your freedom." He set it on her head. Except that it was red, not white, and only bulged out in front, it reminded Amanda of a chef's hat. Not counting her buck teeth, Maria was a nice-looking girl. Even she couldn't make the Phrygian cap seem anything but ridiculous to Amanda. But what Amanda thought didn't matter here. Maria's eyes glowed. The cap might have been odd-looking, but it meant everything in the world to her.

Amanda wondered how long freed slaves had been putting on Phrygian caps in Agrippan Rome. A thousand years? Two thousand? Longer still? Most of the time, she thought old customs held this world back. Here, she dimly understood what this one meant to Maria.

Pulio Carvilio kissed Maria on one cheek. The clerk kissed her on the other. Would they have done that if she were a middle-aged man? Amanda doubted it. But Maria kept on smiling, so she didn't say anything.

Then the brand-new freedwoman kissed *her* and whispered, "Thank you! Thank you! Oh, thank you!" in her ear.

"It's all right. I'm glad to do it," Amanda answered. For about half a minute, she felt really proud of herself. Then she thought of all the slaves in Polisso, in the vast empire of Agrippan Rome, she couldn't free. And that didn't count the slaves in Lietuva and Persia and the gunpowder empires farther east. Rome wasn't built in a day. Slavery wouldn't fall apart in a day, either. *Too bad,* she thought.

Three raps on the door. It could have been anybody. It could have been a neighbor asking to borrow a cup of olive oil. (Sugar, here, was uncommon and expensive—more a medicine than anything else.) It could have been, but Jeremy didn't think it was. He ran for the door as if shot from a gun. He got there half a step ahead of his sister. They grinned at each other.

Jeremy took the bar off the door. Amanda unlatched it. There in front of the house stood Mom and Dad. The next couple of minutes were confused. Everybody was hugging and kissing everybody else. Passersby stopped and watched and called out comments instead of ignoring them the way they would have in the home timeline.

"It's so good to see you!" everyone kept saying over and over.

"Why don't you come on in?" Jeremy suggested at last.

"Good idea," Mom said. Jeremy and Amanda both kept

looking at her. If they hadn't heard, they wouldn't have known she'd had her appendix out. She'd had plenty of time to get better.

"This town took a beating, didn't it?" Dad said, as Jeremy closed the door behind them. "It's in worse shape than I thought it would be."

"Like I told you, the Lietuvans broke in once," Jeremy answered. "The garrison managed to drive them out again." He still didn't say anything about stabbing the Lietuvan soldier. He knew he wouldn't forget it, but wished he could.

Mom and Dad walked out into the courtyard. Dad clicked his tongue between his teeth when he saw the places where the kitchen roof had been repaired. The new tiles were a brighter red than those that had stood out in the sun for a while. "You were lucky," he said. Jeremy nodded.

Amanda went into the kitchen. She came out carrying a tray. "I knew you were coming, so I baked a cake," she said. It was, of course, a honey cake—honey did duty for sugar here most of the time. Along with it, the tray held a jar of wine and four cups.

Everyone poured out a small libation. The cake was sweet. The wine was sweeter. Having the family together again was sweetest of all. "How long till we can go home?" Jeremy asked. Like Amanda and his parents, he was still speaking neoLatin. Voices carried. No point in rousing suspicion.

"Our replacements left Carnuto a couple of days after us," Mom answered, which told him what he needed to know and didn't tell the neighbors anything they didn't need to know.

"The accounts are in good shape," Jeremy said. "We had to collect in silver, not grain, for a while. You know about that."

Dad and Mom both nodded. Dad said, "You did what you

had to do. No one will hold that against you. Sooner or later, we'll turn the silver back into grain."

Amanda stirred. "I used some of the silver to buy Maria's freedom. I liked her before, but we got to be really good friends during the siege. The people we all work for will probably bill us on account of it."

Jeremy thought the same thing. He hadn't said anything to Amanda about it, because he understood why she'd done what she'd done. Even so, he doubted Crosstime Traffic's accounting computers would.

But Dad just shrugged. Mom smiled. Neither one seemed the least bit upset. Dad said, "Don't worry about it, sweetheart. You're not the first person to do something like that, and you won't be the last."

"Really?" Amanda sounded amazed. "When we train to go out into the alternates, they tell us and tell us not to have anything to do with freeing slaves. They say we're not supposed to mess with slavery at all."

"They tell you that to keep you from getting into trouble," Dad answered. "But you didn't get into trouble here. You did everything by the book."

Mom added, "Besides, a lot of the people who teach those training courses have never been out in the alternates themselves. Saying, 'Never do this,' is a lot easier when you've never had to worry about doing it yourself."

"Once you've gone out and seen some of the things people do in the alternates, a lot of the time you *do* want to change it. You can't help yourself. It's ugly," Dad said.

"What exactly are you saying?" Jeremy asked. "Are you saying we shouldn't pay any attention to what they tell us in the training sessions? Why do we have them, in that case?"

He liked authority no better than anyone else his age. If the stuff they fed him was pointless, he didn't want to have to go through it.

"No, I'm not saying that. You do have to pay attention," Dad answered. "But what you run into in the real world—in the real alternates—isn't just the same as what they tell you about in training. When you get out on your own, you have to use your own judgment. Amanda did that. We're not mad at her. We're proud of her."

Amanda looked so smug, Jeremy wanted to hit her. He didn't like her getting praised when he didn't. She probably didn't like him getting praised when she didn't. That wasn't his worry, though. That was hers.

Then Mom said, "We're proud of both of you, as a matter of fact. It sounds like you did a great job here. You're not supposed to be on your own yet. You're especially not supposed to be on your own in the middle of a war."

Dad's chuckle had kind of a nasty edge. "The locals probably figured you bashed out our brains and buried us in the cellar."

"That's not funny!" Amanda stopped acting smug. Her voice went shrill. "They *did.*"

"They sure did," Jeremy agreed. "If they'd been any more suspicious, they would have tried digging down there. That wouldn't have been so good. They would have found all the grain we were storing, and they might have found the concrete over the subbasement." He spoke quietly, so only the people in the courtyard could hear.

"They couldn't get through it," Amanda said.

"No, but they sure would have wondered why it was there," Jeremy said. "Locals aren't supposed to wonder about us at all." He'd learned that in a training session, too. He'd never thought to doubt it, either. It seemed too obvious to need doubting.

By then, Dad's grin had fallen from his face. He poured himself another cup of wine. "I thought I was joking," he said.

"Nope." Jeremy shook his head. "They do wonder about us. We sell things nobody else has. We sell for grain, not silver. They think that's weird, too. I don't know what we can do about it. Move out of Polisso, maybe, and start up again somewhere a long ways off. That would buy some time."

"Less than you think," Dad said. "News doesn't move fast here, but they keep records. They keep records like you wouldn't believe, in fact. There's bound to be a file on us back in Rome. Nobody's ever come out here to ask question, so they can't think we're real important. But if we showed up in Spain or Britain instead of Polisso, news of that would get back to Rome, too. And a clerk who'd seen the one file would also see the other one. He'd wonder why we disappeared here and set up shop there. And somebody *would* start asking questions then. Or am I wrong?"

Jeremy thought it over. He didn't have to think very long. He'd already had his own run-ins with the bureaucracy of Agrippan Rome. "No, you're right. I hope we don't have to pull out of here and start over on some other alternate that looks a lot like this one."

"That would be a nuisance," Dad agreed. "I wouldn't want to have to say we've lost our grip on Agrippan Rome." Jeremy and Amanda both made horrible faces. Dad grinned at them. He had no shame—he was proud when he did something like that. Still grinning, he went on, "We're not the ones who make choices like that, anyway."

"One good thing," Amanda said: "Even if the locals here found out we're from crosstime, they couldn't do anything about it. As long as we could jump into a transposition chamber, we'd be safe."

"True enough *here*," Mom said. "But there are alternates where they have the technology to go crosstime themselves if they ever get the idea. Some of those aren't nice worlds at all. Crosstime Traffic has to be real careful in places like that."

"It might be better if we didn't go to those places ourselves," Jeremy said. "Then we couldn't give ourselves away."

"It might, but it might not, too," Dad said. "If they found out how to build transposition chambers on their own and we didn't know till we bumped into them on some alternate where we were both working . . . well, that wouldn't be so good, either. So we stay and we watch and we try to be careful and we worry. Sometimes—a lot of the time—there are no clear answers, only hard choices."

Jeremy thought about that, too. It reminded him— reminded him uncomfortably—of his own worries after he and Amanda got stuck here. He said, "Things don't seem as black-and-white to you as they do to me, do they?"

Dad and Mom looked at each other. They both started laughing at the same time. Jeremy started to get mad. Dad saw that, too. He held up a hand. "No offense," he said. "Honest, none. It makes us feel good that you're growing up. It really does. It's just that—"

"You don't know how right you are," Mom broke in.

"You sure don't," Dad said. "That's what you'll do between now and when you're as old as we are. One of the things you'll do, anyway. You'll find out how right you are."

"The older you get, the more complicated things look,"

Mom said. "That's not because you'll get smarter. You'll just get more experience."

"You won't get more RAM," Dad added. "But you'll have a lot more programs and a lot more files on your hard disk that you can use and read."

Not all of Dad's comparisons made sense to Jeremy. That one did. He said, "What do we do if somebody from a nasty alternate figures out how to go crosstime?"

Mom and Dad looked at each other again. They didn't laugh this time. Slowly, Dad said, "I don't know. I don't think anybody else knows, either. What do *you* think we ought to do?"

"A lot depends on when we find out they're doing it," Amanda said while Jeremy was still chewing on it. "We can do things if we catch them quick that we can't if they have a chance to spread out."

She was right. Jeremy could see as much. He said, "I just hope it doesn't happen, that's all."

"Well, so do I," Dad said. "But it probably will. It's almost bound to, sooner or later." He raised his winecup in a toast. "Here's hoping it's later."

They all drank to that.

Two days later, the Robinson family came into Polisso. As Jeremy and his kin had before them, they walked in through the western gate. As far as anyone here was concerned, they came from Carnuto. They were all small and dark. For looks and size, they fit in better than the Solters family did. They too had a boy and a girl. The boy, Michael, was thirteen or fourteen. The girl's name was Stephanie. She was Jeremy's age, and pretty enough almost to make him sorry he was leaving. That was all the more true because she seemed very impressed about what he and Amanda had gone through during the siege.

Amanda noticed Jeremy noticing Stephanie. She got him aside and asked, "Well, are you going to tell her all about what a hero you were?"

"No!" He shook his head violently. That hadn't even crossed his mind. He said, "I never even want to think about that again, let alone brag about it."

His sister eyed him. After a few seconds, she nodded. He felt oddly relieved. He might have just passed a test, and an important one. Amanda said, "All right." She started to turn away, then seemed to decide that wasn't enough. "Better than all right, in fact. I wouldn't like it if you got all bloodthirsty on me."

"You don't need to worry about that," Jeremy promised. "I saw that guy get shot when I was up on the wall at the start of the siege. It wasn't movie blood or video-game blood. It was real. I could *smell* it." He shuddered. "And it could have been me as easy as him. Nothing but dumb luck, one way or the other. Anybody who goes on about how glorious war is, should have been there, you know what I mean?"

"Oh, yes." Amanda nodded again. "I know just what you mean. I was there when that cannonball came down by the fountain. That could have been me, too. And you could see the blood in the cracks between the cobblestones for days afterwards. Maybe you still can, if you get down on your hands and knees and look close."

Mr. and Mrs. Robinson were hashing things out with Mom and Dad. They were talking about business, and about exactly how big a snoop the city prefect was. It all mattered if you were going to do business in Polisso. Somehow, though, to Jeremy it seemed to be missing the real point.

And what is the real point, if you're so smart? he asked himself. After a little while, he came up with an answer: *I suppose the real point is that life is cheap here, and you'll get in trouble if you forget it.* He wondered if he should have gone to the beast shows and the gladiator games at the amphitheater. They would have made him sick, but they would have taught him the lesson he needed to know.

He also wondered if he ought to tell Michael and Stephanie Robinson to go. He shook his head. They wouldn't go on his say-so. The locals' blood sports would gross them out, just as they did with him. One way or another, the Robinsons would have to find out for themselves. And, seeing what Polisso was like, they probably would.

In neoLatin, Stephanie was saying, "It smells so bad now that we're in a town again." She was careful about protecting the secret. Michael made gagging noises to show how he thought Polisso smelled. Jeremy hardly noticed the stink any more.

But he noticed the fresher air when he and his sister and his parents left Polisso the next morning. The breeze was out of the west, so it blew away the city stench as soon as he and his family got outside the wall. He looked back in amazement. Somebody might have sent the air through a washer and dryer. He noticed Amanda and Mom and Dad smiling, too.

They walked out toward the transposition chamber in the cave outside of town. A long line of cranes flew past overhead, bound for a warmer, friendlier country. Jeremy waved to the big, long-legged birds. He felt the same way.

No one in sight in either direction. The road west from Polisso wasn't a busy one. The Solters family didn't have to wait before they went up the hillside to the trap door. Even inside the cave, Jeremy had trouble making himself believe the chamber would really show up.

But then it appeared, on time to the second. The door opened. "In you go," the operator said. To him, it was all routine. It wasn't routine to Jeremy. It never would be again. So what, though? This time, everything would work fine.

And it did.